Breaking Free

By

Cadee Brystal

Breaking Free

By Cadee Brystal

CHRISTIAN BOOKS IN MULTIPLE GENRES, JOIN CHRISTIAN INDIE
AUTHOR ~ READERS GROUP ON FACEBOOK. OPPORTUNITIES TO
LEARN MORE GREAT CHRISTIAN AUTHORS.
HTTPS://WWW.FACEBOOK.COM/GROUPS/291215317668431/

Dear Reader,

If you read my previous contemporary Christian romance, *Wide Open Spaces*, you've already met and fallen in love with Shelby and Riley Wheeler. Now it's time to see the sparks fly between Andrew Wheeler and Allison McGuire as they work through letting go of the past disappointments and heartaches, and learning their own Lessons of Love in Miller's Bend.

You'll become better acquainted with the characters who call Miller's Bend home. Cheer for them as they deepen their faith and learn to trust, even as they work through the suspense and terror of the kidnapping of their daughters.

If you enjoyed *Wide Open Spaces* and *Breaking Free,* you will want to be sure to read *Settling Down*, the third love story based in Miller's Bend. Riley and Shelby's friends, Matt Vander Meer and Ashley Nelson each find that they are ready to put down roots and trust one another with their hearts.

Happy reading!
Cadee Brystal

THANK YOU

Thank you to my family members who have encouraged me in my writing. My parents, my husband and our children have been so supportive of my writing. I surely would have kept these stories to myself without their insistence that they needed to be published.

Thanks to my volunteer collaborators, Makayla, Terri, Tammie, Marlys, Jessica, Char and Jennifer; and to my husband who occasionally called me crazy ... but not in respect to my writing.

I love you all!

"ONE GOOD TURN DESERVES ANOTHER."

Cadee Brystal hadn't intended to pen a series,
but it looks as if she's on her way.
She explained that after writing her first book,
Wide Open Spaces, which featured Riley and Shelby,
she just felt that Andrew and Allison
deserved to find happiness, too.

After covering small town news for several years,
Cadee discovered that fiction writing allows
much more freedom. Her writing style fits the life of a busy
woman with a full-time job, husband and teenage daughters.
"I write when the spirit moves me to –
hopefully, I will keep being moved!" she said.

Cadee has maintained the importance of
developing compelling characters who
live out their stories on the pages of
clean, enjoyable books, while delivering
messages of Christian faith applicable
in our contemporary lives.

CONTENTS

CHAPTER ONE

"I will not back off!" Green eyes glittered as the lean woman who had all but taken over the home of Andrew's brother glared at him. "Shelby has been my friend since we were kids and like a sister to me since high school. As long as she wants me here, I'm staying!"

"Well, Riley is my brother and I'm telling you they need some space!" The irritation had been brewing in Andrew for days – ever since Riley confided that he felt unwanted in his own home since Shelby's friend, Allison McGuire, had been staying there. She'd been a guest for a few weeks, and although Riley had acknowledged that Shelby needed some company, the constant presence of another woman and her child lodged additional strain on their relationship.

Andrew had advised Riley to get Shelby alone and simply talk to her about his feelings. His younger brother had refused, saying that he didn't want to come between his new wife and her friends. Now Andrew's instincts told him the opposite was true – Shelby's friend was coming between the young couple.

Andrew's lip curled as his gaze swept the length of Allison's form. "Just what exactly are you trying to do here?" he said with growing concern. Suspicion laced his voice as he added, "Destroy their marriage?"

"Get out!" Allison hissed the response as she wielded a spatula, first swinging it toward the offensive, self-righteous man in her best friend's kitchen and then indicating the door with a flick of her wrist. "You'll upset her!"

"You've already upset him!" Andrew quickly retorted. "And I am always welcome here," he said as he crossed his arms over his amazingly well muscled chest and leaned defiantly against the countertop. "You go," he said lifting his chin toward the door.

The tension built as the two stared, each trying to intimidate the other, until a clearing of a throat drew their attention to the doorway leading to the living area of the cozy house. "Well, isn't this nice?" Shelby said as she looked from one to the other. "I'm thinking you can both go. At least until you can behave." She let go of the door frame and took a faltering step into the kitchen.

Andrew was the first to react. He reached his sister-in-law quickly, and swung her up into his arms. "Should you be out of bed?" he asked as his eyes searched her face. The strain and exhaustion of her condition were clearly written there. He pivoted toward the remainder of the house intending to return her to the bedroom.

"No, wait," she said quietly. "I want to sit out here for a bit," she continued, but her eyes revealed her fatigue. He carried her to the couch instead of returning her to the kitchen. He wasn't at all sure how such a tiny woman would maintain a high risk pregnancy of twins, but she was determined to do everything the doctor had instructed. He had prescribed limiting her activities and adhering to hours of bed rest.

"Riley's a basket-case," Andrew whispered to her as he lowered her onto the couch. "I have to talk to you – alone."

Shelby watched her husband's brother. The man, who most of the time seemed devoid of emotions, appeared to have opened up a floodgate to the place he'd been keeping them tucked away. "Andrew, what's the matter?" she asked as panic flared within her. "What's wrong with Riley?"

Sighing with exasperation, Andrew rose and turned his back to her. "Nothing is wrong with him," he answered with a shake of his head. When he faced her again his deep brown eyes had lost their passion and the blank, flat expression that she'd learned to expect from him had returned. He had closed off his emotions again. Over the past year, since marrying Riley Wheeler, Shelby had learned that Andrew had been married and divorced from Lucy Graves and had gained a step-daughter – make that an adopted daughter – in the process. He dearly loved his daughter, Aurora, or Rori as he called her, but he offered little or no emotion openly to the rest of the world.

In the kitchen, Allison clutched the countertop for a moment to regain her equilibrium. She had always hated confrontations and the surge of adrenaline from the argument with Andrew had the blood rushing in her ears. *I can't believe I told him to get out! It's not even my place.* But then she remembered the way his eyes had raked over her body, not with appreciation, but with loathing. Her face burned with shame as she recalled his accusation that she was trying to destroy her best friend's marriage.

Allison stepped into the living room to find Andrew towering menacingly over her best friend. Shelby lay on the couch, propped up on pillows, looking pale and drawn as she watched her brother-in-law intently. The instinct to protect Shelby blossomed within Allison's spirit. Well aware that she was no match for him physically, Allison decided to bluff. "You want me to call the cops, or something?" she offered with false bravado. "They could throw the brute out of here," she continued, as she pointed to the offending man.

"Oh, by all means," he growled as he advanced on Allison. Pulling his phone from his pocket and thrusting it into her hands, he added, "Go ahead. Call the cops." They were so close she could feel the heat radiating off the man before her.

Ignoring the offered cell phone, Allison let the threat drop. Surprising even herself, she asked, "What have I done to make you hate me so?" He hesitated, but then his gaze traveled over her frame and contempt contorted his features. "Don't judge me," Allison whispered, "you don't know me."

"I don't have to know you. I know your kind," he snapped.

"That's enough!" Shelby interjected. She was on her feet again and advancing on the two. "You," she commanded Andrew, "sit down right now." She pointed to a chair and waited with her crystal blue eyes snapping and brows raised, inviting defiance.

He glared at the raven-haired woman a moment longer, silently trying to banish her before he turned away and took a seat. He zeroed his focus on blue jay feeding on the balcony-mounted bird feeder. Remorse rose up in him as the instinct to protect those he loved subsided. Her words – "don't judge me" – pulsed in his mind. The Bible verse he'd learned as young child flashed in his memory. He refused to turn toward the two women who spoke quietly across the tastefully decorated living room.

Instead he schooled his mind to recall the entire verse.

"Judge not, that you be not judged. For with the judgment you pronounce you will be judged, and with the measure you use it will be measured to you. Why do you see the speck that is in your brother's eye, but do not notice the log that is in your own eye? Or how can you say to your brother, 'Let me take the speck out of your eye,' when there is the log in your own eye? You hypocrite, first take the log out of your own eye, and then you will see clearly to take the speck out of your brother's eye."

Andrew frowned. If he interpreted the words of Matthew correctly then he, himself was a hypocrite. Would that mean that he, Andrew, was trying to undermine his brother's marriage? "No," he said quietly to himself, as he shook off the idea. He was a strong advocate for marriage – for other people – and would never do anything to interfere with the success of any such relationship.

Andrew concluded that his intentions to protect his brother and sister-in-law were completely honorable. He would protect them, their unborn babies and their relationship no matter how many times he had to go toe-to-toe with the conniving woman who had interjected herself into their lives. He recalled with a tinge of bitterness that he had actually liked Allison the first time they'd met.

He stood, but maintained his focus on the bird feeding station. The blue jay had flown away, but he refused to look back to the women. A scowl darkened his expression. Something about that Bible verse was still working on his conscience. *Judge not.* Could he be wrong about Allison? He recalled the frantic drive he and Riley had taken as they rushed to Shelby's side when the two were dating and Shelby had crashed her Jeep in an accident on the interstate. The brothers had arrived to find Shelby resting at Allison's apartment. To allow the couple privacy, Andrew had escorted Allison and her young daughter to the ice cream shop. Although distracted and concerned for her friend, Allison had seemed genuine and interesting. Her daughter, Hope, had been a polite little lady, especially for her age.

Memories seeped unbidden into his mind. He had met the woman again at the time of Riley and Shelby's wedding. He realized that he had truly liked her at that time, but then again, maybe it was a trick of the wedding atmosphere. It's always easier to like someone when there's so much love permeating the setting. Rori had even seemed to enjoy helping care for Hope while the adults had been busy. And even since Allison and Hope had arrived in Miller's Bend to assist Shelby during her bed rest, he'd gotten along well with her, until today.

Andrew startled a moment later when Shelby laid her hand on his shoulder. Concern was etched in her features as he turned to face her. "What's going on, Andrew?" she asked tenderly. "What's this all about?"

Sliding his hands through his hair, Andrew corralled his thoughts and inhaled deeply. "Riley ..." He stalled, not wanting be the one to say the words. *Lord, help me say this right.* "Shelby. You know Riley is crazy about you, right?"

"Uh, huh," she nodded. Confusion flickered in her eyes.

"Right. Of course ... you ... you knew that," Andrew closed his eyes. His own marriage had crashed and burned. What if he messed up his brother's marriage by bungling his attempt to help? Memories of his own feelings rose within Andrew. He had survived as the chasm between himself and Lucy had grown – he recalled the coldness, the distance, and the betrayals. He knew that he wouldn't be able to stand by and watch his brother go through the same painful experiences.

"Andrew," Shelby's faint voice drew his attention again. "You're scaring me."

Glancing past the tiny woman who had captured his brother's heart, Andrew looked toward the kitchen. "Where is she?" he asked with gravel in his voice.

"Allison? I asked her to go to the grocery. Hope is napping," she answered. Shelby faced Andrew squarely and clasped his shoulders in her tiny hands. As his eyes focused fully on her face, Andrew realized again how lucky his brother was to have found this woman. "Now. Tell me what's on your mind. You are acting like a lunatic," she demanded calmly, with a slight smile.

"She's coming between you." Andrew spoke quickly, but stopped abruptly. Did he sound like a lunatic? Shelby's hands snapped away from his shoulders and she pulled herself as tall as possible. "You are wrong," she nearly spat the words at her brother-in-law. "Riley would never … he wouldn't!" As she turned her back toward Andrew, he heard a sob escape from her as her shoulders convulsed.

Andrew quickly moved forward to help her to the couch. Just as his hands closed over her shoulders as her knees began to buckle. *What have I done?* As he returned her to the couch and tried to help her settle there, she batted ineffectively at his hands. "Leave me alone!"

"No," he refuted her command. *Lord, help find the words to fix this.*

"Riley is not the problem here. Allison is the problem." He had spoken the words quietly – almost a whisper.

"Allison is like a sister to me. She would no more try to

come between me and Riley than ... than ... you ... would." Shelby's words faltered as her mind raced ahead. Andrew's marriage had failed. He was always emotionally distant. She wondered if he believed all marriages were doomed and if it was possible that he was trying to "help" Riley be freed from this one. *I can't lose Riley, Lord. Please help me understand what's going on.* She closed her eyes as she tried to calm herself, so she could think clearly.

Andrew had remained silent as Allison's words melded with the verse that had been repeating in his mind. *Don't judge me. If you judge, then you will be judged by the same measure.* While he had thought Allison was interfering in the relationship, now Shelby thought the same of him. Suspicion had darkened her beautiful features and she regarded him cautiously. He hated seeing that look in her expression.

"No," he answered the unspoken question that hung between them. "I'm not trying to divide you. I am trying to help."

"Try harder," she responded with a challenge. "If I don't understand in two minutes, I will call Riley and ask him what's going on." She thumbed the button on her cell phone to check the time before looking back into Andrew's eyes. "I'm listening."

Andrew drew a deep breath and let it out slowly. He had to get her to focus on the change in the behavior between her and Riley since Allison moved in with them. "Describe a typical day and evening for you and Riley a month ago," he said calmly.

Shelby's brows drew together. "Why?" she asked warily.

Andrew rubbed the back of his neck in frustration. "You gave me two minutes. Please just do it."

"Fine. We'd get up, get ready for work; have breakfast
…"

"Did you talk?"

"Well, of course!"

"Then what?"

"We'd go to work."

Silence. Andrew cleared his throat. "How about lunch?"

"Riley would pick me up and we'd come home … and
eat," she replied.

"And …"

"And go back to work," she said primly. She felt a blush
rising as she wondered if Riley had ever mentioned to his
brother that they sometimes did other things on their lunch
breaks.

"After work?"

"Andrew, I don't understand what this has to do -"

"You will. I hope," he cut her off. "Could you pick up the
pace here? I'm running out of time."

"Fine. One of us would make supper. The other would do
some bookwork or research. Whatever we needed to do. We
would eat together and talk about our days," she spoke more
slowly as she realized that she hadn't had an evening like that
for weeks. She closed her eyes as she continued, "Then we
would sit together or cuddle on the couch. Watch TV or a
movie. Talk about the babies and the future. Talk about our
dreams." She sounded sleepy.

Andrew knelt beside the couch. Very quietly he urged
her, "Tell me about yesterday."

"We got up. I went to the kitchen to have milk and cereal
with Allison and Hope …" her forehead wrinkled as though
she was trying to make sense of something. "Riley got ready

15

and popped into the kitchen. He grabbed his coffee. Kissed me on the cheek and sat down. Allison asked what he wanted for breakfast ..." Shelby's eyes flitted open and she struggled to sit up. Andrew gave her a hand getting righted.

"What happened?"

"He said he wasn't hungry. Then he got up and went to work."

"What do you and Allison and Hope do all day?" he prodded.

"We talk. She cooks and cleans. Takes care of Hope. Runs out on errands."

"Does Riley come home at lunchtime?"

"He ... hasn't for a while," she said with a frown.

"And what's it like here in the evenings?"

"Allison usually has supper ready. Sometimes the three of us eat early, if Hope is hungry," she explained. "Then Riley can eat in peace when he gets home." She stopped talking and Andrew let her absorb what had been said.

"After you've all eaten, then what?"

"Allison, Hope and I watch TV or play Wii or read, but Riley says he's busy and disappears into the kitchen or bedroom," she looked into Andrew's eyes and waited.

He waited. He said nothing. Shelby squirmed slightly.

"You know being on bed rest is really boring, Andrew. I'd be going nuts if Allison and Hope weren't here," she said defensively. "And she cooks and shops. And she cleans. If she wasn't here, Riley would have to do all that. He would have to do all that after he gets home from work."

Andrew took Shelby's slight hands in his. "I know you would be bored and lonesome if you were here alone all the time. But you have to be able to see that you and Allison and

Hope are forming a family that leaves Riley on the outside."

Shelby dropped her gaze to her hands and shook her head to dispel the thought. "He's choosing to distance himself ..."

"No. Shelby. Listen to me," Andrew said as he raised his right hand to gently lift her chin. "Look at me, and listen to what I'm telling you. Riley loves you more than I ever dreamed he would love anyone. He is totally devoted to you and your babies. He has not chosen to distance himself. You – or Allison – or the two of you together are pushing him away from you."

"No we aren't!"

"Think about it. Think about how you feel when you remember the way the two of you were together before Allison's arrival. Then think about the way you feel together now," Andrew said. "You are tearing him apart Shelby. He misses you. He misses his family. He needs to be the person who is taking care of you."

Cadee Brystal

CHAPTER TWO

A light knock sounded at the bedroom door. The sound repeated more loudly. Shelby stretched slightly as she gave up on taking a nap. Rubbing her eyes, she rolled herself from her side up into a sitting position. She glanced at the clock – after four o'clock – Riley should be home by six. Andrew's words had disturbed her. She had tried to sleep, but it had been a wasted effort. As she lovingly caressed her swollen body she realized how restless and exhausted she felt. Guilt rippled through her conscience, too, as she wondered whether Allison's presence really could be damaging her marriage.

"You okay in there, Shelby?" Allison called through the closed door. Concern laced her voice as she pushed the door open a crack and peeked inside. "Oh, good! You're up," Allison answered on Shelby's behalf.

Shelby only nodded. She didn't have the strength to deal with any additional stress. *If Andrew is right, why hasn't Riley said something to me? Is he afraid I won't listen? Or doesn't he care if we drift apart?* The calico cat that had arrived at the Wheeler home a few weeks earlier popped up onto the bed beside Shelby and pushed up under her forearm.

"Hey, Puzzle," Shelby said quietly. "How you doing?"

"Aunt Selby!" came the cry of three-year-old Hope as she followed the cat into the bedroom and saw Shelby perched on the edge of the bed. "All done napping?" The cheerful little girl always raised Shelby's spirits. The round faced child bounded over to Shelby as her red braids bounced on her shoulders. She deftly pulled herself up onto the bed before wrapping Shelby in a huge hug. "I wuv you."

"Ah, Sweetie," Shelby said as she returned the hug. "I love you, too."

"I like living with you," the child replied as she tightened her hold on Shelby.

"I like having you visit us, too," Shelby responded with another quick hug. But her eyes had moved to her friend's face. Allison dropped her gaze to the tan carpet and took a step backwards and pivoted.

Out of sight, she called, "I better check on supper."

Hope wriggled away from Shelby and stood before her with a very serious expression. "Guess what?" she whispered loudly.

Shelby's mind was processing Allison's hasty retreat upon the mention of "living" with Shelby and Riley. Suspicion niggled at Shelby.

"Guess what?!" Hope repeated loudly.

"Oh. What, honey? What?" she asked absently.

Rubbing her protruding toddler tummy, Hope announced, "I'm going to have a baby!" She smiled proudly and waited.

"You are? A baby?" Shelby responded with wide eyes and a brilliant smile. Then rubbing her own tummy, Shelby asked, "If you are having a baby, what am I going to have?"

Without missing a beat, Hope announced cheerily, "Puppies!" Then she ran giggling from the room.

"Well, how about that? I've got puppies in here," Shelby said quietly to her extended abdomen as she continued to run her hand lovingly over the surface.

Allison stood distractedly in the middle of the kitchen thinking about the pickle she had gotten herself and Hope into. Visiting her best friend had seemed like the perfect short-term solution to her own problems when she found out that Shelby was on bed rest for the remainder of her pregnancy. It was a perfect situation until things started happening. Things like the uneasy feeling that she was being watched. Things like Andrew popping in demanding that she get out. And things like Hope saying she likes living here. Suddenly Allison felt guilty, like she was doing something wrong. Like she was taking advantage of her friend. Like she was telling lies and sneaking around.

Hope bounded into the kitchen with giggles bubbling up and trailing along behind. "I help, Mommy?" she offered as she wrapped her pudgy arms around Allison's leg.

"Yes, Baby, you can help Mommy," she replied. Kneeling to hug her daughter, she whispered, "Please remember not to tell anyone we are living here. It's important." She rose, pulling the child up onto her hip. "Okay?"

Serious green eyes met serious green eyes, and Hope nodded. "Yes, Mommy. I sorry I forgot."

"It's okay, Baby Girl," Allison said, as she clutched the child to her.

Hours later Shelby glared at the clock as her stomach rumbled. *Riley, where are you?* She had only snacked while Allison and Hope had supper because Andrew's words had struck a chord with Shelby. Conceding that they might have been making Riley feel left out, Shelby had decided to dine with her husband when he arrived home. Only he hadn't yet arrived. It was already eight o'clock and Allison was putting Hope through her bedtime routine already.

The phone lay on her rounded abdomen that periodically rippled with the movement of their unborn babies. "I sure wish your Daddy would come home," she said absently as she caressed a protruding knee or elbow. Then her hand slid up and clasped the phone. She had left him a couple of messages already and he hadn't returned her calls. She ran through several possibilities: Maybe he's at the shop working. Maybe he's with someone. Maybe he's just that mad about the way things were between them. Before she realized that she'd even made the decision to do it, she had pressed the speed dial for help in locating Riley.

Matt answered as he always did with a drawn out "Yellow?"

"Orange," Shelby replied sadly. Her heart just wasn't into fooling around right now, but it was her habitual response to Matt's distorted greeting.

"Shelby?" he said perking up. "What's up, sweetheart?" Matt was one of Riley's very best friends. Together with Tyler, the trio comprised what the townspeople of Miller's Bend referred to as "the posse". In their younger days the trio had been known to liven things up in the sleepy little town on the plains of South Dakota. But since their return from vocational school they had all been taking on responsible roles in the community.

"Hey, Matt ..." she chimed. Then paused as she wondered how to ask where Riley was without sounding desperate. "So, have you seen Riley and Ty today?"

"Yeah."

"Recently?" She prodded. *Is he with you? Can I stop worrying?*

"You okay?"

"Yeah," she sighed and looked at her rippling belly. "No. Do you know where Riley is right now?" she asked as tears pooled in her eyes.

The silence stretched as she waited an eternity for Matt's reply. She imagined Matt, wherever he was, looking around the room for an escape. Among the Wheeler brothers and the posse members, Matt was the most shy of the lot. He hated hard questions and tough situations – like the one he was in right now. Maybe he knew where Riley was, maybe he didn't. But apparently he knew there was a problem looming between them. *My husband told you what's bothering him and he didn't tell me?!* Shelby's concern swirled with the new irritation, and then blossomed into anger. *How could you, Riley?!*

"Look, Matt, I'm worried about him," she offered soothingly. "I haven't seen or heard from him and it's past eight. He's not answering either his cell or the shop phone."

"Shelby, you know I'd like to help you guys, I just don't know ..."

"I'm in no shape to go hunting for him, Matt. If he won't answer my calls there's nothing I can do but ask for help. If I can't get it from you, then I'll call Ty."

"Don't bother with that. Ty's here with me," Matt sounded trapped. After a pause he added, "We'll ... we'll see if we can locate him and send him home. And Shelby, don't get yourself worked up. I'm sure he's safe."

"Thanks, Matt. When you find him tell him I'm worried and he should come home ..." She paused before adding, "Tell him I think I understand and I'm sorry. And I love him."

"Okay. Don't worry. Bye," Matt said, and then pushed the disconnect button before she could reply.

Matt slid the phone into his pocket and turned to face his companions. "She says to tell you she's sorry and she loves you," he relayed. He drilled Riley with a disapproving glare before he continued, "So, you can either haul yourself home right now, or *I'll* haul you home. Let's go."

CHAPTER THREE

Miller's Bend was a small town and it didn't take Riley long to arrive at his home. A riot of emotions swirled around within him as he approached the door. He'd been so low, sitting with his friends, not able to bring himself to share his fears with them, but needing someone to understand his despondency and desperation. Dread had kept him from going home after work, so he had headed over to his buddy's place. Matt was a quiet person who would let a friend just hang out without forcing an explanation.

At least that's what Riley thought until Matt received that phone call from Shelby. Whatever she said caused a transition in Matt that was almost annoying. Quiet, passive Matt had all but pushed Riley out of the apartment and then followed him home! Riley shot a scathing look at the friend striding beside him up to the door. "You can go now," he growled. "I made it home safely."

"Uh, no."

"I need to talk to my wife. Alone."

"Exactly."

Riley shook his head with bafflement and advanced toward the burgundy side door on his cozy two-bedroom ranch home. He'd been so filled with pride when he and

Shelby purchased the house, he recalled. Having Shelby in his life was helping him accomplish dreams he had not even admitted to himself. Until recent weeks he had been enjoying a charmed life with a wife who he thought adored him, a nice home, successful business and twins on the way. Now his life seemed unbalanced, and it all hinged on Shelby's feelings. He felt as insubstantial as a scrap of paper tossed on the currents of the wind. His future depended on Shelby and he hadn't been able to talk to her for weeks – he hadn't been able to read her at all. Fear wrapped around his heart as he grappled with what he would do if she didn't want him around anymore.

Riley stood in the kitchen – didn't remember opening the door and walking in, but there he stood. "Come on," Matt said quietly as he pushed the door closed behind him. "I'm sure she's in the living room." A hand on his shoulder nudged Riley into motion again. He moved woodenly deeper into the house until he saw her lying on the couch. She looked so frail, except for the huge mound where their babies grew. Concern swept through Riley as he watched her.

"Shel? Honey?" he spoke quietly as his focus on her still form intensified.

The light touch of a female hand on his arm startled him. "She's finally sleeping," Allison whispered on his left. Riley's head dropped, as did his spirits. He had hoped that when Matt told him Shelby understood and was sorry, that it meant Allison would be gone from their home – at least in the evenings so they could have their lives back. At least tonight, so they could talk.

"No, she's not," came a weak argument from the form on the couch. "She's waiting for her husband."

"Oh, Shelby," he said as he moved to the side of the woman he loved. "You look so tired," he added as he skimmed her cheek with his fingertips.

"Riley, I love you," she offered. "We need to talk."

"Yeah," he replied sadly.

Realizing that she wanted to sit rather than lie on the couch, Riley helped her reposition. Shelby looked at her friend, "Allison? Can you … could you …?" Shelby was clearly uncomfortable with whatever she was about to ask. "We need to speak privately," she finally said.

Allison, who had stepped forward apparently ready to help with anything her friend might ask, looked shocked. And uncertain. "Of course … I'll just …." Her voice trailed off as she glanced around. While it was a nice home, it was also small. It would be impossible to leave them in complete privacy, no matter which room she went to. As her gaze skittered around the room, it landed on Matt who had been leaning quietly against the door frame. He looked uncomfortable, like he wanted to run.

Tension pulsed in the room for a moment. Then Riley, without looking up, cleared his throat before saying quietly, "Matt. Maybe you could take Allison to the café? Maybe have coffee and a dessert. Bring her back in a while."

Matt's body language and spoken response were in discord. He stepped backwards, retreating and shaking his head, even as he spoke the words "Yeah. Sure." He looked at Allison. It was clear that he didn't want to spend time with her any more than she wanted to spend time with him.

"Maybe you guys could talk tomorrow?" Allison offered with desperation sounding in her voice. "I could go on an errand run then?"

"No," Shelby and Riley's voices blended in response. "We have to do this now," Shelby continued solo.

"What about Hope?" Allison's discomfort had escalated into alarm. "What if she wakes up?"

"Then we'll take care of her," Riley said reasonably. "Please, Allison. Leave us alone for a while."

Allison looked nervously toward Matt, and back to Shelby. The plea was clearly written on her face, "Don't make me go."

Shelby nodded. Anxiety filled Riley and he held his breath. *Please. Please don't choose her over me.* And then she did it. "Okay, Allison ..." Shelby began. Riley closed his eyes and clenched his jaw, as he anticipated the next words. But they weren't the ones he feared. "I know you are apprehensive, but Matt will take good care of you. You go with him. Riley and I need to clear this up now. Tonight. It can't wait."

No one spoke as Allison slowly nodded. "I'll just check on Hope and grab my jacket," she said to no one, and to everyone.

Moments later, Matt politely walked Allison to his car. He opened the door for her and closed it gently when she had settled inside. He landed silently in the driver's seat and started the engine. He spared her a glance as he pulled away from the curb. They rode in silence to the café. Once inside, silence wrapped around the pair. Allison glanced around, noting that it was really slow in the little restaurant, especially for a Friday night.

"You don't have to babysit me," she said quietly after the waitress had taken their orders. The sullen man across the table swung his gaze to Allison's face. He studied her without speaking. Gauging her, considering her, learning about her. But she didn't see any judgment in his expression. Not like when Andrew had looked at her.

"You can take me back to the house. I'll just sit in Riley's truck until they tell me it is okay to go inside," she offered.

"No."

Allison focused on their waitress. She was average height and curvy. Her strawberry blond hair was swept up in a bun and her eyes were a strange blue green. Allison thought that was the unique color that could appear to go either way, depending upon the girl's clothing choice. She was young, maybe 20, and cute in the way one can be when the world hasn't dumped on you yet. Cute and naïve.

The waitress returned to their table. She seemed irritated and avoided looking toward Matt. The young woman gently placed a mug before Allison and filled it with coffee. She then thumped a mug down on the table in front of Matt and deposited the coffee carafe next to it. She turned and left abruptly.

Allison watched the waitress retreat before glancing at Matt. His gaze followed the waitress. Allison looked back and forth between the two, noting the way the young lady kept her body turned away from them. She noted the look of longing and regret in Matt's face and the red flush on his neck and face. "Oh," she said with a start. "You like her."

His attention was brought back to Allison. "What are you doing here?"

She glanced down at her coffee, and then looking him in the eye she retorted, "Being held against my will."

"That's not what I meant and you know it." Matt watched her intently as he pressed on, "Why are you here in Miller's Bend. Why are you interfering in Riley and Shelby's lives?"

"Interfering?" she echoed as her forehead creased. "I'm not -"

"Yes. You are."

"I'm helping my friend." *And hiding out.*

"You are. And you aren't," he said. "Can't you see that you are coming between them? Or don't you care?" He paused. Icy blue eyes scanned Allison's features for a second before he continued, "Or is that what you want?"

There it was. Again. "I swear! Is everybody in this town so suspicious?" Allison slapped her hand on the table, startling Matt.

"Everybody?"

"First that brute accused me this afternoon. Now you accuse me," she said as she straightened her spine. "I am not trying to do anything to Shelby and Riley. She's my friend and I'm helping her out for a while."

"What brute?" Matt asked as he narrowed his eyes on the woman across the table. "Someone was at the house today?"

"Would that be a problem?" she teased.

"I'm serious," he responded. "Who was there?" The muscles in his jaw flexed as Matt watched Allison intently. There was no question that she was a beautiful woman. The question in Matt's mind was could she be trusted? He shifted in his seat, leaning against the backrest of the booth, and spreading his arms across its length. "Why don't you tell me about yourself? But first tell me about the person who accused you."

30

The waitress returned carrying two plates – one with cherry pie which she placed dangerously close to the edge of the table in front of Matt, still managing not to look at him; the other, laden with a slice of "death by chocolate", she set gently in front of Allison before turning away.

"The brute?" he prompted when they were alone again.

"You are serious," she replied as she picked up the silverware and unwrapped the utensils from the napkin. "He's ..." she paused, considering teasing Matt further. "He's Andrew. Riley's brother."

Confusion flickered across Matt's featured. "Explain."

"Not big on whole sentences, are you?"

Matt didn't offer a comeback.

"Fine. Andrew came by the house today and tried to exile me," Allison said as her shoulders drooped. "He seems to think I'm trying to drive a wedge between my best friend and her husband." She looked at Matt. He was watching her without signs of judgment. He was listening without comment.

Matt very deliberately cut into the pie and forked a bite into his mouth. Allison's emerald eyes followed his movement. She was mesmerized as she watched the obvious appreciation of the pie. He swallowed and she looked at her own dessert. She sipped her coffee before looking up again. He was watching her expectantly.

She carefully took a small bite of her dessert. It really did look like enough chocolate to kill a person – but she supposed there were worse ways to die. She swallowed and sipped the coffee again. "That's a really good dessert. How's the pie?"

"Pretty good," he answered, as his blue eyes continued to assess her. "Go on."

"Go on?"

"You were going to tell me about yourself," he reminded quietly.

"There's not really much to tell," she said flatly.

"What's your last name?"

"What's that matter?"

"Just conversation."

"I'll bet."

"You're awfully suspicious for someone who is what they claim to be," he taunted.

"You want my social security number?" she asked as she leaned forward and glared at the man across the table. "It'll make the background check that much easier." She tilted her head in a spunky defiance.

"That's not necessary. Just level with me," he said. "Tell me why you are here."

"It's none of your concern ...," she snapped. She realized it was the wrong tack to take with this man even as the words left her lips. Of course he would think it was his concern. Just like Andrew had thought it was his concern earlier that day. "Wait!" she said as she held up her hands in the gesture used to stop traffic. "That's not what I meant. Just give me a second."

"Okay." He took another bite of the pie and rinsed it down with a drink from the coffee mug. She watched him with a wary expression. He could almost see her calculating how much she would have to tell him.

"First I should thank you for behaving in a civil manner," Allison looked into his face again and was distracted by blue eyes – blue like the crystal waters she imagined one would find on a cove on a tropical white-sand beach. A beach she would never see in person, but loved to daydream about regardless. Matt grew restless before her and he narrowed his eyes on her again.

"Why wouldn't I be civil?"

"Well, Andrew wasn't. He just assumed that I'm some sort of evil wench who's come to wreak havoc on my friends," she explained. "You seem close to Riley -"

"Close?" he laughed then. "Lady, you haven't got a clue!"

"So I'm a clueless evil wench?" she countered with a playful smile.

"Jury's still out."

"So you two are close?"

"We *three* are like brothers," he finally broke loose with a little information. "Tyler, Riley and I. Then of course there's Andrew, who actually is a brother. So you've got quite a defensive line here, ready to help Riley out when we see trouble," he paused. "And you definitely look like trouble."

Sadness flitted over her features, and she pushed the chocolate dessert away. "I'm not." Then silence fell over them.

Presently the waitress appeared beside their booth and waited patiently for either patron to look up. It was Matt who final did so. "Hey, Lauren," he greeted her with a shy smile.

"Hey Matt," she replied with slightly less ice in her voice than Allison would have expected considering the body language the girl had been throwing all evening. "You and your ... date about done? It's almost closing time." She waited. She rocked back and forth, rolling her right foot to the side and back. She bit her lower lip. And she gazed at the tall, lean, blond man seated in the booth.

"Yeah, Lauren. We are done here," he said. She dropped the ticket on the table and turned away. Allison noted the dejected look, the sagging shoulders and the slow steps as the girl retreated.

She kicked Matt. Hard. In the shin.

"Ouch! What?!"

"You can't let her think we are on a date, you dope!"

"I can't help what she thinks," he said in exasperation.

"Just like I can't help what you think?" she challenged.

"You can! All you have to do is tell me what's going on!" he whispered loudly.

"You can, too! Tell her this is not a date!" Then she kicked him again. It made her feel good.

By the time they had paid the bill and Matt had stuttered his way through explaining to Lauren that he was most definitely not on a date, Allison had begun to feel bad for kicking him … the second time.

CHAPTER FOUR

When Allison awoke the next morning, she thought about the strange outing with Matt before getting up to prepare breakfast. Even though Matt was clearly in Riley's camp if there was to be a battle, he was a calm man, a thinking man. He seemed to be a man willing to wait for more facts rather than judge someone. He was a man very unlike Andrew, who had unreasonably accused and condemned Allison without asking any questions.

She shivered slightly as she recalled Andrew's repulsion when he looked at her. "I know your kind," he had said with disdain. It was disheartening to her to think that Andrew had no idea what "her kind" was, and didn't care enough to find out. She sighed sadly as she tried to rub the tension from her forehead. Matt hadn't reacted like that. He had asked questions and tried to listen to her answers – but she hadn't really given him any answers. She frowned as she recalled the way she had danced around his inquiries.

She reflected that Matt had respected her enough to give her the chance to explain and she had responded to that by dodging his questions. Allison decided that, depending on how things went between Riley and Shelby last night – and how the morning conversation with them would go – she would need to contact Matt and apologize. And, she would give him some straight answers. She owed it to him to be honest with him. At least to a point.

Allison's mind finally registered the fact that there were voices coming from the living room. Or was it the kitchen? She quietly pulled on jeans and a T-shirt and stepped into the hall hoping to slip into the bathroom unnoticed. She pulled the door closed behind her and when she looked up, she was facing the unhappy countenance of Riley's brother. Her breath stopped as adrenaline coursed through her system. He simply watched her. She swallowed hard and pulled up a smile from somewhere deep inside. "Good morning, Andrew," she said.

She thought she detected the slightest twitch of the corner of his mouth, but his eyes stayed flat and cold as he assessed her. Finally, he inhaled deeply and let the air rattle out again. "Morning." Then he stepped aside and let her pass through the hall.

Everyone stopped their chatter when Allison joined them in the living room a few minutes later. She froze in midstride as she realized that Andrew was not the only early morning guest. Riley was seated on the couch, near the end, and he cradled Shelby's head and shoulders on a pillow in his lap. Their intertwined hands lay across her billowing belly where, their babies were growing and developing rapidly. He stroked her hair as he listened to the noise around them.

Allison was relieved to see that they had apparently reconnected, and she sighed. At least she hadn't single-handedly destroyed their marriage after all. Glancing around, she saw Matt and smiled to him. "Good morning," she said quietly. She nodded to Andrew, as they had already exchanged greetings. She then extended her hand toward the other man in the room as she stepped forward. "Hi, I'm Allison," she said, hoping that she was reading the room right.

The man was physically opposite of Matt. He was the shortest of the men in the room. He sported long, wavy hair that was nearly as dark as her own, but it was his eyes that really made her take notice. The color was a strange silvery gray, but they felt warm as he looked into her face. "Hi," he answered as he clasped her hand in his own, "I'm Tyler. I'm guessing you've heard of me." His smile was warm and friendly, and accentuated by deep dimples. He released her hand and stepped back toward the wall.

"Yes. Actually, we met at the wedding," she added as she glanced to the couple on the couch. Riley was helping Shelby shift into a seated position. While everyone present was friends – with the exception of Allison – they seemed to be restless and perhaps a bit confused as they waited for something.

Riley wrapped an arm protectively around Shelby's shoulders and she leaned into him. Allison felt a twinge of something – maybe pain, envy, loneliness or even guilt – and it made her glance away. *Have I been coming between them?* She tried to remember if she'd seen them like this since her arrival, but couldn't come up with the image.

"We asked you all to come over this morning because ...," Riley paused and looked to Shelby. She nodded and smiled up at her husband, encouraging him to proceed. "You all know that we were having some problems. Most of you knew it before we did." He looked from face to face. No one spoke. No one looked away – except Allison. She couldn't hold his gaze, instead she studied a spot on the wall behind Riley. He cleared his throat before continuing, "Yesterday and last evening, we were victims of an intervention. And we want to thank you – *all* of you – for helping us."

Allison shifted her focus to Riley's face where tears shimmered in his caramel-brown eyes. He nodded toward her, "Yes, Allison, you helped, too. You gave us the time we needed last night to talk through what was happening. And we appreciate it."

"But … I thought …," she paused and glanced at Andrew, then back to Riley. "Don't you blame me?"

Shelby broke into the conversation then. "Allison, I love you. You are like one of my sisters and I know you wouldn't try to interfere in our relationship," she said in a quiet tone. "I am responsible for how I spend my time and my energy, not you."

"Allison's presence here …," Riley began speaking again and then paused to look into his wife's eyes. "Well, she was a distraction. For Shelby – not for me," he explained then kissed Shelby tenderly on the forehead. "I just let the closeness between the two of you make me feel left out. And I didn't want to interfere with your friendship, so I … drifted," he explained.

"But it is because I'm here," Allison said as a tear slipped onto her cheek. "I could have ruined your marriage." She closed her eyes and leaned against the wall, "Andrew was right." There was a rustling of clothing, people shifting and moving, clearing throats and swallowing. And then a hand rested on each of Allison's shoulders and she pulled her eyes open slowly to see the same clear blue eyes that she had looked into across the dining table last night.

"He was not right," Matt said quietly as his eyes searched her face. "Do you hear me? My instincts tell me Andrew wasn't right about you."

Her gaze escaped the hold Matt had on them and flickered toward Andrew. He had turned away and was intently watching the birds at the feeder outside. Drawn back to Matt, she said, "Thank you. And thank you for your willingness to talk to me last night. I'm sorry that I was … evasive. You deserved better."

A warm smile curled his lips invitingly, "You're welcome." Then he leaned closer and whispered, "When you decide you can share your secrets, you can call me." He dropped his hands and stepped back, retreating to his previous seat.

"We just want all of you to know that we appreciate your love and support. And the help you gave us in seeing what was going on," Riley spoke quietly again. "Andrew, thank you for listening to me. And for acting when I failed to," he paused. "But we want you to know that the trouble was between Shelby and me, and it happened when we quit communicating with each other." He looked to his brother and waited for eye contact. Then very deliberately he said, "Allison is not to blame." A long, consuming look passed between the two men. Everyone seemed to hold a collective breath and then Andrew nodded ever so slightly before he dropped his gaze. His glance quickly bounced to Allison's face, but she forced herself to look away.

Riley cleared his throat again. "The Bible told us that a man shall leave his father and his mother and hold fast to his wife," he said as he shifted to face Shelby. Taking both her hands in his and looking into the face of the woman he loved, he continued, "I didn't hold fast. When something else tugged at you, I just let go. I never should have done that."

"It'll be okay, Riley," Shelby said reassuringly. "We'll get back to solid ground. God will help us find our footing again."

"So, will she be moving out?" Andrew's low voice rumbled from near the window.

Every head turned toward Andrew. Every eye assessed him.

"Oh man, Andrew. Lucy really messed you up, didn't she?" Tyler asked when no one answered. "Not every woman is like her. You have to know that. You have to get over it."

Andrew stepped toward Tyler, "This," he said swinging his arms to include the whole household, "isn't going to magically get better if she keeps staying here."

"This," Tyler replied swinging his hands in an exaggerated echo of Andrew's gesture, "will get better because they are aware and willing to change."

"Wrong. You can't have three people in a marriage," Andrew seethed. "And I would know."

Riley stepped between the men, facing his brother. "Andrew." He waited for his brothers eyes to lock on his own. For a second Riley saw his brother's agony swirling in their depths before the emotions stilled. "You and I are not the same. Lucy and Shelby are not the same. Our marriages did not start out the same. And ours will not follow the course that yours did."

"It could, if she continues to live here," he countered, as he tried to make his brother understand. Then looking to Allison, Andrew's expression softened and he directed the next comment to her. "I'm sorry about the way I attacked you yesterday. But if you love Shelby the way I love Riley, you have to be able to see that they need their lives back. They need to spend their time and attention on each other. You have to understand that we need to find you a place of your own."

40

"We appreciate your concern and your help in getting us to understand what was going on here. But we need Allison. Shelby needs her here," Riley spoke quietly again. "And we think she needs us. God set this up and we need to go with it." He looked to his wife for affirmation.

Shelby nodded, "Trust in the Lord with all your heart and lean not on your own understanding, and He will make your paths straight. We have greater awareness now, thanks to you," she said. Her gaze swung to her friend who seemed pinned to the wall. "But Allison is staying as long as she wants to and is able to."

The room was silent once again and Allison waited. Blood rushed in her ears. *God set this up? Hah! When has God ever set up anything good where I was involved?*

The bedroom door creaked open and a bleary eyed little girl wandered into the pulsing room, dragging a rumpled blanket, and followed by the calico cat. After a few steps she stopped and looked around, until she found Allison. "Mamma?" she said in a very serious voice, "Did I miss the party?"

Allison knelt to catch her daughter as she trotted over to her. "No, Baby Girl, there was no party. But we should get breakfast, don't you think?" The red head bobbled affirmatively.

"I can help," she replied seriously. Then she looked around at all the faces, her gaze fastened on Andrew. She marched up to him and touched his hand. When he looked down into her eyes, she said, "I can help."

Andrew looked into the innocent eyes of the little girl and felt some of the anger and regrets over his own disappointments of the past slipping away. She was young and sweet, with no sins tallied against her. Her optimism should be encouraged and cultivated. Wondering whether he had become too cynical, he lowered himself to one knee and rested an elbow across the other. "I'm sure you can, Big Girl. I'm sure you can."

Allison swept the girl away from Andrew and escorted her down the hall to the bathroom. As Allison returned to the living room, Matt and Tyler both left, explaining that they had already eaten and needed to get started on the day. Andrew also said he couldn't stay because Rori was home alone, and she should be getting up soon. As he reached for his jacket, Riley asked quietly, "Could you stay a while longer?" He paused and then looked to Allison. "Would it be okay if Andrew takes Hope outside to play for a little while?"

A look of caution crossed the features of the dark-haired woman and her gaze shot to Shelby. Shelby serenely nodded. "The three of us need to talk. Candidly," she explained. "I think you might be more comfortable if you aren't worried about Hope overhearing." Shelby waited while Allison processed the request. It was clear that Allison didn't want to let her little girl leave her side. The trio had been constant companions since the pair had arrived. It was then that Shelby realized that even when Allison went to do errands, she hadn't been taking Hope along, but having her stay with Shelby. *Oh, my gosh! She's been inside the house for weeks!* Shelby narrowed her gaze on her friend. What is going on?

Andrew analyzed Allison's response. She was so tense that she practically vibrated with energy. And she was trapped. She had to respect Riley and Shelby's request to talk alone with her, but there was no way she wanted her little girl going anywhere with Andrew. She looked desperately around the small house for some other option. She did not look at Andrew. Finally, she sighed. "I'd rather not ..." she said before her voice choked off. "Okay," she finally said with a short nod.

Andrew felt a twinge of empathy as he realized what a heavy load of responsibilities she carried. He had been married with a step-daughter whom he had adopted, and had been divorced for over a year now. Struggling to balance quality time with Rori, manage the household and run his financial consulting business, sometimes left him totally drained. He couldn't image the difficulties a young woman raising a baby alone had faced.

Just when he felt his heart softening toward Allison another thought crossed his mind: *Maybe she's not a single mother. Maybe she has left her husband and stolen Hope away from him.* Irritated with himself, Andrew tried to focus out the window again, but there was nothing there to hold his attention. Silently, he vowed to learn as much as he could about Allison.

His gaze had wandered back to the mysterious woman. Beyond the fact that she had been Shelby's friend for years, Andrew knew little about her. The two met while Riley and Shelby were dating. They spent some time together during Riley and Shelby's wedding and reception. He had talked with her superficially partly because they were seated at the same table during the reception. He even danced with her a couple of times. On various occasions since then, they had been thrown together, and Andrew had thought Allison was a very nice person and he enjoyed Hope's antics. But, he had taken the woman at face value. He hadn't been evaluating her. She hadn't been a threat to his brother's happiness at the time.

Andrew scoured his mind for any details that would support his gut feeling that Allison was a manipulative woman, after something, hiding something. He failed. In every image he pulled to mind, she looked guarded, worried, maybe lost. She had appeared happy for her friend, but also carried a deep sadness and caution which underlay her persona. It could have appeared that she was aloof, but as Andrew recalled her behavior earlier and watched her across the room now, he considered the possibility that it was really a cool reserve designed to hold people at a distance. Today, however, she looked so young and vulnerable that Andrew began to wonder what was really going on in her life. Again he wondered what was truth and what was image.

For a moment, no one spoke. Then long buried words came to Andrew, as if in response to his mental questions: *Carry each other's burdens, and in this way you will fulfill the law of Christ.* A sense of shame washed through Andrew. Maybe, just maybe, the tall slender woman and her cherubic daughter needed assistance. He had been pushing her, judging her and accusing her based on … based on his own experiences with Lucy. His actions were probably making the situation worse for her.

Andrew feared that the way he had gone about confronting Allison had been all wrong. He looked at Shelby and Riley and saw the strain of the past hours and the drama he had stirred up. Regret sliced through him. He had handled the situation badly and the repercussions could have been devastating to the couple. Silently he offered thanks to God for holding them together.

"Oh, Lord!" He said as he turned away to face out the window. There were still no birds out there, but it was the only place to look while he gathered his thoughts. Another phrase swept into his consciousness: *All of you, live in harmony with one another; be sympathetic, love as brothers, be compassionate and humble.*

"I ..." he started to speak as his eyes remained fixed on the pane of glass.

"What?" Concern laced his brother's voice which was soft and low, and close to Andrew's ear. "Are you okay, Andrew?"

He heaved another heavy sigh that seemed to break free from the depths of his soul and ripple through him. He'd had his emotions locked down since Lucy's betrayals, but his feelings had been floating to the surface in recent days. It was confusing. And humbling. Turning to face Riley, Andrew said, "I think ... I think I messed up." He hadn't realized it, but both women flanked his brother. He glanced from Riley to his sister-in-law, to her best friend. His eyes locked on the emerald wonders that hid her secrets, and he had to say it. Couldn't stop himself. "I'm sorry, Allison. I don't know ..." he stalled and swallowed hard. "I shouldn't have ..." He stopped trying to talk. The right words weren't there. He didn't even know if they existed. He just gazed into those eyes – into her.

Cadee Brystal

CHAPTER FIVE

When Andrew left Shelby and Riley's house a short time later, Allison had watched with growing wonder. She was amazed that he had attempted to apologize for the previous day's verbal attack. He'd been so cocksure and arrogant when he confronted her in Shelby's kitchen and accused her of interfering that Allison was having trouble justifying the man from that scene with the one who had expressed fears and regrets this morning. Thanks to the comments of Tyler and Riley, she now knew that Andrew's irrational accusations were rooted in his own relationship with the woman named Lucy. Allison also had come to realize that Andrew's actions were driven by love and concern for his brother.

Andrew had shown extreme care and tenderness toward Hope, who went happily with him to play in the backyard. As she absently watched Andrew's gentle interaction with Hope, alarm had rattled through Allison's system as she contemplated where she could live other than with Shelby and Riley. She hadn't really feared her best friend would send her and Hope away. But she had begun to consider where they would have gone. She supposed that Ashley was the only other person in the world she could turn to for help. Of course it would be very difficult to explain why she needed help when she wasn't even sure herself. It was just a feeling. It was a feeling that shook her to her core.

The trio had entered a heart-to-heart discussion, but Allison had managed to hold back the most compelling reasons for being in Miller's Bend. She had shared with them that the State's budget cuts to the university had resulted in the closure of the campus laboratory where she worked as a biologist. Her position had been eliminated and she was without a job. That unfortunate twist had allowed her the freedom to pack her belongings and come to Miller's Bend to help out when Shelby was ordered to bed rest.

She had let her apartment go and was adrift in the world. She didn't mention the bone-deep instinct that she was being observed. Followed. Watched. She didn't understand it herself – hadn't been able to verify it. She just felt the need to hide herself and her daughter away.

Riley and Shelby were now focused on their need to reconnect and strengthen their bond as a family. Allison finally understood that her continuous presence in the household had unintentionally pushed the young relationship to near a breaking point. She even had to concede that Andrew had identified the problem. Although, she hoped that eventually he would realize that he had taken his interpretation of the situation way too far. One of the last things in the world that Allison would want to do was to come between any couple who loved each other.

The obvious love between Shelby and Riley contrasted with Allison's own experience. Four years ago, she had thought she loved Brody, but had never been confident that he returned her sentiments. And then he'd been killed. His life had ended violently and brutally, right before her eyes. In the months that followed, as their baby grew within Allison, the heavy cloak of sadness and longing had settled over her. And loneliness.

Since she and Hope moved to Miller's Bend to stay with her friend, Allison had become acutely aware of just how lonely she was. Living alone in the college town after her friends graduated and moved on had seemed logical, but now she wondered if it had been the right move. But where else would she have gone? The image of the aunt who raised her slipped to mind. Had things between the two of them really been so bad?

Allison pulled her thoughts to the present. She and Riley waited awkwardly in an uncomfortable silence in the sitting room of an exquisite Victorian home which belonged to an elderly white-haired lady. Shelby had stayed behind in the couple's home to catch up on her rest.

The woman's buoyant voice called out from beyond the doorway, "Do you take cream in your tea, dear?" Allison looked to Riley and he raised his eyes to hers as he came out of his revelry. He was clearly exhausted, ruffled and unshaven, but an aura of kindness surrounded him. He raised his eyebrows in question and Allison shrugged.

"Yes, she does," he called in reply to the old woman's query. Then quietly to Allison he whispered, "She brews it strong enough to take the hair off your chest ... you'll want the cream."

A smile touched her lips but no response came to mind. A moment later the hostess glided into the room carrying a silver tray laden with refreshments. "I woke up this morning and I just had a feeling I would have guests, so I whipped up a batch of sugar cookies," she explained as Riley met her and relieved her of the tray.

He placed the tray on the coffee table and began to pour tea and pass the delicate China cups and saucers to the ladies. Allison's dismay shown in her expression and Riley laughed,

"What? You've lived with us for weeks and you didn't know I could serve tea properly?"

Embarrassment flooded Allison and her cheeks burned. "I'm sorry, Riley. I'm sorry I didn't get to know you better while I was a guest in your home. And I'm sorry for the trouble I caused."

"It's alright, Allison. As long as we make the necessary adjustments, we'll be fine. If Mrs. Holmes is willing, this may work out after all," he replied as he presented the plate of cookies first to Allison and then to the hostess.

Allison shifted her attention to the woman. MaryAnn Holmes was old – maybe a hundred, Allison thought before silently laughing at herself. A serious assessment had her pegging the woman in her late 70s or early 80s. She was slight, almost frail looking, but with a strength and self-assuredness that emanated from deep within. Intuition told Allison that this woman was a force to be reckoned with, but at the same time a profound sense of peace surrounded her.

Riley had introduced the two women when he and Allison had arrived on the stoop of the massive Victorian home a short time earlier. Mrs. Holmes welcomed him like a family member, and greeted Allison with warmth and acceptance. She'd seated them and hustled off to prepare the refreshments. Now as they sipped and nibbled, Riley cleared his throat.

The ghostly silver eyes of the host lifted to his, "How can I help?"

Allison choked and sputtered as she swallowed wrong. Her look cut to Riley as she wondered what he had told the mysterious Mrs. Holmes.

"Oh, dear. There's no need to be so jumpy," Mrs. Holmes said as she shifted her attention to Allison. "I'm sorry. It's a habit of mine. I just cut to the chase."

"Mrs. Holmes, as I said when we arrived," Riley began. He glanced at Allison to try to reassure her. "Allison is Shelby's friend from … well from way back … and she's been staying with us for a few weeks."

"Since Shelby's had to stay at home?" the elder asked as she sipped her tea.

"Yes. You know she'd go crazy locked up at home alone all day every day," he glanced at Allison again. "It's been a Godsend having her here for Shelby, but …"

Allison piped in, "It's getting kind of crowded. The house is small, and with four of us -"

"Four?" the woman asked. She'd set her cup and saucer delicately on the table and was looking intently at Allison. "You're married?"

"Well, no, ma'am."

"What then?"

Allison hated this part. She hated telling people that she was an unwed mother. She hated seeing the assessment and judgment in their eyes. She wasn't ashamed of her daughter and never would be, but the reactions of people varied greatly, and for some reason she cringed at the thought of disappointing this woman. Straightening her spine Allison looked into the face of the hostess and said, "I'm not married. I have a three-year-old daughter, whom I love very much. She is the greatest treasure in my world."

Energy pulsed in the silence for a moment. "You are a lucky woman," Mrs. Holmes responded. "Children truly are a gift from God. Some people never receive that blessing, and others don't recognize their children for the treasures they are. I'm glad that you have that kind of love in your life."

Surprise ricocheted through Allison. She'd expected a woman of this generation to look down on her for her status as an unwed mother. "Uh. Thank you?" she stuttered.

"Don't get me wrong. I don't approve of that sort of thing, but I can't condemn you or the child. Tell me about your daughter?" she prompted.

Allison began hesitantly, "Her name is Hope. She's three …" She stopped and glanced at Riley wondering how much to tell the woman.

"She's an absolute gem, Mrs. Holmes," he took over the conversation. Appreciation shown in his expression as he continued, "From what I've seen, she's cheerful and helpful. I never knew a child that young could be so easy to have around. In the time I've spent with her … well, she's very sweet. I hope our twins are as agreeable and well-behaved when they are that age."

Allison stared at Riley. Did people really see Hope that way? Of course Allison thought wonderful things about her daughter, but that's just a mother's perception isn't it? "Thank you, Riley. I didn't realize …"

Mrs. Holmes was watching Allison. "Well, where is she? I'd like to meet her?"

"Andrew has Hope this morning," Riley offered as he thought of the two of them playing together in the yard. His brother had looked happier than Riley had seen him in several months as he'd frolicked with the little girl.

"Well, that should be good for him," the elder commented absently as she sipped her tea. Turning her attention to Allison, she concluded, "I'll meet her soon, no doubt."

"Yes, ma'am."

"How's Shelby doing?" the silver eyes were on Riley again. "You look like you've been pulled backwards through a funnel, my boy. I hope she's in better shape than you appear."

"We've had a long couple of days, but I think we've got some things ironed out now. She's resting at home," Riley replied. "I've come to ask a favor of you ..."

His voice faded as he recalled the summer when he was a young teen and had been fast on the road to serious trouble. Mrs. Holmes had caught him vandalizing her property and had hauled him inside. He'd expected anger. He'd expected police. Instead she had shown him love, and understanding. Over time they built a strange friendship and eventually she had guided him to his own acceptance of God in his life. He was eternally thankful to this woman, who just over a year ago had helped him and Shelby recognize that God had put them on the paths which brought them together. He already owed her so much and now he was going to ask a favor of her.

"Ask and ye shall receive," the hostess offered encouragingly. Allison frowned, where had she heard that phrase? She tried to recall ... it seemed like a church thing.

"We were wondering if your apartment is open. Allison needs a place to stay. Live. For a while," Riley said as he faced the old woman. "She and Hope would still spend the days with Shelby, but they need a place to go home to at the end of the day. So Shelby and I can ... have time alone together, too." Allison watched Riley while he humbly made his request. She realized that he had been man enough to swallow his pride and ask for help in order to assist her and Hope. Allison was thankful that he had made it appear that he was the one who needed Mrs. Holmes' assistance, rather than

Allison. He added quietly, "She doesn't have a job right now
…"

"Oh, dear," Mrs. Holmes responded slowly. She frowned
and looked perplexed for a moment. "I don't usually make
mistakes like this," she said distractedly. "Let me see …"

Riley looked to Allison and they waited.

"Of course you and Hope are welcome to stay here," she
continued. "I can prepare a room upstairs for you and you can
help me out with some projects in exchange for your room
and board."

Allison felt apprehensive and confused. "What about the
apartment Riley mentioned? I'd rather not be underfoot …"

"I'm afraid I rented it to a young woman just last week,"
Mrs. Holmes looked troubled. "I have plenty of room here.
You can stay upstairs. And I'm serious about your helping me
with some projects."

Allison was short on options. She couldn't impose on
Shelby and Riley any longer and she needed to keep a low
profile until … when? She didn't have an answer to that
question.

Gratitude washed over Allison as she began to
understand that these people – friends of a friend – were
willing to help her. "I'm grateful for the offer Mrs. Holmes.
I'll be glad to do whatever work I can for you. Thank you."

CHAPTER SIX

The mother and daughter packed up their belongings the same day and by Sunday afternoon, they had moved into the well-maintained three-story home. It had turned out to be a busy day as there had been a steady stream of visitors all afternoon. Riley had dropped in to deliver a fruit basket that Shelby had insisted on sending over as a gesture of thanks to Mrs. Holmes. While he was there, he asked if she was ready to have her yard cleaned for springtime, or if Allison needed any heavy furniture rearranged in her room. Shortly after they decided that the following Saturday would be an excellent day to complete the yard work, he left, saying that he needed to get back to Shelby.

Tyler was the next to arrive. Allison determined that the sole purpose for his visit was inventory control on the cookies. No sooner had his vehicle pulled into the drive, than Mrs. Holmes placed a plate of chocolate chip cookies on the table and poured a glass of milk. "These boys of mine," she'd crooned in soft affection, "They may have grown up, but they still come back regularly."

Confusion rang in Allison's voice, "Your boys?"

"Yes dear. Riley, Tyler and Matt," she confirmed with a nod. "And Andrew to an extent, as well." Allison nodded dumbly as Tyler burst through the kitchen door and hugged the old woman tenderly.

"I heard that you have an excessive supply of ... ah! There they are," he exclaimed as he turned toward the cookies. "Hi, Allison," he added absently as he pulled out the chair and claimed a seat. "Where's Hope? Could she have a cookie with me?"

"Um. Sure," she replied hesitantly as Hope peeked into the kitchen. "Hey Baby Girl. Do you want a cookie with us?"

The foursome enjoyed light conversation as the cookie supply dwindled. Allison searched the faces of Mrs. Holmes and Tyler, wondering if they were related somehow. There were few similarities, but the haunting eye color that they shared indicated there could be a link.

After Tyler's departure, she turned to Mrs. Holmes. "Is there always so much traffic around here?"

"Oh, it ebbs and flows, but there's usually someone to help keep me alert," the older lady answered. "Chases away the loneliness when you have so many who care about you."

"Do you have relatives nearby?" The question had flown from Allison's lips before she was aware. "I'm sorry. It's none of my business."

Mrs. Holmes responded with a sad smile before turning the tables on her houseguest. "Do you have relatives nearby, child?"

Allison's black pony tail swung as she shook her head, but it was Hope who spoke up in response to the question. "Just me and Mamma," she said quietly. "But we will be a family one day. Won't we, Mamma?"

Tears pooled in Allison's green eyes as she dropped her gaze. "That's right, sweetie. One day we will," she responded quietly. She hugged her precious daughter to her, while the little girl squirmed to be released. "Do you want to go play with your dollies for a while?"

"You come, too?"

"In a bit," Allison answered as she released Hope. "You go ahead."

After Hope danced from the room, Mrs. Holmes turned a watchful eye on Allison. "Your parents have passed?"

Allison nodded. "I was very young. I don't remember them," she confided.

"Who raised you?"

Something about the woman's demeanor assured Allison that she had a genuine interest in her story. "My aunt raised me. I went to school with Shelby and spent lots of time with her family. My aunt and I were both happier when I was with the Sweetin family," she remembered sadly.

Mrs. Holmes look was a bit skeptical as she digested Allison's words. "Do you suppose that if you could look at the relationship through your aunt's eyes, you would assess it the same way?"

Allison's forehead creased as she considered the question. "I'm not sure what you mean."

"I mean, you were a teenage girl," the older woman explained. "Perhaps it wasn't as bad as you felt it was at the time. Perhaps you should talk with her again."

A quick knock on the door announced the arrival of yet another guest. Allison rose and pulled the door open and found herself face to face with Andrew. "Hi," he offered as his gaze skittered past her. Allison stepped back to allow him to enter.

"Come in," she replied as she turned to address the landlady, but discovered Mrs. Holmes had silently disappeared from her spot at the kitchen table.

"MaryAnn's been baking again, I see," Andrew's low voice rumbled as he gestured toward the plate which still held the remaining cookies. He snagged a few and tucked them into his pocket. "For Rori."

He lifted his gaze to Allison who fidgeted near the doorway. "I'll get Mrs. Holmes for you," she spoke quietly as she began to move toward the living room.

"Wait."

"Why?"

"I stopped by to see you ... to talk to you," he explained quietly. "I was out of line when I accused you of trying to come between Riley and Shelby. I'm sorry."

He waited as the green-eyed beauty regarded him coolly. She seemed to be waiting for something more from him, as well as gauging him. Finally, she relaxed slightly and nodded. "I believe you are sorry."

A sigh escaped him as he glanced out the window. "I'm not normally like that with people. It's just that I was scared for Riley. I pray he never has to endure ..." His voice trailed away. He shook his head slightly as if to clear the thought and he turned again to face Allison. "I'd like – I mean, do you think you could forget that and we could just move forward?" he asked earnestly.

"I don't know," she replied slowly. Shelby had always spoken well of her brother-in-law and had asked Allison to forgive him for his combative behavior if the opportunity ever arose. Her senses were alert to his mannerisms as well as the words Andrew spoke. He seemed genuine, but she'd always been cautious about people and even more so since she'd misjudged Brody. Andrew's verbal aggression had left fresh bruises on her confidence, but her best friend's appeal on his behalf tugged at her conscience as well. "I doubt I will forget it, but I think I understand – at least partly. Maybe if we got to know each other better, then you wouldn't be so suspicious of me," she offered at length.

"I'd like that," he sighed. "I promise you – I was only concerned for Riley and Shelby. I realized later that I could have really made a mess of things for all of you. I hope you will forgive me," his voice rose slightly which made the statement into a question. His expression pleaded for understanding and Allison felt her resolve to be tough melting.

"Part of what you said and did was right," she conceded. "I was coming between them. It's just that Shelby and I didn't realize it. And it was far from intentional – that's where you went wrong. Accusing me was wrong."

"I know. And I'm sorry," he repeated. "I came by to see if you've settled in alright," he diverted the conversation and Allison was glad for the change.

"Yep. We seem to be fine here," she said with some enthusiasm. "Mrs. Holmes is a wonderful lady to take us in."

"She's got a great track record," he replied with a smile. "I'd better be going. I'm taking Rori – my daughter – to the park for a while." He took a few steps toward the door before pausing. "Would you and Hope want to join us?"

When he glanced back over his shoulder, Allison was shaking her head. "Thanks. But not today. Maybe another time," she added with a smile.

"Okay," he said as he pushed the screen door open. "By the way, if you ever need someone to watch Hope, Rori and I would be happy to have her for a while." When he'd disappeared through the doorway, Allison continued to stare at the empty space wondering what had just happened.

After spending time in their room, reading and playing together with Hope, Allison heard Mrs. Holmes calling to her. Hope ran to the top of the stairs and Allison hurried after her. "Oh there you two are!" Mrs. Holmes exclaimed. "Come on down, we have more company."

Hope maneuvered down the steps leading with the same foot all the way. "Who here?" she asked excitedly.

Allison swung Hope up onto her hip as she answered, "Must be one of Mrs. Holmes' friends. Let's go see who it is." She stopped in the doorway to the kitchen as she recognized Matt seated at the table. The hostess was slipping a pot of coffee from the coffee maker and turning to pour a cup for the new guest.

"Do you drink coffee, dear?" she asked Allison. "I know what each of the boys likes, but I haven't had a chance to find out what you like."

"How many boys do you have?" Allison asked just before she felt a blush rising in her cheeks.

Matt laughed lightly before greeting her. "Hi, Allison," he said warmly. "Good afternoon, Hope. Care to join us?" he asked as he rose and moved to pull out the chair adjacent to his.

Allison set Hope gently on the chair and moved to the cupboard to retrieve tumblers for herself and her daughter. Backtracking to Mrs. Holmes' question, she responded, "I'll just have water, thanks, and I'll pour some milk for Hope." She glanced at the table, fearing that she would find a freshly loaded plate of cookies, but instead there was a bowl of fruit salad.

Matt's bowl had been filled with the colorful bits of fruit, and she noted three more bowls waited. "Well this is nice,"

Allison commented, "I don't think I could eat another cookie today."

"So the others have all been here already?" Matt inquired with a knowing smile.

"Indeed," the older lady replied. "You're the last to stop by to see me today." She set her China tea cup down and regarded Matt for a second. "Or didn't you come to see me?" she asked playfully.

Matt's attention snapped to Mrs. Holmes. "Of course I came to see you – you're my best girl and you know it," he replied smoothly, but his focus shifted back to the black-haired woman seated across the table. He tossed her a grin and a wink before looking back to Mrs. Holmes. "Have you planned the work day yet to get the yard ready for spring?" he asked.

"You bet. Riley will be over on a Saturday and imagine he'll bring Andrew. I forgot to mention it to Ty, but you can let him know," she quickly brought him up to speed. Allison watched the exchange as she and Hope enjoyed their fruit salad. Well, Hope enjoyed the strawberries out of her fruit salad before discretely sliding her bowl over to Allison.

"Who are you?" Hope asked, directing her question to the man beside her. "Do you have a little girl? I need a friend to play with," she continued.

"Nope, I don't have any kids," he answered the last question first. "My name is Matt -"

"He's a friend of Aunt Shelby and Riley," Allison offered quickly.

His icy blue eyes danced with mischief as he leaned close to Hope and whispered, "I'm a friend of your mom, too."

"Why don't you eat cookies?"

"I like foods that are healthier," he said plainly. "I like to eat fruit as a treat instead of eating cookies," he concluded.

"Like cherry pie?" Allison added with a teasing smile.

"Not exactly. That was a special occasion," he responded as he returned the smile. "It was worth breaking my training rules though."

"So you actually have rules?" Allison laughed. "I thought the four of you boys were all rebels."

"Oh, we are," he confirmed with a grin.

"Training rules?" Hope echoed his words. "What that means?"

Turning his attention to the child, he explained, "I have an easy job that doesn't burn up the foods that I eat very fast, so I have to eat things that don't make me fat. And I have to exercise – like going for long runs – to burn up the energy."

"You burn?" Hope asked with wide eyes. "Mamma?" she scrunched her eyebrows in confusion as she looked to Allison.

"No, honey. Not burning with fire. It's just the way we say that he has to work hard so he doesn't get chubby," Allison explained carefully. "No fires. Okay?"

The preschooler nodded solemnly. "No fire," she repeated. "I go play?"

Wiping Hope's hands and face, Allison released her. "You can go back to our room and play."

"I believe I'll escort her," Mrs. Holmes chimed. "Will I see you Wednesday evening at church, Matt?" she asked as she stood.

"I imagine so," he drawled. "Who would you sit with if I don't show up?" he teased.

"Don't you dare stand me up, young man," she admonished playfully. "I'll see you then." Mrs. Holmes slipped from the room to follow Hope upstairs.

After a moment of silence, Allison looked up to see Matt regarding her. She sensed he was about to start asking questions, so surged to ask her own. "Do you all stop by every Sunday to see Mrs. Holmes? Or was everyone checking up on me today?"

The lean man popped a strawberry into his mouth and chewed thoughtfully before swallowing. He rocked his chair back on two legs – the way Mrs. Holmes had admonished him thousands of times not to – before he answered. "I can't speak for the others." He dropped the front of the chair to the floor and leaned forward. "As for me, I came for both reasons. I do stop by to see Mrs. Holmes at least once a week, and I wanted to see how you are doing," he confirmed.

"Oh."

When that was all she offered, he asked, "So, how are you doing?"

"Fine."

"Not big on full sentences?" he teased, reminding Allison of her own words when they had been at the restaurant.

"We are fine. I think it'll work out alright," she finally said. "Mrs. Holmes has some painting for me to do in the evenings."

"You and Hope are sharing a room upstairs?" he asked, although he apparently knew the answer. She nodded in response, but didn't comment. Allison wasn't sure who to trust yet, although she was beginning to see that if you were a friend of Riley's, then you also got Matt, Tyler and maybe Andrew in the bargain as well. And it was reassuring somehow to have more people who were looking out for her.

Changing the focus away from herself, Allison queried the man before her. "You said that you don't work very hard in your job … what is it you do?"

He laughed at that. "I work plenty hard. It just isn't physical labor. If I ate like Riley and Ty, I'd be the size of a sumo wrestler," he explained without answering the question.

"I understand," Allison nodded as she spoke. "When I worked in the lab, I had the same problem."

Matt blushed as he looked away. Very quietly he said, "I can't imagine you as a sumo." He stood and began clearing the table. As the dishwater filled the sink, he plunged the dishes into the sudsy water. He heard Allison moving around behind him, putting things into the refrigerator.

"I'll rinse and wipe," she offered as she stepped beside him. He simply nodded and set the first dish into the rinse. "You didn't tell me what you do ..." she gave a verbal nudge. "Do you want me to guess?"

He shook his head and passed another dish into the rinse. "You'd never guess it, and you'd probably embarrass both of us by trying," he answered as he turned to face her. "I'm an artist." He waited for her to laugh, but she didn't. Instead the black-haired woman turned to gaze at him before nodding. Her focus dropped to his hands, then back up to his face.

"If I had to guess which discipline – and apparently I do have to guess – I'd say either musician or sculptor," she spoke quietly.

"You don't think that's weird?" he asked as he went back to washing the dishes. "That I'm a sculptor, I mean?"

"No. Do you think it's weird that I'm a scientist?" she countered.

"Well, no," he replied steadily. "But that's a nice, normal job." The comment reminded Allison that she no longer had her nice, normal job and that she would need to find employment soon if she was going to stay in Miller's Bend.

The two finished up the dishes with minimal discussion and Matt made a quick exit.

Mrs. Holmes had reappeared in the kitchen with Hope and a board game. Hope chattered about Shelby's kitty as the grandmotherly woman began setting up the game. "Do you have time to play a round or two of Candyland with us?" she invited.

They hadn't played long, when Allison heard a car door slam followed shortly by a light knock on the door. When the door opened, a young woman stood in the space. "Hi, Mrs. Holmes," she greeted before her gaze landed on Allison and slid quickly to Hope. The color drained from her cheeks. "Oh!" she stammered. "I ... I'm sorry. I didn't realize you had company." She was handing a package to Mrs. Holmes and backing away simultaneously.

Allison looked up at the woman and was struck by a sense of familiarity. The sense that they had met niggled at Allison, but she had made a point of not going out – not being seen. She wracked her brain trying to remember where or when she might have seen the woman. Allison let her eyes slide over the woman's features as she tried to place her.

"Lauren? Won't you come in, please?" Mrs. Holmes offered invitingly. "I'd like for you to meet my new friends and houseguests."

The woman ceased her retreat, but didn't move forward until Mrs. Holmes reached out and grasped her hand. "Come on in, dear. You look as though you've seen a ghost." The kindly old woman fairly pulled Lauren into the room and pushed the door closed. "What did you bring?" she asked as she glanced at the carton in her hands.

The woman – Lauren – looked shaken, but was quickly pulling herself together. The color was back in her cheeks; in fact, she had a slight blush now, and Allison began to wonder if she was alright. "Here," Allison offered as she jumped from her seat. "You should sit down. I'll get you a glass of water." In a few seconds she had pressed the younger woman into the chair and was running cold water into a glass.

"Thanks," the girl mumbled as she took the glass and sipped from it. "I ... I don't know what happened there." Then she looked to Mrs. Holmes who was peeking inside the carton. "It's a Key lime pie. I thought it would be a nice way to say thank you for letting me stay here," she spoke to the older lady, but her focus was on the preschool girl seated across the table from her.

Hope's green eyes, so like her mother's, regarded the newcomer carefully. She finally leaned toward Allison while keeping her focus on the woman across the table, "Who she, Mamma?"

Mrs. Holmes had placed the pie into the refrigerator and finally addressed the awkward group. "I'm glad you stopped by when you got home today, Lauren. This way I can introduce you, since you are bound to be seeing a lot of each other."

First the kindly woman informed Lauren, "I'd like you to meet Allison McGuire and her daughter, Hope. They are staying in one of my rooms in the upper level."

"I'm so glad to make your acquaintance," Lauren said carefully. She glanced nervously between mother and daughter. Allison extended her hand in greeting and Lauren shook it lightly. She mimicked the process with the child. When they released hands, Lauren asked, "How old are you?"

"I'm three!" Hope responded with pride. "I get to go to preschool next fall." Allison laid a proprietary arm around her daughter and pulled her close. Something made her stomach tighten and the hairs on the back of her neck stand up. She didn't know what caused it, but she wasn't going to just ignore it.

Suddenly Mrs. Holmes was addressing Allison and Hope. She indicated the strawberry-blonde with a wave of her hand, "This is Lauren Martins. She is the renter of the apartment downstairs."

The last name repeated in Allison's mind. Martins. That was similar to Brody's last name – Martinson – but similar is not the same. Just a coincidence. Regret and pain seared through her as she remembered Brody – Hope's father. They'd been so young. Why did he have to die?

Later, in the privacy of her apartment, Lauren spoke quietly, but distinctly into the mouthpiece of her cell phone. "I'm telling you – I think I found her." After she listened to the response, with her voice cracking, she continued, "The girl is the right size and age. Red hair that curls and green eyes. She's even got dimples, like ..." Lauren couldn't speak for a moment as she thought of the man who had likely sired the child – his devilish smile, the deep dimples and the playful glint in his eye. Tears pooled in her own eyes at the thought that he was gone forever. *Oh, Brody. I miss you so.*

The raspy voice on the other end of the call pulled Lauren back to the present. "How soon should we come?"

"Not yet. I want to get to know her, so she's not scared," Lauren replied. "I also want to get more information about the woman," she added distractedly. Which, she thought, should be easier since she lives right upstairs.

The kindly old lady, Mrs. Holmes, had helpfully introduced Lauren to Miss McGuire, right there in the kitchen of the grand Victorian house where they both rented living space. Little did the old woman know just how pivotal that information was. Lauren had marveled at the good luck she'd had in finding the girl. Now she had to figure out how to insinuate herself into the lives of the black-haired woman and the little girl. Brody's little girl.

CHAPTER SEVEN

Andrew knocked lightly on the kitchen door to Riley's home and waited. Glancing at his watch, he realized he was a quarter of the way into his lunch break as he wondered why no one was answering the door. He knocked again – a bit louder this time – and waited. Finally, he turned the knob and pushed the door open. "Hello?" he called, just as a calico streak shot past him into the yard. He snagged Hope as she tried to follow the wayward feline to freedom. It had been several days since he'd seen her, but she wrapped him in a big hug as he swung her up into his arms. He asked playfully, "And where do you think you are going, young lady?"

"I want to play," she insisted as she wiggled to free herself from his hold. He deftly shifted her to a hip as he stepped into the house and closed the door.

"Where's your Mamma?" he asked.

Hope let her lip jut out and pulled her brows low over brooding green eyes before pointing toward the living room. Andrew noted a simmering pot of chili on the stovetop and his stomach rumbled. "Let's go see her," he said. "And stop squirming."

"Everything okay?" he asked as he surveyed the scene in the living room. Shelby was seated on the couch and appeared to be fighting off a fit of laughter, so he figured she was fine. Allison was on her knees trying to vacuum potting soil out of the carpet with a hand-held cleaner. It was apparent that several potted plants had been overturned and she was working to clean up the mess. Andrew let out a low whistle which was designed to express awe over the disarray in the room – there was even an overturned chair for goodness sake. However, the whistle seemed to be taken in a different way by Allison who was instantly on her feet, facing the intruding man.

Indignation and embarrassment danced across her features before she began laughing. "This must look horrible!" she exclaimed. As her expression softened and relaxed, his attention was drawn to a smear of dirt near a dimple on her flushed cheek.

"I wouldn't say that," he responded with a smile as his gaze lingered on her features. Shaking off a wayward thought, he added, "It looks like someone was having too much fun, though." With a stern expression, he looked to Hope. "Did you cause this mess?"

The pouty lip had disappeared and sad eyes looked to the dirt on the floor as she dejectedly nodded her head. The tight red ringlets bounced. Over the years he'd spent with Rori, Andrew had schooled himself not to smile when a child needed to be reprimanded. "Well, then you'd better get in there and help clean it up," he said as he gently set Hope on her feet. "I'll tend to the lunch," and he strode from the room as Allison gaped after him.

After the living room was back in shape and they'd all eaten, Allison apologized for the chaotic scene Andrew had walked into. She explained that Hope had been restless and demanding all day and had taken to chasing the cat, which of course had caused the chair and plants to be overturned. Shelby was still suffering from outbursts of laughter as the adults discussed the events. "It's the most excitement I've had for weeks," she commented as she excused herself from the table. "I better check on her – she's been alone for too long in the other room. Oh, and I'll put these papers on Riley's desk, too," she said, indicating the envelope that Andrew had brought to the house.

He checked the clock, "I need to be getting back to work–"

"Hope!" Shelby's squeal interrupted his thought. He and Allison rushed to see what was happening in the other room. The restless preschooler had squeezed shampoo and conditioner into the bathtub, and was adding a measure of toothpaste to the concoction when the adults burst into the tiny bathroom. Shelby was seated on the closed stool, trying not to laugh. Allison, who had entered the room ahead of Andrew, covered her face and turned away so Hope wouldn't see her laughing. In doing so, she found herself face to face with Andrew, and her breath caught. When there was laughter in his eyes, he was an amazingly handsome man.

His focus shifted to her face and Andrew's attention caught there. Beautiful. For a delicate moment, he was embroiled in a twist of emotions, but the main thought that he captured was that he needed to kiss Allison. His expression grew serious as he stepped back.

Turning back toward her daughter, Allison said in a strangled voice, "Baby Girl, I don't know what I'm going to do with you for the rest of the day!"

Inspiration hit and before Andrew could take the time to think it through, he offered, "I could take her to my house and Rori could watch her. Maybe they'd burn off some energy."

"Isn't Rori in school?" Allison asked.

"No classes today," he countered. "Teacher in-service training."

"Oh ... I guess ..." Allison's voice faltered. A few weeks ago she would have been immobilized by fear at the very idea of letting Hope go with a stranger. But, that had been when she felt so alone. She was no longer alone – the people of Miller's Bend were becoming her friends, and she and Andrew seemed to have moved past a rough spot and had begun to form a friendship. She knew that he was kind and that Hope would be safe with him and his daughter. But old habits are difficult to overcome, and Allison looked to Shelby who shrugged.

"She'd be fine," Shelby said reassuringly. "Rori is very responsible."

About ten minutes later, Andrew stepped into his own home and closed the back door. Standing in the kitchen while he set Hope gently on her feet, he could hear voices coming from the living room. "Rori!" he called out. "We've got company." He was kneeling on the floor, struggling with the stuck zipper on Hope's jacket, when she stepped backwards, pulling away from him. As he glanced to the child's face, he read apprehension, just before she launched herself into his arms. She made a strange noise and buried her face in his shoulder.

A second later he saw the reason for her reaction: Lucy. His ex-wife stood in the doorway between the kitchen and the living room. Rori wasn't in sight. "Snagged yourself another one, Andy?" she purred.

"Why are you here? Can't you just leave us alone, Lucy?" he countered. Even as her name left his lips, Andrew was slapped with remorse for his hasty reply. Exchanging barbs with the woman had never resulted in improving his outlook, or his standing. "Look, I'm sorry. It's been a tough couple of days."

Her sly smile was slowly spreading as she registered his state of mental disarray. "Well ... Honey, I could relieve some of that pent up stress for you ..."

Not in a million years! Andrew ignored the suggestion and turned his body as though he could shield Hope, whom he clutched tightly to his chest. "Just have a seat. Here. In the kitchen," he said as he fled into the living room. Realizing that Rori wasn't in the main floor of the house, he took the steps two at a time moving to the second story as he tried to distance himself and Hope from the woman in the kitchen. "Rori?"

"I'm in here, Dad," came a hesitant reply from beyond the bathroom door. The door slowly opened and dark eyes filled with suspicion scanned the hallway. "Is she gone?"

"She's in the kitchen," he said with a sad shake of his head.

The door opened wider, and Rori surveyed the child in her dad's arms. "What's she doing here?" she asked, nodding toward the girl who clung to him. For a second Rori felt stung that he would hold another child with such care.

Pulling the clinging little girl back slightly to expose her face, he said, "I've brought Hope to our house for a while." The irony of the words hit him as he realized that "hope" had been in low supply. He knelt on one knee and rested the preschooler on the other as he spoke to her. "Do you remember my little girl? This is Rori."

Andrew silently willed Rori to be the cheerful, helpful young lady he knew she could be for the following few hours, rather than the insolent, angry preteen that she was equally capable of portraying. He waited as the rich brown, sometimes brooding, eyes of his twelve-year old daughter assessed the hesitant child perched on his knee. He was losing circulation in that leg, and beginning to wonder whether Lucy had remained in the kitchen as he had directed her.

Finally, Rori sighed and reached a hand toward the red-headed child. "Hey, Hope. Let's go play in my room," she said with a smile.

Hope tentatively took Rori's hand and slid from Andrew's knee to stand on the floor, remaining in the shelter of his body. Alarm shown in her eyes as she looked back and forth between the two. In a low whisper she cautiously asked, "Crew Ella?"

Andrew was confused and looked to Rori, "Did she say 'Cruella'?"

Rori's eyes danced now as her shoulders began to shake as a case of the giggles overtook her. "Do you mean Cruella de Vil? From the movie?" she asked Hope.

Serious green eyes peered at Rori. Hope's hair bounced as she nodded vigorously. "Cruella live here?"

"Oh, mercy, no," Andrew answered too loudly before catching himself. "I mean, no. Honey, that lady does not live here."

Rori hadn't yet regained her composure.

Andrew turned Hope to look at him. "Can you stay upstairs with Rori and play while I go talk to Cru ... to the lady downstairs? Will that be alright?"

Hope regarded him carefully. "She not Cruella?"

"No, honey. She's not."

"She not live here?"

"No. She doesn't live here."

Pointing to the older girl, she asked, "She nice?"

"Yes, she's very nice. And responsible," he answered earnestly.

"Okay," Hope finally answered with a nod. "I stay here."

"Thank you. Both," he replied as he made eye contact with first Hope, and then Rori. He rose and headed downstairs.

When Andrew entered the kitchen he found his former wife rifling through the cabinets. Coffee was brewing and the woman was slamming cupboard doors. "I swear. Don't you have any Bailey's or anything to put in the coffee?" She had her back to him and was stretched up on her tip-toes. The too-small mini-skirt was inching dangerously higher, and he looked away. For what could have been the thousandth time he wondered how he had been so wrong about Lucy.

"You know I don't."

"A girl can hope," she replied with a whine as she turned to face him with a too-big smile.

"You know there's no alcohol here." Andrew stepped forward and assumed an authoritative stance, crossing his arms across his chest. "What do you want?" he asked.

She dropped her chin and pushed her lips out in a very unattractive faux pout before replying, "You."

"Outta the question."

"Ah, come on," she purred as she advanced on Andrew. She sported a tight, low-cut sweater that was stretched out of proportion. "You know you miss me ..."

"Like an IRS audit," he replied through gritted teeth, just before he moved around the small kitchen table. He reached for a coffee mug for himself, but didn't offer her one. "You need to leave."

"But you just got home," she countered while executing well-rehearsed doe eyes.

Andrew filled his cup with strong coffee even though it hadn't finished brewing yet. He returned the carafe and turned to find the minx had moved in too close to him. His back was to the kitchen countertop so he started sliding to the left. She reached out as if to touch his cheek but he deftly blocked her advance with his wrist. "Don't!" His eyes glittered with anger, and his lip curled in disgust. "Don't touch me. Ever," he hissed.

Lucy retreated. True emotional pain flashed across her features, but was quickly replaced with hostility. "You know," she huffed, "For a while after we married, I actually almost thought you cared about me."

"We've been down this road too many times, Lucy ..." he sighed as he ran his hand through his hair with agitation. "When you had me, you didn't want me. Now that you don't have me ... well, look at yourself." He gestured toward her, from her spiked ruby heels, to her coppery blond hair piled high on her head, and repulsion rose in his throat.

"Andy ... don't be mean to me," she whimpered. "I need your help."

All his patience was drained. His emotions swirled within his heart. Memories swirled within his head. "Why did you come here?"

Sensing Andrew's intolerance for her ploys, Lucy crumpled onto a kitchen chair. "Fine. I need money."

"No."

"Just a little – you have plenty."

"No," he repeated.

"You wouldn't miss a few thousand," she purred.

"A few thousand?" he choked as he slammed the coffee mug down on the table between them. "Why would you need a few thousand dollars?"

"For Aurora."

"No."

"Please, Andy ... Andrew," she begged. "I need to get her some stuff and I'm all out."

"What stuff?"

"Things for ... school."

"Lucy, I'm not dumb enough to give you money," he answered. "Give me a list of what she needs and I will pick it up for you."

She sniffled. "But, you have to give me the money!"

"You better go. Now." Andrew commanded. He didn't look at Lucy. He turned and walked into the living room. He heard the angry clicking of her spiked shoes as she stormed past him to exit through the front door. The door slammed behind her. Framed pictures rattled on the wall. Andrew trembled as he moved to a chair and sunk slowly into it. With elbows on his knees, he cupped his face in his hands. "Dear God," he sighed. "I need your help."

Cadee Brystal

CHAPTER EIGHT

Nearly two weeks later, Allison reflected on the new normal in her life and marveled at how comfortable she had become. She and Hope were ensconced in the home of the kindly Mrs. Holmes. They were living in a large room on the second floor of the house, and had settled into the routine of going to Shelby's around nine in the morning to visit and help out. They would return to Mrs. Holmes' around three each day. Allison had begun repainting the hall and rooms in the upper level of the house. In the evenings, Allison would spend time with Hope and help prepare the evening meal. The three would dine together.

Allison had been surprised the first evening when they were all seated at the kitchen table and Mrs. Holmes had reached over and grasped her hand. Allison had instinctively tried to flinch away, before realizing that the woman had extended her other hand toward Hope as well. The child had eagerly clasped onto the skinny wrinkled hand and beamed up into the face of the old woman. Hope had turned to Allison and reached out, "Come on, Mamma. We're like a family now." Allison's sinuses had begun to tingle and tears sprang to her eyes, as she took her daughter's hand in her own.

Even though she hadn't been one to believe in the unseen entity that some people worshiped, she had spent enough time with Shelby over the years to recognized when a person was about to pray. Respectfully, she closed her eyes and dropped her head. As Mrs. Holmes began to give thanks for the meal and for God's influence in bringing Allison and Hope to her home, Allison felt a strange sensation. It was a warming. It was a lifting. It was confusing.

When Allison and Hope had returned from the Wheeler's that first Wednesday afternoon, Allison had begun preparations to paint in the upstairs hallway only to be stopped by Mrs. Holmes. "My dear, why don't you just rest this afternoon? You will barely get started before it will be time to head out to the church," she had said.

"Oh," Allison had stalled. "I ... um ... I don't do church."

Those silver gray eyes of the landlady perused Allison. "Well," she said after a moment, "It can't hurt to try something new. And it might help."

Allison was aware that everyone she knew in Miller's Bend would be attending the activities at the church that evening. "There's no one to watch Hope," she said. "I'll have to stay home."

"Nonsense!" the older woman replied. "There are ample activities and classes for the children, even the ones as young as Hope. She'll have a great time. And she will benefit from the lessons about our Lord."

Allison acquiesced. After all, there would be nothing lost in attending worship with the others. What would it hurt to go to church, just this once?

It wasn't until a few days later that Allison understood that it wouldn't be "just this once". That she would be called upon to attend church services and activities with Mrs. Holmes regularly. Apparently, in their haste to get Allison and

Hope set up with economical lodging, everyone had neglected to inform her of the house rules. Mrs. Holmes had a history of taking in young people whom she deemed to be "in need". "In need" of what, hadn't been made clear. Neither had the rules.

"Oh dear," Mrs. Holmes had said. "Didn't we go over the rules?"

"Rules?" Allison had echoed in bewilderment.

A quick run-through by Mrs. Holmes revealed that pets were acceptable; overnight male guests were not acceptable; drugs were not acceptable; alcohol was not acceptable. The same was true for swearing and "raucous" music. "And you and I will go to church together every Sunday morning and you will accompany me to Bible study or services Wednesday evenings," Mrs. Holmes had concluded.

In an adolescent streak of rebellion, Allison had argued weakly, "What about the renter downstairs? She didn't go with us Wednesday night."

Mrs. Holmes gently touched Allison on the hand before saying quietly, "The reason she hasn't made it to church with us is because she works at the restaurant and hasn't been able to get scheduled off for Sunday mornings or Wednesday evenings." The older woman added kindly, "It's best to have one's own house in order, before concerning ourselves with what other people are or are not doing."

Mrs. Holmes' had been right of course. There was a classroom for preschool aged children and Hope had been delighted to meet some children her own age. They had left her in the hands of two young women who would oversee the kids while trying to teach them lessons about God and stories from the Bible.

Allison followed Mrs. Holmes into the sanctuary where, a few rows ahead, she spotted Shelby nestled between Riley and his parents. His right arm wrapped lightly around her shoulder, his body rotated toward hers. Their heads dipped close together in conversation. Allison felt a sweet yearning as she noted the way her friend leaned into Riley's embrace. Shelby had the kind of love and support that Allison had desired for so long.

A masculine voice rumbled quietly near Allison's left ear, "It's nice, isn't it?" She knew without turning that the speaker was Andrew, and that he was seeing the same emotional setting she was seeing. She looked away from the woman sheltered and protected by the man who loved her, and her gaze landed on Andrew's face. Surprise swept through her as she recognized a longing in the dark eyes that watched his brother. "They're lucky," he said before touching his hand lightly to her back to nudge Allison into motion again.

They caught up with Mrs. Holmes in a few strides, and she latched onto Andrew's elbow. He quietly escorted them to the pew of Mrs. Holmes' choosing before Andrew handed first Allison and then the older lady into the pew. Allison found herself seated comfortably between Mrs. Holmes and Matt, with Tyler seated beyond him. She smiled and whispered a quick, "Hi" before the pastor began the short service. Glancing around, she found that Andrew had taken spot beside Riley. A fleeting thought had her wishing she was seated with them.

As the brief lesson concluded, Allison marveled at how comfortable she had been attending the informal mid-week service. She hadn't felt pressured and had felt emotionally safe seated between Matt and Mrs. Holmes. She'd opened her mind and listened as the middle aged, gray headed pastor had casually delivered a message that seemed applicable to many young people. Allison's scientific instincts had her examining and reexamining the points he had made.

She didn't realize that Mrs. Holmes had risen and moved out of the pew until Matt nudged her. "We can go to the fellowship hall now," he said in a low voice. "Or if you want to, you can sit in on one of the adult study groups." He watched her idly as he waited for her response.

She glanced around, trying to take a cue from the people she knew. "What's everybody usually do?" she finally asked. "I'm new to this."

"Everybody?" Matt asked as his eyes tracked her line of vision to Andrew who was visiting with the pastor just outside of the sanctuary. All the others had quickly moved out of the sanctuary in preparation for the various study groups, leaving Allison alone with Matt. "I've been going to a class for singles. You are welcome to sit in as a guest if you want to," he continued.

A faint blush tinted her cheeks and she shifted her focus to her hands that were clasping the pew ahead of her. "Thanks, but I don't think so."

"Why not? You'd be welcome," Matt declared quietly.

"I don't think I'm like a normal single. I have a three-year-old and a past," she explained as she raised her chin stubbornly and captured his gaze.

"Hey," he said as he laid a gentle hand on her shoulder. "Everybody has a past. It doesn't define us." She nodded but didn't comment. "And Hope is a blessing to everyone who knows her. You shouldn't be ashamed that you have her."

Allison's head snapped up and she glared at the tall man beside her. "I am not ashamed!" she clarified. "It's just that normal singles don't have to deal with the things I do. It takes a lot of energy and time and money to care for a child alone. Your old interests just aren't important anymore. Everything you have is focused on your child," she explained.

"Whoa! I'm sorry. I guess I didn't say that right," he apologized as he leaned back. "I didn't mean to insult you. I'm just trying to understand."

"Trying to understand what?" Andrew's voice broke in from the pew behind them.

Allison startled because she had thought they were alone and hadn't heard anyone approaching. Matt didn't show any signs of surprise as he stood. "Nothing," he directed his comment to Andrew. Then turning his attention back to Allison, he said, "I'm sorry if I upset you. My class is about to start. You're welcome to join us." He waited a second for her answer, although he could see in her expression that she would turn him down.

"Thanks, but I'll pass ..." When he started to move away, she stopped him, saying, "Matt. I'd ..." her words trailed away as she wondered what to say. "I'd be willing to listen and discuss what you are trying to understand, if you want to sometime," she finally said quietly.

He caught her gaze and nodded. "Thanks. I think I'd like that," he replied. Then he turned and began striding away.

Moments earlier, Andrew had been visiting with the pastor when he realized Allison had stayed inside the sanctuary and he'd started back inside to see if she was alright. Curiosity had gotten the best of him when he recognized Matt seated beside her and, although there was a chance he'd be interrupting a private conversation, he was pulled to return to her.

Allison was still gazing after Matt's retreating form with an expression of confused concentration, as though she was trying to solve a riddle. Andrew rose from the pew where he had alighted. "Did I interrupt something? What was that all about?" he asked mildly.

She raised her face, and the colors cast by the last rays of evening sunshine flowing through the stained glass windows played across her features. So beautiful. The fleeting thought disturbed Andrew and the realization that followed shook him: it hadn't been curiosity that had led him to Allison, but a flare of jealousy – he wanted to be the one that the lovely raven-haired woman sat alone with. He wanted to be the person she spoke to in hushed tones.

"I'm not certain," she said absently before recovering. "He asked me to join the singles Bible study class and I declined." Moving into the aisle, she looked quizzically to Andrew, "Don't you go to a class now, too," she asked.

He shook his head. "Normally I would, but the class I attend just finished up a series and we won't start a new group of lessons for a couple of weeks. I'll join the others in the fellowship hall until Rori gets out of her class," he explained. They proceeded slowly down the aisle and Allison somehow felt Andrew's touch even before he placed his hand lightly at her back.

She liked the sensation of being guided by Andrew. Her instincts urged her to slow her steps; to encourage him to let his hand linger; to stay close to the man who escorted her now. But her mind clamored, reminding her to recall her mistakes of the past. She couldn't afford to let another man fool her. Stopping abruptly and shifting to one side, Allison broke the contact and turned to face Andrew. She was about to tell him to stay away from her – to never touch her again, but a soothing feeling washed through her as her eyes swept over the man before her.

Other than the fight they'd had in Shelby's kitchen, she'd seen him as a kind and gentle person, always ready to give of himself to help others. Everything Shelby had ever told her reinforced that Andrew was a nice guy – a good man. That was part of the problem the day they faced off in the kitchen. From what Allison had known about him and her own brief meetings with him, she wouldn't have expected that behavior – not in a million years.

If Brody had done something like that, it wouldn't have surprised her, Allison thought with amazement. She'd seen him being belligerent, and even down right obnoxious to both people he knew and strangers, such as wait staff at restaurants. Forcing her mind back to the time she'd spent with Brody she tried to recall whether he had ever put his own needs behind someone else's. The answer had her frowning.

Andrew's rich chocolate-colored eyes had been assessing Allison as her mind raced through the comparison between the two men. He let his hand fall away from the contact he'd had at her back when she'd stopped suddenly. She'd worn the look of determination as she had pivoted to face him, but the determination wavered. Certain that she was working through some internal puzzle, he waited, hoping she wasn't going to lash out as she had in Shelby's kitchen. Of course, Andrew recalled, he had pushed her that day. He had tried to evict the woman from someone else's home, he remembered sadly. And he had accused her of … well, awful behavior. Since getting to know her better, and praying about it, he realized how wrong he had been.

Concentrating on reading the woman with whom he stood alone, he decided to take the risk of reaching out to her again. "Is something wrong?" he asked in the low, almost whispered voice that made Allison want to move closer to Andrew.

Opening her mouth to deny it, she remembered that they were in the House of God – a god she didn't want to acknowledge, but one Andrew clearly had a strong belief in – and wouldn't it be wrong to tell a lie here? She also had to admit to herself, that she wasn't given to fibbing or dodging issues no matter what the venue. Straightening her spine she declared, "It was uncomfortable for me ... I mean, I don't think it's proper for you to be touching me under the circumstances."

He regarded Allison solemnly for a moment before the corner of his mouth lifted slightly, "And what exactly are the circumstances, under which I cannot touch you?" he asked with a note of teasing in his voice.

"I'm serious," she declared as she smiled back at Andrew. "I don't want –"

"I got that. You don't want me to touch you," he interrupted. "But I know you think scientifically, so when you specify 'under the circumstances' I'm pretty sure that you have them well defined in your mind. It's only fair that you share the details with me, so that I can comply with your wishes," he concluded. The smile was back in his voice, she noted. Was he teasing her?

"You are audacious."

"I'm a lot of things," he replied with a smile. "But the ones you need to be concerned with are that I'm honest and sincere. If you don't want me to touch you, then I won't."

The surge of victory she felt was quelled by a sweeping disappointment. Perhaps he read something in her expression. Perhaps he was just feeling playful, but it thrilled Allison when he leaned close to her ear and his breath tickled her delicate skin. "If you ever change your mind, just give me the sign," he whispered. She shivered in response and nodded obediently.

Then shaking her head negatively she asked shakily, "What sign?"

His eyes danced with merriment as he stepped back, "You'll figure it out."

He started for the doorway again only to be stopped by Allison's voice. It wasn't her normal voice, but had a timid childlike quality to it.

"Can I ask you something?"

He sensed that they were done playing around and this would be serious. "You can ask me anything," he replied as he returned to the spot where she stood. She looked scared, or maybe overwhelmed, and he yearned to embrace her – to help steady her spirit. But she'd set the rules and he'd abide by her wishes, so he slid his hands into his pockets as he faced her and waited.

CHAPTER NINE

"Why do you – all of you – spend so much time at church?" Allison's eyes were wide with wonder and sincere curiosity.

"So much time?" he parroted. "Just Sunday morning and Wednesday evening. That's not so much time." Andrew regarded her carefully as the truth began to filter through his mind. Carefully he asked, "You don't normally attend church." But it wasn't really a question and he could tell by her body language that he had guessed right.

Allison realized that Andrew had assumed she was a Christian, and his disappointment in discovering she wasn't a believer was all too visible. She didn't like that it mattered to her what he thought. *I've gotten along all my life without your approval,* she thought rebelliously.

"I'm only here because of Mrs. Holmes' rules," she replied in a flare defiance.

Andrew had been about to say something that surely would have pushed her away from him, and possibly further away from God, but he stopped himself. His personal disappointment meant nothing in the scope of things. He'd been given the opportunity to help open the eyes of a non-believer and he was going to make the most of the chance.

He pulled up a smile and looked again at the woman before him. Like a stranded swimmer, she silently pleaded for a lifeline. Whether she realized it or not she was asking him for a reason to come to God. He looked around, silently wishing for an older, wiser member of the Christian family to handle this – he desperately wanted Allison to accept God's love and welcome Him into her life, and into Hope's life.

"So, you want to know why we spend time in God's House?" he began slowly. "Well, Sunday morning is fellowship, the service – where we receive the message, and attend Sunday school classes. And Wednesday evenings, we share a meal and have a short service, like we did tonight, and the kids have classes. Some of the adult classes meet, too." He paused and looked to Allison. He hadn't answered her question at all, he realized. She needed the "why".

Her brows furrowed. "But … Why not just come to the service Sunday and then go your way?"

"Let's sit," he said as he gestured toward a pew they were near. She nodded and slid into a seat. He settled near the end and turned to face Allison. He closed his eyes for a second as he asked the Lord to guide his words. When he opened them, she was studying him.

"When you were a student at college," he began slowly, "did you attend your classes?"

"Of course."

"Did you also study outside of class?"

She nodded affirmatively. Andrew watched her long black tresses slide forward over her shoulders as she leaned toward him.

"Were there study groups available for your disciplines?" he continued.

"Yes."

"And you signed up for the sessions didn't you?"

"Yes. But what's that got to do with church?" she asked impatiently.

"It's very similar if you consider it for a minute," he spoke quietly. "Think of the Sunday service as the class. If you only attended your biology classes at the university, you would gain some of the knowledge – maybe a great deal of knowledge, wouldn't you?"

The waves of black hair rippled as Allison shook her head in denial. "That's not enough," she said. "You only get a superficial understanding in the classroom. You need the labs to experience the theories that are lectured about. Without the hands-on experience, it just doesn't … click."

Andrew smiled widely, "Now apply that to faith. You can hear the teachings on Sunday morning, but you need more in-depth study and discussion to really apply what you've heard."

"Okay," she said slowly. "That's a start. Nice analogy, by the way."

"Thanks," he smiled as he let out a sigh.

"But what about all the fellowship? How does that help?" she countered.

Again, Andrew silently requested guidance in his conversation with Allison. "Being together with others who also believe in the Lord God as our Savior, it strengthens our own beliefs," he said with a strange awkwardness. "Does that make any sense?" His brows furrowed as he reviewed the words in his mind. "I guess it's a little like the saying 'the family that plays together, stays together'," he added. "The more things you do together as a group, the stronger the group is. But the individuals also become stronger … in the case of religion, they become stronger in their faith."

"But if you only fraternize with like-minded people, don't you close yourself off from discussion of other options and ideas?" she asked earnestly.

"In today's world, there's no way to be isolated from other points of view," he answered without thinking. "It's inevitable that people will question your beliefs and try to tell you that living for your own wants and needs is more rewarding than living God's plan for you."

"How do you know God has a plan for you?"

"Faith."

"Faith?"

"Allison. God has a plan for everyone," he said as he began to reach out to her. He pulled his hand back and let it drop to his thigh. Allison's eyes followed the movement.

She wished for a second that he would go ahead and touch her, but he apparently was a man of his word and he wouldn't until she gave him the sign. Whatever that was. "Not me. He doesn't even know I'm here," she lamented softly.

"Yes. He does and He wants you to come to Him and ask Him into your life," Andrew's voice took on a pleading quality. "If you don't …"

She latched onto his words. "You think He wants me? I had …" she swallowed hard and started again. "I've made bad decisions. I doubt that he wants me. He probably doesn't even remember that I exist."

"Don't kid yourself, Allison. He knows and He's trying to help you find your way to Him and the Kingdom of God. It's written in the Bible, that five sparrows would be sold for two pennies, and not one of them is forgotten before God. That means every creature, even one as insignificant as a sparrow, is on His radar," he explained. Andrew's focus bored into Allison's eyes as he continued, "You and Hope are infinitely more significant than any sparrow. He's offering you a chance to come into His Household. All you have to do is turn to Him and ask for His love and forgiveness. And offer Him your love and obedience in return."

A calm quietness reigned for several moments as Allison digested the words Andrew had spoken. Silently, in her mind, she refuted parts of what he'd said. She didn't want to argue with Andrew, and she could tell that he believed deeply the message he was trying to deliver to her, but she had questions and doubts. Finally, she remembered that she wasn't completely satisfied with the answer to her original question.

"What about the time commitment?" she asked abruptly. "I don't like the idea of having to be here all of Sunday morning and Wednesday evening, too."

"Do you like sports?"

"What's that got to do with anything?" she asked warily.

"Do you?"

She nodded.

"Did you play on a team in high school?"

"Basketball and volleyball," she confirmed with a nod.

"Did you have to tryout to make the team?"

She shook her head. "It was a small school and they needed all the bodies they could get to fill the squad."

"Were there kids who just showed up? Or was everyone dedicated to the team?"

She recalled how upset she would be with those who didn't care about the game. "Oh, yeah. There were kids who were there just so they didn't have to go home or have jobs," she said. "They didn't really help out at all."

"Can you relate that scenario to the idea of 'God's Team'?" he asked. "There are people – Christians who think just being 'on the team' is good enough. They just show up for the Sunday service or just drop their kids off for Sunday school, but don't invest themselves in their beliefs."

He continued, "I'm not judging them. Maybe that works. But I believe - and so do my family members and closest friends - that we need to make a bigger investment in our faith. We don't want to just be 'on the team'; we want to be 'in the game'."

The vehemence in his declaration startled Allison. She stared as he turned away from her, as though he needed to shield himself after being so open to her. He clasped the end of the pew and rose, but before he could step away, she stopped him. "Andrew?"

"Yes?" he answered but didn't look her way.

"Andrew." She waited for him to turn and focus on her before she continued, "Thank you for … for sharing that with me."

He nodded, stepped into the aisle and waited for her to precede him as they left the sanctuary in silence.

CHAPTER TEN

The little river that curved endlessly through the valley widened out and gently poured fresh flowing waters into the picturesque lake. "Is Lake Ketchum a Native American name?" Allison asked as she looked to Andrew. "Sounds like a sportsman's paradise."

They had fishing lines in the tranquil water and their bobbers rested lazily on the water's surface. Andrew didn't respond to her comment as he watched the steaks sizzling on the grill. Children's laughter soothed Allison's nerves and the sounds of the birds nearby offered relaxing background noise. "It's nice here. Thank you for inviting us," she said quietly as she began pulling drinks and dishes of foods from the cooler.

She had been uncertain when Andrew and Rori appeared at Mrs. Holmes' door after work. The two shared a conspiratorial look as Andrew handed a folded piece of paper to Allison without a word. Her hand had shaken slightly as she opened it to see the words printed in youthful handwriting:

The pleasure of your presence is requested Friday evening beginning at 5:20 p.m. and continuing until dusk, or such time as deemed necessary to return to your abode. You and the guest of your choosing will be treated to an exquisite dinner, serene atmosphere and tantalizing company, should you choose to accept. (over)

Allison glanced at the clock – 5:18 p.m. She looked to Rori who had been watching expectantly. "Turn it over," the preteen whispered with urgency. Allison's gaze shifted to Andrew's which held amusement and contained excitement – he seemed as eager to learn her answer as his daughter did.

Allison flipped the invitation over and on the back it read: This message will self-destruct in 10 seconds.

She looked at the man before her. He simply raised his eyebrows and waited for her answer. She looked at the girl, who bounced excitedly. "We have to get going. And you only have five seconds left until that thing self-destructs," Rori reminded as she glanced at the piece of paper Allison still clutched.

"Okay," Allison said decisively as she dropped the paper to the table. "Just let me go get Hope," she said as she passed into the next room. When she'd returned with Hope, the invitation was gone. The four arrived a short time later at the tranquil picnic area on the little lake.

The low rumble of Andrew's voice broke through Allison's thoughts. "How do you like your steak?" he asked. A little shiver went through her as she turned and caught a strange expression on his face. He'd been watching her and she hadn't even realized it. The thought reminded her that when she'd first come to Miller's Bend, she'd been sure someone had been watching her – following her, but she hadn't felt the sensation since moving into Mrs. Holmes place. She frowned wondering how she could have forgotten to be careful. "It's not that hard of a question," Andrew prompted. "How do you want your steak done?"

"It doesn't matter," she said dismissively. Her mind was on the perceived threat and the fact that she had become less vigilant.

"Of course it matters," the deep voice spoke from beside her now. "What are you thinking on so hard?" he asked as he reached out as if to touch her cheek.

She turned to face him again. His gaze was intense and she felt herself being pulled toward him. Neither moved, but she felt … lost, but safe; crazy, but calm; and although she was still alone, she felt supported. She was reminded that since moving to Miller's Bend she had developed friendships with people who really cared about her.

A question hung between them and Allison struggled to focus on it and answer. What had she been thinking on so hard? "Ghosts. I guess it was old ghosts," she finally sighed. The flames on the grill flared and Andrew jerked his attention to the steaks.

"I guess we'll both have well done steaks," he laughed as he flipped the meat. He added wieners to the cooking surface so the kids could have hotdogs. Allison quietly finished prepping the table and called the kids.

As the four sat around the picnic table, and clasped hands to offer thanks, Allison was struck by the feeling of family. *Oh Lord, is this what it's like to have a loving man to share your life with?* Her skin was warmed where she held a child's hand in each of her own. Tears pooled in her eyes as she kept her head bowed and listened to his words.

"Heavenly Father. Thank you for the bountiful gifts you have given us and for the food we are about to receive. Thank you for this beautiful spot that you have created in nature for our enjoyment. And especially, thank you for the tantalizing company that we share this evening," he paused. "And please help each of us find healing in the old wounds we may have. Amen."

A chorus of "Amens" combined melodically. Allison kept her head down a moment longer as she tried to compose herself. She wasn't aware of anyone praying for her before, but she was certain that Andrew's final comment had been directed to her and her ghosts. He was watching her intently when she opened her eyes and looked up. He leaned slightly toward her and whispered, "Your burned steak is getting cold."

After they'd eaten, Andrew assigned Rori the task of repacking their supplies into the cooler. The request was met with an exasperated sigh and a whiny "Why me?"

"Because we all chip in and help," he had replied with a smile. "But if you would rather check the fishing lines, you and Hope could do that instead."

Rori hugged him quickly. "Thanks, Dad. That's a way better job," she yelled as she dashed toward the water's edge. The preschooler zigzagged behind her, leaving a trail in the sand.

Allison started to follow but Andrew stopped her with words spoken in a low voice. "She'll be fine. Just keep an eye on them," he said with quiet confidence. "The water's still cold, she won't wade into it and we are right here. I can be there in a few seconds if need be."

It was an alien feeling for Allison – the idea that she wasn't solely responsible for Hope's health and well-being. "You're sure?" she asked skeptically.

His gaze met her's. "I'm sure," he confirmed. "But, it'll make you feel better if you keep a close watch," he indicated the girls at the shoreline with a lift of his chin. "I've got this if you want to join them."

She watched the girls for a moment longer before giving a delayed response. "No. I trust you," she said. "If you think it's alright, then it is."

He laughed, realizing how deeply he appreciated her easy acceptance of his statement. In short order, they had placed everything back in the vehicle and Andrew had made sure the fire was completely extinguished. He appeared beside Allison with a blanket which he dropped onto her shoulders without touching her. She remembered that he'd promised to wait for a signal from her and she wondered again what that signal would be if she decided that she wanted his touch.

"Thanks," she said with sincerity. "Do you think the kids are getting chilled?"

"Not likely," he replied as he settled next to her on the bench of the scarred picnic table. He seemed to be examining the varied markings as though they held the secret to some great mystery.

"How's Shelby doing?" he asked at length. "I haven't seen them since Wednesday. They seemed happy ..."

When he didn't finish, Allison brought her gaze to his. He was agitated and in need of reassurance. She nodded. "They're fine, Andrew. Shelby's anxious to have the babies. She's tired of being pregnant – it's been really hard on her body. And the bed rest is hard on her spirit. But, once Riley comes home, she's like a whole new – tired – person," she said in response to what she believed the underlying question to be.

"You're sure? They're solid again?" he asked. "I mean as a couple."

Nodding, and with a twinge of envy inspired by the devotion shared by the pair, she replied, "Oh, yeah. Rock solid." Then she saw once more the deep sadness in Andrew's expression. "You helped them out. They are both thankful to you for pointing out …" She saw uncertainty flash through his eyes and stopped talking as she considered his point of view.

"It's just … I could have made things worse. You know, planting the idea in a person's mind that their spouse is looking elsewhere can be a dangerous thing," he cradled his head in the palm of on hand as he dropped his other fist to the table. "My actions could have opened a chasm between them and ripped their marriage apart."

"But it didn't," she spoke confidently. "They both knew that you had their best interests at heart. They know with absolute certainty that you were only concerned with their relationship."

The sincerity with which she spoke helped reassure him, and he let the topic drop since he didn't wish to dwell on it further. "We should call the girls in and head back," he said as he raised his head to locate the children.

"They're over by the rocks," she offered. "But wait. Before you call them, can I ask you a question?"

Reluctantly he faced Allison again. The sun was setting, and the warm glow behind her combined with the light reflected off the water to play games with his mind. She seemed to shimmer before him as though she might fade and disappear. The notion was whimsical and he wasn't given to whimsy. He frowned as he answered her reluctantly, "Sure."

"Would you be willing to tell me why you were so accusatory toward me?" she asked timidly. "Why would you assume something so nasty, when you didn't know me that well?"

"You know," he replied with exasperation. "I apologized – more than once – for that. Can't we just leave it alone? Please."

Sad green eyes blinked tightly before she turned away. "Okay. I was just trying to understand," she said quietly.

He couldn't stand the dejected attitude she projected. Knowing her life wasn't easy, he didn't want to add strain or stress for Allison. But he really didn't want to go into details about his life with Lucy either. The evening had been very pleasant and he didn't want that to change. But Allison deserved some sort of explanation. With a heavy sigh, he offered a vague response, "It wasn't really you." The vulnerability was back in her eyes as she waited, expecting a more complete explanation. "I know it doesn't make sense, but, unfortunately, I'm afraid it was a reaction to my experiences with my former wife," he added, hoping that would be adequate. He didn't want thoughts of Lucy and their relationship infringing on the evening.

Her expression was sad and curious, but she didn't respond. Merely shrugging, she started folding up the blanket that had been wrapped around her shoulders. It dampened her spirits to think that Andrew still didn't trust her enough to share more with her. She moved to the SUV and dropped the blanket inside. When she turned to call out to the children, Andrew hadn't followed but watched her intently.

"She was … unfaithful," he choked out. "I didn't realize it … at least, not for a long time." He wasn't looking at her any longer, though he faced Allison. "I couldn't stand the thought that Riley could be forced to go through the pain of a failing marriage." Anguish twisted in his eyes for a moment when he pulled his gaze to her face, but he quickly recovered and closed off the evidence of emotions.

Disbelief strangled the words that had been forming on Allison's tongue. What kind of woman would betray this man? Her heart demanded the answer, but her mind stopped the words from breaking free. He was clearly distressed and digging into his personal wounds would serve no purpose. Instead, she stepped closer to him – probably too close – and whispered, "Oh, Andrew. I'm so sorry."

CHAPTER ELEVEN

When the promised yard clean-up day rolled around the following Saturday, the project included a variety of tasks completed by Riley, Andrew, Matt and Tyler, with assistance from Allison and Lauren. Allison felt clumsy and awkward when she was near Andrew. She had tried to visit with him about the mundane, but he was silent and seemed to want to be left alone.

She felt better when working with Matt or Tyler, either of whom seemed happy to have the help and the conversation. She worked hard, while keeping an eye on Lauren. Allison didn't understand why, but the woman seemed uneasy. Matt seemed to be keeping an eye on the shapely redhead too, but Allison was certain it was for entirely different reasons.

She recalled the shy looks he would cast in the waitress' direction the night that he had taken Allison out for dessert so Shelby and Riley could talk. Had that really been only a few weeks ago? So much had happened since then. She considered how reserved Matt was, and how he had been content to let Lauren think he was on a date that night. It was clear that Matt and Lauren had an interest in each other, but neither was admitting to it. Inspiration hit and before she thought out the implications, she bumped into Matt with a shoulder as they raked side by side.

"Why don't you go over there and help Lauren with cleaning up in that flower bed?" she prompted.

"Nah," he answered with a shrug as his blond curly hair danced in a light breeze.

"Fine."

Allison marched over to where Lauren and Tyler worked together in the perennial flower bed. From Andrew's vantage point on a ladder, he couldn't hear the exchange, but he had sure taken notice when the raven-haired woman had pushed between the two and sent Lauren rather unceremoniously toward Matt.

Andrew's hands stalled from their job clearing debris and leaves from the gutters. He watched when Allison laughed at something Tyler said as she joined in the work in the planting area. She seemed at home in the yard and glowed under the late spring sun. Suddenly, he longed to be down there working beside Allison instead of isolated on the ladder. She'd tried talking with him, but he'd brushed her off and now he had what he'd wanted – to be alone with his thoughts – but he still wasn't happy.

He remembered the peaceful outing that he and Allison and their daughters had enjoyed together at the lake. It had felt great – being together like that, he reflected. Everything had gone well until he got in too deep … shared too much.

He'd been embarrassed after their open conversations that evening. He regretted sharing with her that Lucy had cheated; he regretted having let his emotions be seen. He had an additional regret as well. He had asked his friend, Mason Alexander, to investigate the woman before he had confronted her at Riley's home. When he'd returned home from the lake that night, there was a call from Mason, saying they needed to talk about the results of the investigation.

If there was one thing Andrew was certain of, it was that Allison would be furious with him. But he knew that he had to tell her the truth. She had a right to know what Mason had discovered. Telling her might drive her away from Andrew. But his greater fear was that it might drive her from Miller's Bend all together. And it would be his fault.

He scowled as he looked again to the area where Allison worked. She was bent low, working around some perennial plants, and a strip of nearly white skin was exposed where her shirt had slid up, away from her waistband. Have mercy! A low growl of frustration emanated from his throat as Andrew drove his hands back into the rain gutter. He flung moldy, wet, fermenting chunks of barely distinguishable gunk down to the ground below with an unnecessary violence.

Allison and Hope had been attending Sunday services with Mrs. Holmes regularly, and if a person counted the Wednesday evening church activities as well, the total time spent in worship was pushing Allison to more church in the past few weeks than she had attended in the past several years. She was feeling rebellious again, especially since Lauren seemed to be immune to the church attendance rule.

Allison didn't feel like going out this morning. She didn't feel like obeying. She didn't feel like hearing more about a God she hadn't begun to know until recently and, this morning, she didn't want to know. *He's never been there for me. Why should I be at church for Him?* "Hey, Baby Girl," Allison called to Hope, "Want to stay home this morning and watch cartoons."

Hope, who had put on her festive yellow sundress and matching hat looked curiously at her mother. "Toons, Mamma?"

"Yep. Let's watch cartoons, okay?" Allison promoted the idea. "We could eat popcorn too, if you want!"

Confusion shown in Hope's face, "But, we go to church first?"

"Nope," Allison said shaking her head in denial. Then she leaned down so her face was even with her daughter's and in a conspiratorial whisper she said, "We'll skip church."

Hope grew very serious for a moment. Then perkily replied, "I want to go to church, Mamma."

"Why?" The question was out of Allison's mouth before she could catch herself. She really didn't want to go and wished that Hope would have sided with her. The realization that she was trying to use a three-year-old to reinforce her own actions clarified in her mind, and for a second, Allison felt shamed.

"Because it feels good," Hope answered earnestly. She then added cheerfully, "I have friends there, too." And she bounded away, out the bedroom door. Allison heard her daughter's footsteps thumping down the stairs.

"Well then, I guess we go to church," she replied to the reflection in the mirror.

Hours later Allison stared blankly out the passenger side window. She didn't see the houses that the car moved past. She didn't register where they were going. Her mind was replaying the Bible verse that the pastor had read, "Then little children were brought to Him that He might put His hands on them and pray, but the disciples rebuked them. But Jesus said, 'Let the little children come to Me, and do not forbid them; for of such is the kingdom of heaven.'"

Allison had nearly choked when the pastor had read that passage during the service. The very morning that she had tried to keep her own child away from church had to be the same morning the pastor spoke about interfering with children's religious exposure, education and opportunities. He had followed with more examples and finally with an additional Bible passage saying, "Whoever causes one of these little ones who believe in Me to sin, it would be better for him if a millstone were hung around his neck, and he were drowned in the depth of the sea."

Allison was only beginning to learn about God and religion. Her friendships with Shelby, and later with Ashley, had been her only exposure over the years. Shelby hadn't hidden her own religion, nor had she apologized for her beliefs. But she hadn't forced her views on Allison either – a fact for which, until this morning, Allison had been glad.

Until she moved in with Mrs. Holmes, Allison had been confident in her belief that she created her own destiny that everything was exactly as it appeared here on Earth, and there was nothing beyond that. No Heaven. No Hell. No consequences.

The time spent in church, counseling with the pastor, socializing with Andrew and with Mrs. Holmes had sparked a change in Allison, in her heart, and in her mind. And now she had opened a mental door, allowing herself to question her belief in non-belief. *What about Hope? What if I'm wrong?* Allison wasn't just risking her own soul, her own eternity … she was risking Hope's as well. She weighed two options in her mind: believe in nothing and risk damnation or believe in God and risk … what was the risk in believing? Salvation?

She closed her eyes tightly. A moment ticked by as she repeated the thought in her mind. She thought of Mrs. Holmes, of Shelby and Riley, and their friends who clearly embraced the Christian faith. They all seemed to have an element in their lives that she was beginning to think she may be missing. Was the element faith in God? Allison didn't know. She was confused. Drifting and alone – well, alone with Hope – until arriving in Miller's Bend, she now was beginning to feel like she belonged when she was with these people.

Is God making a difference in my life? What if ...? She inhaled deeply, and as she felt the vehicle come to a stop, she whispered quietly and earnestly, "Please, God, help me find my way to you. For Hope."

With her face still turned away from Mrs. Holmes she opened her eyes, expecting to be in front of the Victorian house. Instead, her focus pulled to the muscular man who had just closed the car door behind a preteen girl who stood beside him. He placed a hand on her shoulder and began to steer her toward the entrance to the restaurant. When he noticed Allison peering out of the car window, he hesitated and then waved in greeting before continuing on his way. Andrew.

"That's Rori!" Hope shouted from the back seat. "That's Rori! She's my friend!" Hope was pulling at the straps of her car seat. "Mamma … Mamma! I get out."

Shaken, Allison didn't respond immediately. It was Mrs. Holmes who addressed the child, "Take it easy, honey. We'll get out in a minute." Allison could feel the older woman's gaze on her, but didn't turn her head. She closed her eyes again and breathed. *Breathe in. Breathe out. Repeat.* It had been her mantra. When life goes crazy, when things get nuts, just breathe.

When Allison finally opened her eyes and looked to Mrs. Holmes, she saw concern, understanding and more. "Are you okay, child?" she asked tenderly.

Allison nodded. "Why are we here?"

"At the restaurant?"

Allison nodded again.

"For lunch, dear."

"Oh." Allison answered numbly. She climbed out and opened the door to the back seat. "Hey Baby Girl," she said cheerily. "Want to get some lunch?"

Hope shook her head vigorously. "I see Rori," she said as she pointed toward the door of the restaurant.

Allison worked to unlatch the belts that held Hope securely in place. "How about mac-n-cheese? Or maybe chicken strips? You like those ..."

"I like Rori," Hope replied as she smiled broadly.

"I know, honey," Allison conceded. "She's here with her family. But, you can go over to their table and say 'Hi' to her. Okay?"

The odd trio proceeded in silence to the interior of the bustling restaurant. The waitresses were rushing to seat patrons, take orders and deliver food to the tables where customers waited. As they waited to be seated, Hope pulled away from her mother and trotted to the table where she had spotted Rori.

Allison caught up to her just before she reached her destination. They were too close to pretend she hadn't seen the family seated there. She swung Hope up onto her hip and greeted Andrew with a smile, "Good morning. I'm sorry for interrupting, but Hope wanted to come over and see Rori."

Hope wriggled in Allison's embrace like a worm on a hook. She was impatient and she wanted to get down! She reached her chubby arms toward Rori and leaned as if willing herself to be transported into the older girl's lap. Andrew stood and relieved Allison of the squirming child. "Good morning, Big Girl. How are you today?" he asked as he looked into her face.

The motion stopped and Hope blessed Andrew with a full smile. She touched a hand to his cheek and replied, "I want Rori."

"Okay. I get it," he said with a laugh. "I'm not good enough for you, huh?" He handed her gently onto his daughter who had appeared by his side. He pulled two dollars out of his pocket and gave them to Rori, "Why don't you take her and see what's good in the vending machines?"

"Sure thing, Dad." And the two disappeared before Allison could intervene.

Andrew noted the stern look in Allison's eye. "I'm sorry. I hope that was okay?"

"I don't let her have candy much," Allison replied in a tone she hoped sounded neutral. She was intently aware that Andrew's parents were watching the scene. Mrs. Holmes had caught up, too.

"She won't get candy," he assured her. "More likely temporary tattoos or bouncy balls. But I can go call them back if you want me to."

"No, it'll be fine," Allison replied she distractedly tracked the children's progress to the lobby area of the restaurant.

With a sweep of her hand, Mrs. Wheeler, indicated two empty chairs. "Won't you join us?" she offered.

"Why, yes, thank you," Mrs. Holmes replied. And before Allison had fully processed the words, the wisp of a woman had planted herself in one of the open chairs. The one farther from Andrew.

Allison shook her head. A few weeks ago, the last place she would have wanted to be was in a busy restaurant with

Hope exposed to prying eyes. Today, however, it seemed like a wonderful opportunity to enjoy fellowship with some of the people she was getting to know, beginning to feel close to. Feeling thankful that Hope had led them to the Wheeler's table, Allison was still concerned whether Andrew was sharing the feeling.

While she and Andrew had engaged in several close, candid conversations, he had made it clear that he wanted to be left alone yesterday while the group worked in the yard. And while he was warm and caring toward Hope, he seemed cool to Allison.

Andrew cleared his throat and relief blossomed in Allison as she heard his words, "Allison? You remember my parents?"

Her eyes locked on his and for a second, she thought she read amusement there. The old Allison would have been concerned that Andrew was enjoying her discomfort. But, then his expression warmed, and she felt a sense of security. He was genuine and welcoming as he continued the introductions. "My mom, Beth. And my father, Lawrence." Then to them, he explained "This is ..." he paused as if he'd been about to interject a description but decided against it. A half second later he concluded with, "Allison. And the little cherub with Rori is Hope, Allison's daughter."

Lawrence had risen and extended a hand in greeting, "Of course we've met. Glad you can join us, Allison."

She took his hand and returned the greeting. Then looking to Beth she said, "Nice to see you again, too."

Andrew had been caught off guard when Hope and her mother had rushed up to the table where he and his family were seated. He wondered why she would approach him after the way he had dismissed her yesterday while everyone was working to prepare Mrs. Holmes' yard for summer. He was well aware that he had been moody and distant yesterday, and he hadn't yet figured out how he was going to tell her what Mason had learned. He would have to talk with her alone. Soon.

That conversation would have to wait. He was no longer worried about the woman who was so deeply embedded in the lives of Shelby and Riley. With the new information, he was now more concerned about Allison herself. He pulled out the vacant chair and helped slide it forward as she took her seat.

The waitress approached to take their orders just as Andrew was settling back into his own spot. "Hi, ya' all. What can I get for you today," the redheaded waitress asked cheerily.

CHAPTER TWELVE

The meal was served and conversation floated around the table. Andrew's every instinct was to grill Allison to find out more about her, but instead he listened intently to the women's friendly conversation, and actually learned more than he expected.

She was 25, and had grown up without her parents. She had lived with an aunt in the same little town that Shelby lived near. They attended the same school ... something that starts with a "B", but he didn't catch it. She hadn't really stayed in touch with the aunt after graduating from high school. She'd majored in biology and had stayed in Brookings to work in a campus laboratory until state budget cuts had eliminated the position.

She viewed the situation of Shelby being prescribed bed rest and herself being out of work at the same time as coincidence. Andrew wondered if it was more – maybe God was at work in this. Or maybe it was the devil at work, he thought wryly. When he and Mason had gone over Mason's report, Andrew had felt a sense of dread – as though something very bad was going to happen, but he couldn't figure out what.

He was going to have to talk to Allison. "Why don't you and Hope come over to our house this afternoon?" he said before he even realized that he'd intended to. Surprised by his words, Andrew waited for her response.

Allison's gaze cut to Andrew's face and the buzz of conversation stopped abruptly. "I'm sorry? I don't think I heard you right?" she said quietly.

Hope was suddenly bouncing on Rori's lap as she chanted "Yeah! Yeah! Yeah!" Rori was looking at Andrew with a bewildered expression that was very similar to the one Allison was still directing toward him.

"Well ..." he drew the word out as his mind raced for a reason. "Hope ... Hope hasn't seen Rori for a while and I thought it would be nice for them to play." Rori's demeanor told him that was the lamest thing she'd ever heard. Allison was better schooled at withholding her thoughts, but he saw confusion and hesitation there.

"The two of you can ride with us from the restaurant and then I'll take you home whenever you are ready," he continued, even as he tried to understand why he was doing this.

Allison had been lulled into a sense of comfort as they had sat in the restaurant, dining and chatting in the way she knew some families would on a Sunday afternoon. She had actually begun to enjoy it. She'd dropped her guard and now she swallowed hard as she considered what motivation Andrew could possibly have for trying to get her over to his place.

She had made it her practice to stay away from men ever since Brody. She didn't need them. She didn't trust them. If she rode over with him, she'd be stranded there. She would be vulnerable. She dropped her gaze as she prepared to turn him down, but her eyes rested on Hope. Poor Hope. She was so

excited at the prospect of spending time with another child –
even a near-teen child. "Ah, Baby Girl, I know you want ..."

"Peeze, Mamma!" Hope pleaded. "Peeze, I wanna play."

Andrew held his breath. He wasn't going to push Allison,
but he hoped she would decide to accept his invitation. And
he hoped she wouldn't.

"Would it help if you have a car, dear?" Mrs. Holmes
said quietly. "Perhaps if you drive yourself ..."

"Oh, of course!" Andrew's mother broke in. "We could
give MaryAnn a lift and you could take her car."

Allison looked unconvinced. "We wouldn't be
imposing?" she asked to no one in particular.

"Well, I guess that could work," Mrs. Holmes answered,
more to Beth than to Allison.

"It's settled then," Beth stated authoritatively. "Andrew
and Rori will lead you and Hope to their place. Lawrence and
I will get MaryAnn home eventually." She smiled to the older
woman, "You don't feel like a shopping trip, do you?"

And that is how it happened. That's how Andrew ended
up escorting a quietly reflective Allison, a mildly brooding
Rori and an obliviously exuberant Hope to the front door of
his home a few minutes later, after a short drive from the
restaurant. Allison kept glancing back toward Mrs. Holmes'
older Cadillac as though she longed to be seated behind the
wheel, speeding away from this place. Speeding away from
him.

Once inside the home, Andrew closed the door behind
them and moved through the living room with Allison
following numbly. "It's turned out to be pretty warm today,"
Andrew said as led the trio of ladies. "Maybe we should sit
outside and enjoy the sunshine." The last part was addressed
primarily to Allison, which was good because he realized

when he glanced behind him that the girls had immediately headed for the steps leading to the second story.

"We're going to bring the Barbies down here and watch a movie while we play," Rori yelled back over her shoulder.

"Sounds like a plan," he replied. A smile touched his lips briefly before he turned his attention back to Allison. "So, yes?"

She blinked. "Sorry, what did you ask?" He was moving again, toward the kitchen.

"Do you want to sit outside?"

Allison strode silently to the window that overlooked the back yard. It was enclosed in privacy fencing. They couldn't be seen from the street. The sun shown warmly in spots around the yard and mature elm and linden trees cast other areas into shade. "You have a nice home," she offered. "You locked the front door?"

"No, but I can if it makes you more comfortable," he replied as he assessed the woman before him. "Actually, I don't usually lock it when we are home. But I would have guessed you would feel ... confined ... if I had thrown the bolt."

"I'd appreciate it. I mean locking the door," she said. Then she rushed on in nervous explanation, "If we are going to be outside, I wouldn't want Hope to slip out the front."

"No problem," he replied quietly. He wanted to ask Allison why she was so scared, what made her behave this way? But instead he said, "I'll just go lock it and tell the girls to be sure they don't open it." He disappeared through the doorway leading into the living room.

When he'd left the room, she expelled a huge breath. The deep rumble of his voice soothed Allison from the other room as he explained to the girls to stay inside. He hadn't questioned her, although he had watched her intently and with speculation. He was an interesting person.

Allison remembered the first time she'd met him, when Shelby had been hurt and Riley raced to Brookings to take her home. Andrew, who had accompanied him, had been the calm, rational balance to Riley's frantic reactions. Andrew had invited her and Hope out for ice cream so Shelby and Riley could talk. At the time, she had the impression that Andrew was a sweet man. He was good with Hope, but she knew now that he'd had years of experience with Rori. He'd been kind to Allison and attentive to both of them.

She contrasted that image of him with the one she'd faced down in Shelby's kitchen a few weeks ago. A brute. The man had been bullheaded and obnoxious. He was bossy, self-righteous and infuriating. She didn't realize that she'd been scowling until Andrew stepped back into the kitchen. "What's the matter?" he asked. He stepped toward her and she automatically avoided him by backing away.

"Nothing," she replied, shaking her head.

"You're safe with me. You must know by now that I'm not going to hurt you," he said.

She settled into a kitchen chair, dropping her bag onto an adjacent chair. Tracing a pattern in the wood grain, she spoke, barely above a whisper. "I thought … It was so nice when we've talked," she began slowly. "I was starting to think we could be friends. You helped me with some of my questions about church and faith." She looked up into his expectant face, seeing eagerness and hopefulness gave her the courage to continue. "You shared with me your pain about the past … at the lake that night."

The muffled voices of the children in the room filtered through. There were high pitched fake voices for the Barbies, kid-powered car noises and the sounds of a popular movie. It all worked together to rattle Allison's nerves. She'd longed for a family for so many years, she began to wonder if she was interjecting herself into Andrew's family in some sort of tormented attempt to form a family. She stood suddenly as the notion flared in her mind.

"None of that should make you think that I would harm you," he said in rising concern. "I've enjoyed our discussions, too," his eyes swept her form before flickering toward the door leading to the living room. "Rori and I really enjoy having Hope around, too."

"But you did hurt me with your indifference yesterday," she retorted as she raised her chin and glared at him. There was a challenge in her glorious green eyes – a challenge to deny her statement.

It was then that he stepped close to her. Dangerously close. He filled her senses and she found herself wishing that Andrew would take her in his arms and help her feel loved and safe. In the past she had dreamed of having a strong, caring partner – someone she could lean on or support, someone she could love or be loved by, someone she could pamper or be pampered by. Since Brody's death it had been a nameless, faceless abstract figure. In this moment it was Andrew. It was all Andrew.

He wouldn't reach for her though. He wouldn't embrace her. She knew instinctively that he was a man of his word. And he had pledged that he wouldn't touch her until she gave him a signal.

"I was hoping that I hadn't," he whispered from his position inches from her. "I hope you can understand that the closeness we shared that evening … scared me a little." He'd had his eyes focused on her face as he'd begun speaking, but had let them drop while he tried to explain. The rich brown eyes had slowly followed the contours of her cheeks, trailed down her neck and continued the journey. He liked what he'd seen as he let his eyes wander over her curvaceous form, but when he realized what he'd done, embarrassment welled up within him and he turned away.

He breathed deeply as he regained his focus. "I'd never told anyone outside of my family what happened with … my marriage," he said quietly. "I needed some distance and time to think things through. I'm sorry if that confused you or hurt you."

Mesmerized by the man, she had followed when he turned away. Now standing there, listening to his quiet explanation, she felt a confusing mix of emotions. Her mind warned her to protect herself, urging her to walk away. Her heart told her to reach out to him and offer support, kindness and understanding. Before she realized it, her hand was on his back, stroking gently to try to sooth his stress away.

She thought she felt a slight tremor in the muscles beneath her fingertips before the man leaned into her touch. Nothing was said for a moment, until he turned slowly to face her. The contact between them remained, but her hand slid around his shoulder as he pivoted and then down his well-muscled arm. When she would have let her hand drop away from him, he caught it in his own. His eyes searched hers intently. "Do you know what you are doing?" he rasped out.

She was caught – like a moth that flies toward the light of the candle, but then suddenly finds itself too close to the flame. At once lulled into feeling the security of the light, and panicked at feeling the pain of the searing flames dancing around.

Without blinking or flinching, she met his gaze for what seemed like an eternity. Emotions, fears, disappointments and spirit-deep cravings passed between them silently. Finally, she let her eyes drift slowly closed like some ethereal beauty. The faintest of sighs slipped past her lips as she slowly began to shake her head. "I've no idea," she whispered.

Then she let her eyes travel the length of his form. Neither spoke as she took in his neatly combed short haircut, clean shaven face, broad shoulders, and muscular torso. She swallowed, but her eyes continued their travels ... narrow hips, strong thighs encased in dress pants ... when she got to his casual shoes, she made her gaze follow the design in the floor covering over to the cupboard and up to the sink. Then back out the window into the yard. There was no way she could look him in the eye after that perusal. Her cheeks burned with embarrassment as she waited to see what would happen next.

If Andrew had been shaken by the closeness the two had shared Friday evening, the past few minutes had been the equivalent of the walls of Jericho tumbling down. For two years he had slammed the gates closed, believing he could protect his heart, as the citizens of Jericho had believed the walls around the city protected them. He hadn't realized the effect that Allison's presence was having, but apparently she'd silently been circling, like the soldiers in the Bible story. Not with a shout, but with a whisper at just the right moment, she'd sent the walls around his heart crashing into nothingness. He was totally defenseless.

"I'm not sure I know either," he said solemnly. He assessed her silently as she had turned to face Andrew once again. Leaning back against the counter, she crossed her arms protectively across her torso. Finally, he nodded as though conceding some internal battle.

"So we'd best go outside," he suggested. "What would you like to drink?"

"Water's fine."

"You're sure? I have fruit juice pouches in several flavors, soda pop, milk, coffee, tea. Nothing alcoholic though – I won't have the stuff in the house ..." his voice trailed off.

"No. Thank you. Water will be fine," she reiterated. Before heading out the door to the back yard, Allison peeked into the living room to see Hope and Rori sitting on the floor. They played with a half dozen Barbies – doll clothes were sorted into neat piles, cars were parked side by side under the coffee table, the movie played in the background, and the girls were laughing. It really was good for Hope to spend time with another child.

A pang of regret clenched at Allison's heart. If things had been different, maybe they would have a family now – a husband, another child. Maybe she would have finally had the thing she'd longed for in her own childhood: a stable, loving family. She hated thinking about "what could have been." To distract herself from the morose thoughts and lighten the mood, she took a stab at humor. "Do you routinely lure women to your home?"

He chuckled as he filled two glasses with cold water. "Oh, yeah," he joked, "A different woman every night."

Allison accepted one of the glasses of water that Andrew held. He ushered her through the back door and closed it. They walked in silence toward a seating area in the sun. She supposed later that it had been nervousness that prompted her to make the sad attempt at levity, but even she was surprised when the words slipped past her lips. "So ... a different woman every night, huh? And no alcohol in the house. Sounds like you have some pretty serious addiction issues," she had said with a laugh. Andrew had stopped short and she knew in a heartbeat that she'd made a mistake.

An old pain chased across his features, followed by enduring sadness as memories surged to the forefront in his mind. He shook his head as though in denial, as he responded, "Not mine. Lucy's."

"Lucy?" In a half-second she recognized the name and realized she had accidentally conjured memories of his wife. "Oh, Andrew … I'm sorry. I was only joking around," she said softly. "I didn't mean to …"

He didn't respond. Thoughts and memories swirled and battled for prominence in his mind as his rich brown eyes avoided the woman beside him. He wanted to think about the present and the future – he longed to move forward. Maybe with Allison and with Hope. If only he could repair the damage done from his mistakes.

His silence elevated Allison's nervous prattling, he realized as he began to focus on her words. When she uttered the statement that he must have loved Lucy very deeply, the words snapped him back to the here and now. "Allison. Stop," he demanded.

The abruptness of the command and the harsh quality in his voice made her freeze. Eyes wide, like an admonished child, she watched him and waited.

"I …" Andrew's mind blanked as he sought the words to explain his relationship with Lucy. "This sounds awful. So awful that I hate to say it, but … we didn't love each other. Ever. We'd been friends for a long time, but we never were in love. I married Lucy to protect Rori."

Allison didn't respond although he could read the confusion in her eyes. Questions – maybe dozens of them – danced through her agile mind. But she waited for him to tell her what he needed to. She just continued to watch and listen. Andrew hoped, prayed, that she would listen with her heart, not just her analytical mind. He liked her presence in his life, in Miller's Bend. He hoped she would stay after Riley and Shelby's babies were born.

"Lucy ... had ... problems before we married," his voice had lost any trace of personal inflection or emotion. He didn't meet Allison's gaze, but looked beyond her, past her shoulder. Allison didn't know what he might be seeing behind her, but she was certain his focus was locked on something in the past. "I probably shouldn't have married her, but I thought it was the only way I could help Rori."

"That's sad," Allison spoke quietly.

"Yeah," he agreed as he pulled his focus back to Allison.

"You know what?" she said. "That's kind of noble – trying to protect Rori. But it's also kind of twisted."

"I'm not going to explain the whole thing now," he said in a businesslike manner. "I just don't want you thinking I'm pining over the loss of some great life-long love. It wasn't like that. I did what I had to for Rori. I guess I expected some loyalty and respect from Lucy in return and she stabbed me in the back."

"So you say," Allison spoke quietly. "I'm no expert on love, but I think you must have loved her on some level in order to feel as bitter as you do over the betrayal. She's got you more than a little messed up."

Andrew set his glass on the table as defensive instincts scrabbled to the forefront. "You think I'm messed up?" He started walking. Allison fell into step beside him.

"It wasn't an insult. Just an observation."

He snorted and kept walking. Allison focused on the landscaped pond ahead. It was beautiful. There were rocks and plants all around the small, shallow pond and some of the early bloomers were showing color in the buds. Soon it would be a spectacular sight.

"Look," she said as she laid a hand on Andrew's forearm, to get his attention. "Everyone has a past. We have to deal with it and then we break free from it." He didn't look at her. He couldn't risk exposing his insecurities, his demons. "If we don't," she continued earnestly, "then we are stuck wallowing in our history and we don't get to live our present and we deny ourselves positive futures."

"I'm not wallowing," he said defensively. "I just don't want to risk making the same mistakes again."

"That's understandable," she said as she raised her gaze to his. "Just don't assume that everyone is like Lucy."

She turned and started toward the next feature in the yard. He followed her in silence for a few strides. The instinct to defend himself rose up and boiled out in a hissed statement. "I don't assume everyone is like her."

Allison stopped abruptly and turned to wait for Andrew. He had caught up and nearly collided with her.

"You said to me 'I don't need to know you – I know your kind.' Were you not assuming that I am like Lucy?" she asked without emotion.

"I was worried about my brother."

"And assumed that I would behave in the same way you think Lucy would," she stated.

"Maybe," he finally admitted. Agitation radiated from Andrew – Allison could feel it coming off him in waves. She stepped back. Her foot lodged unexpectedly on a rock, throwing her off-balance. Before she realized that she was in danger of falling, Andrew had reached out and pulled her upright again. She was certain from the look in his eyes and the way his hands lingered on her arms that he wanted to pull her close and hold her. That's what she wanted, too. But before she could figure out what the signal was, he had released her.

"Thanks," she said as she rubbed the spots on her arms where he had clasped strong hands around her to steady her. "I'm sorry. I didn't mean to upset you," she said quietly.

Cadee Brystal

CHAPTER THIRTEEN

Allison and Andrew let the emotional analysis drop. Both were relieved to move the conversation to more mundane topics as they strolled around the yard. Allison marveled at the landscaping and special hidden features in the yard. "Did you do all this work yourself? It's magnificent!" she exclaimed. She was examining a planting area that spotlighted shade-loving plants which were just beginning to thrive in the early spring warmth.

"Thank you. I'm glad you like it," Andrew answered. "I wish I could say I did the work myself, but I had it hired."

"Who did the work?" she asked even though she would never be in need of a landscaper, at least not in the foreseeable future. "It's distinctive. Don't you think?"

"I do. He does excellent work," Andrew pulled his attention from a bird feeding station back to Allison. Her expression was relaxed and she seemed to be truly enjoying herself. "You appreciate gardening? Do you do any yourself?"

The sunshine danced on Allison's raven hair, she had closed her eyes and raised her face to the collect the sun's rays. A smile touched her lips before she replied. "I love being outdoors. And yes, I love to work in the garden. It was where I always felt welcome growing up." Her posture let her long hair cascade back and exposed her neck. The second he realized that he wanted to hold her close and bury his hands in her hair, he turned away. He felt the blush rushing up his neck to his cheeks.

The muffled rustling of retreating footsteps in the grass caused Allison to open her eyes to find that Andrew was near the table where they had set their drinks. She followed slowly. When she neared the table, she backtracked in the conversation. "You never said who did the work?"

"Hmm?" Andrew stalled as he looked up from his drink. He'd been thinking about the image Allison presented moments before. He'd been thinking that a woman really ought to be aware what an image like that can do to a man. He'd been thinking that she'd looked like a piece of artwork – a masterpiece molded, or maybe painted, by a skilled artist's hands. The thought had brought Matt to mind. Matt was a local artist working to make a name for himself and Andrew thought a rendition of the scene he had just taken in would go a long way toward making Matt famous. He thought about how well Matt and Allison seemed to get along when he'd seen them together. And that thought irritated him even more.

Andrew shook his head to clear the thoughts of Allison posing for Matt, while he crafted an image of her. He grimaced, "What did you say?" Trying to focus elsewhere, he took a drink of water.

Confusion flickered in her eyes, "I asked who did your yard work. You said you hired it."

"Oh, yeah. It was Tyler Schuster," he replied absently.

"Tyler's a landscaper?" she seemed amazed. "I didn't know that," she said before pausing. Glancing around the yard again at the various features, she began to smile. "Do you have his number?"

"You live in an apartment," he said without addressing her question. He didn't want her posing for Matt or calling Tyler.

"So?" she replied with genuine innocence. "What's that got to do with anything?"

"Clearly you don't need a landscaper for your one-room apartment." Annoyance crept into his voice and she picked upon it.

Placing her hands on her narrow hips, she glared at the man seated before her. "Why are you so … analytical about everything?" she huffed. "All I did was ask for his number."

"Why do you need a landscaper?" he persisted. He rose to face her again, not realizing that he had taken an aggressive stance.

"I don't need a landscaper, Andrew," she said stepping closer and standing taller. "I need a job!"

A job. Of course she would need a job. Andrew's mind raced. "What about Shelby? I thought you were dedicated to being her assistant?"

"She's going to have those babies any day now," she replied. "Then she won't need me around." She dropped her head as she turned a quarter turn. Birds flitted around. Robins hopped along the edge of the empty flower bed reserved for annual plants that would bloom later. It had yet to be planted for the season, making it a perfect hunting ground for the worm-eating harbingers of spring. "Besides, my savings are dwindling. I need to get back to work."

"You are a biologist," Andrew pointed out.

"You think there's a lot of call for biologists in Miller's Bend?" she said with a sigh. "If I'm staying here, I'll have to take what I can get."

"No ...," Andrew countered as he beat down a strange sensation. Why had he been alarmed at the "If I'm staying here" part of her statement? He chose to ignore that question. "You should never settle for taking what you can get." After a long pause, he offered a suggestion, "You know, the cheese plant is at the edge of town and there are three ethanol plants within an hour's drive. Wouldn't those be businesses that would have positions for biologists?"

"I've applied at the cheese plant. And at the closest of the ethanol plants, but there's nothing open right now," she shared. "They'll keep my application on file," Allison said as she looked to Andrew with bright eyes and a false smile. "In the mean time I need to find something else."

"You could work for me," he declared, even as he tried to understand the things that were coming out of his mouth. "Yeah. I need some extra help at the office," he sounded like he was justifying the idea to himself. "It would be flexible hours ..."

Allison had that look again – the one that said "You're nuts." Disbelief and wariness were evident as she regarded him before replying, "I don't think that's the best option. But thanks for trying." She waited a minute longer before continuing. "Maybe you could just give me Tyler's phone number?"

Andrew had to concede, if only to himself, that the suggestion had been born of desperation. "Sure." With a sigh, he began scrolling through his contact list ... Schuster, Tyler ... He read the number to Allison, who entered it into her cell.

"Thanks."

Allison looked toward the house. "We should probably be going ..." she said, although she really didn't want to go.

She felt … not comfortable, but something else … sheltered, maybe.

"Not yet," Andrew responded as he stepped forward as if to reach out to her. "I mean … there is something I have to tell you."

Allison's spine stiffened and it was clear to Andrew that she'd taken his request as an order. He reacted quickly to counter her assumption. "Please stay a little longer," he said quietly as his focus locked on her rich, emerald eyes. "There's something I need to tell you. It may help you in sheltering Hope," he finally added as the clincher to sway her to stay.

"What about Hope?" she demanded as her demeanor changed. Fear and desperation simmered within the beautiful woman. She pivoted as she glanced all around the yard. This time she wasn't looking at the landscaping though. She was looking out – beyond the top line of the fence – scanning the area for something out of place. Searching for some perceived threat.

Andrew noted the behavior and mentally logged it as confirmation that she was aware that someone had been watching or researching her and Hope. And the worst part of that thought was that she knew she was being monitored. "What are you looking for?"

Her attention snapped back to the man who had questioned her. Her mind raced. *He's not your friend. He's not your ally. He's nothing to you and you are nothing to him.* Each silently assessed the other for a moment. Allison longed for someone with whom she could share her unspoken fear, someone who could tell her she was being unreasonable, someone who could help fortify her own strength, someone who could protect her and Hope from an undefined threat that she sensed. But more important than her wants, was her most primitive need to protect her child: she needed to get Hope to safety. She needed to flee Miller's Bend. And she needed whatever information Andrew had.

He watched as her uneasiness grew, building and churning with in her like a summer storm cresting the distant hills. Her trepidation grew into a jumpy, reactive kind of fear. Narrowing his eyes, he asked, "Who's after you, Allison? Who are you hiding from?" Her anxiety quickly morphed into fear and defiance. A split second later, she bolted for the back door of the house.

Andrew's powerful strides had him to the back entrance of the house before Allison reached for the door knob. He stood facing the frantic woman, with his back to the door, and waited. "You have to let me in," she yelled as her attempts to push him out of the way ended in futility. She couldn't move him – he was solid. Solid like a statue. In frustration Allison fisted her hands and swung them forward toward the muscled wall of man that stood between her and her precious daughter. Andrew had seen or sensed her move and had captured her wrists in his hands before they made contact with his torso. He gently manacled her in an attempt to deflect the assault without hurting the woman he held.

Allison struggled and thrashed, trying to get free of Andrew's hold until the words he whispered broke through her panic. He spoke quietly, rather than yelling. It was a soothing cadence, and it was words she'd longed for all her life. "It's alright, Allison … I want to help you … It'll be okay … We'll take care of this … Let me help …"

Slowly the fight went out of her and Allison found herself looking up into the deepest, richest, most enthralling set of brown eyes she had ever seen. She registered a myriad of emotions swirling there in their depths before he looked away from her and gently pushed her body back, away from his own. When he refocused on Allison's face, his eyes were neutral and his demeanor was business-like. Allison reached for the door knob again. Again, he stopped her.

Keeping eye contacted, she turned the door knob and said, "I need to see Hope. I have to check on her and be sure she's okay."

His hand closed over Allison's as he shook his head in denial. "You'll scare her if you go bursting in there. Let's both step into the kitchen, you can make some popcorn for the girls and I'll go talk to them for a minute. When the popcorn is done, you can bring it into the living room. That'll give you time to calm down."

Considering his words, Allison realized that Andrew was right. He had done her a great favor by intervening when she had attempted to dash to her daughter. She nodded slowly and dropped her gaze. Studying the cracks in the concrete step, she admitted quietly, "That's a … reasonable plan."

"Okay. Ready?" concern sounded in his voice. "Allison. Look at me …" When she raised her eyes to his, he added with quiet confidence. "She's fine. They are playing. Just like when we came outside. I promise."

Allison had a measure of difficulty in accepting his words, but something about his quiet confidence spread into her consciousness, soothing her. Inhaling deeply, she answered, "Okay."

Stepping inside the home, Allison could hear the TV and the sweet sounds of two girls laughing. Andrew was right. Hope was fine. After checking on the kids and providing them with the snack, Allison and Andrew returned to the kitchen to talk.

With the two seated along adjoining edges of the kitchen table, Andrew cleared his throat and glanced at the clock. Not that he needed to know the time. It's just that he didn't know where to start this conversation. Knowing his words would upset her again, but resigned to what must be done, he cleared his throat again and brought his attention to Allison's face.

"I don't want to scare you and I don't want to make you mad," he began. "You remember that I was ... concerned about your intentions involving Riley's marriage?"

Allison nodded.

"Well, I did something that I'm not proud of ..." he said before his gaze skittered away from her. Noting her rising anxiety, he forged ahead, "And I'm sorry that I did it. Except that's how we found out ... And I think it's important. So I guess it's good that I did it, because otherwise we wouldn't know ..."

Allison's brows furrowed as she tried to follow Andrew's monolog. A sense of foreboding swept through her, "What is it Andrew? What did you do?"

"I hope you won't hold it against me, but I ..." he stopped speaking and swallowed hard. His eyes locked on hers. "I'm sorry. But I had my friend, Mason Alexander, investigate you. He's a lawyer."

"You?" she whispered. "What?"

Disbelief. No more words were spoken.

The clock ticked loudly. Muffled sounds drifted from the living room.

Finally, Andrew touched Allison's hand, which jerked away reflexively.

"No."

"I'm sorry." His voice was dry and the words choked from his lips. "I didn't mean to upset you. I just had to protect Riley ..."

Tears pooled in Allison's eyes. "You really thought that poorly of me?"

"I didn't know you," he said. His voice was still rough. "There are twisted people out there; doing demented things ... I just wanted to know that ..."

"That I wasn't one of them?" she finished the sentence with indignant anger rising in her voice. "You seriously thought I would interfere in my best friend's life?" She looked at him again with a mix of hurt and animosity.

He raised an eyebrow in an unspoken question. She responded, "Well, okay. I did interfere. But it was accidental. Not on purpose." The admission broke some of the tension that had been building. "But to have me investigated? Really! Don't you think that's going a bit far?"

Chagrined, he spoke quietly, "Yes. And you don't know how sorry I am. Except ..." He paused before meeting her gaze again. "Except that's how we found out that it looks like someone is tracking you and Hope."

Allison's world stopped spinning. She couldn't breathe. She couldn't think. She couldn't stay. Blindly, she reached for her bag. "I ... We have to go."

Cadee Brystal

CHAPTER FOURTEEN

"I'm going to be moving on," Allison said sadly to Shelby a few days later. "We've ... I've overstayed my welcome." She sniffled and swiped a tear from her cheek, before looking away.

The babies had been born on Sunday and now they and Shelby were at home. Everyone was doing fine. Everyone, except Allison. Sunday had been a big day for her – she had asked God to be in her life; she had gotten to know Andrew better only to learn that he had been investigating her; she'd learned there was proof that someone actually was hunting her and Hope, and she'd gotten a job.

Oh, yeah, and her godchildren had been born. Jacob and Isabelle had been born a little early, but healthy. Everyone in the Wheeler's circle of friends had openly thanked God for seeing Shelby and the babies through the pregnancy and delivery safely.

A dozen times since Sunday, Allison had started to pack up her belongings. Ready to run. And then words would come to her - words of encouragement from Shelby or Riley, or from Andrew or Mrs. Holmes. Even Tyler had told her a story about how much easier life is when you share your burdens with people who love you. He had concluded by saying that Christ has directed his followers to bear one another's burdens, and so "we are all in this together."

Shelby grasped her friend's hand and squeezed. "You could never overstay your welcome, and you know it," she said earnestly. "We love having you in Miller's Bend and you're making friends. You've got a new job. And Hope is happy." Her eyes searched Allison's face. "You should stay."

"They are your friends, Shelby. Not mine. And the job is working in a greenhouse and doing light landscaping ..." Without conviction, she continued, "I should go ..."

"Where?"

"Ashley ..."

"Ashley is on assignment somewhere and no one knows when she'll be back," Shelby said narrowing her eyes on her friend. "You can't outrun this. You need to stand and face it."

"We don't know who it is! We don't know what it's about!" Allison countered. Baby Isabelle stirred. "Sorry ..." she whispered as she glanced at the baby.

"Andrew's got Mason monitoring you and whoever has been tracking you," Shelby reminded her friend in a soft low voice. "They are looking out for you."

"I know. But ... I'm so scared," she replied. Allison's features were drawn and she looked exhausted as she paced to the window and back to stand before her friend. "The only thing in the world that matters to me is Hope. What if something happens to me so I can't take care of her? What if something happens to her?" Despair and concern dominated the woman. "I don't know where to turn!"

Shelby raised her brows as she looked at her friend. "Don't you? Really?"

Allison stilled and her eyes searched Shelby's face as her brows drew down in confusion. "The police?"

"No," she paused. "Here, take Isabelle, so I can get up," she said extending the child in her arms to Allison. "Thanks."

Allison tenderly cradled the baby as she moved to the bassinets that had been placed side by side in the living room. Jacob slept soundly in his, but Isabelle preferred to be held as she slept. Allison silently thanked God again for the healthy babies her friend had delivered. And as she placed the baby into her bassinet, Allison felt a warmth sweep through her.

Shelby had scooted to the edge of the chair and pushed herself into a standing position. The effects of the pregnancy, combined with lack of exercise during the period of bed rest had left her weak and out of shape.

Focusing on her friend, Shelby knew she needed to help Allison see the bigger picture. Picking up the conversational thread they had suspended, Shelby said, "You talked to the police already, right?"

Allison nodded. "They can't do anything because no one has threatened me," she said. Shelby knew that. Andrew and Mason had persuaded Allison to go to the police, even though all they had for proof was the paper trail showing that she was being monitored. Riley had gone with them to see the Chief of Police, Jeff Schuster – Tyler's father.

Shelby took a deep breath. She was about to cross into new territory with her friend. *Father, help me steer her to your help.* "Allison. You know that I'm Christian? And you've seen God's hand in my life?"

Allison's reflex a few months ago would have been to sigh, roll her eyes and lead the conversation elsewhere. But today she simply nodded as she listened to her friend.

"I've never tried to bring you into religion. Or religion to you," Shelby said quietly. "I should have. But I didn't want to risks losing your friendship over it. And I guess I sort of thought you would come around to God eventually … on your own."

"Shelby," Allison almost hummed the name as she stepped close to her friend and embraced her. They held each other for a minute before Allison continued speaking. "You could never lose me. You and Ashley have been my family for years. And Hope, of course."

"Don't forget Riley," Shelby added. She beamed at her friend, "And I suppose Andrew, too. He's part of our family!"

Allison let that comment pass as she guided Shelby into the kitchen and settled her at the table. "I'll make some tea," she said unnecessarily as she began heating water and pulling mugs from the cupboard.

Soon she was seated across the table from Shelby and each woman's hands encompassed her steaming mug of tea. Neither spoke for a moment. Then Allison sighed and sat up a little taller. "So, Shelby ... You were going to tell me what? That God can solve my problems? That bad things don't happen to Christians?"

Shelby shook her head and her golden hair swayed gently left and right. "That's not it." She looked into her friend's eyes. "It's not that having God in your life, keeps the bad things out of your life. It's that if God is in your life, then when the bad things come along, you have the means to deal with it better. You have help and guidance. You have love and support."

"But He still doesn't stop the events and traumas," Allison replied as her eyes began to fill with tears. "He didn't keep Brody alive. He didn't stop the stalker from attacking you ..." She stood and grabbed a kitchen towel to wipe her eyes. "I ... never mind."

Shelby was quickly beside her friend. "No, He didn't. You are right about that. But people have free will. We make decisions and people have to live with the consequences."

"My point exactly," Allison retorted as she crossed her arms in a display of stubbornness. "He didn't help."

"But He did help!" Shelby exclaimed. "When you lost Brody, He helped by giving you someone else to love. It was God who gave you Hope. And when I was being stalked, God made sure that Riley's path and mine crossed. God gave me Riley to watch my back. And he gave me to Riley."

"But …"

"But what?"

"But … how could God help with this? I don't know who is behind it. I don't know what they want. I just feel so vulnerable," Allison said quietly. "I feel so … lost."

"You are lost, Allison. I know you've chosen to believe in non-belief, but I'm afraid for you," Shelby squeezed her friend's arm. "And I don't just mean about your mystery tracker. I mean about your whole life. Let God guide you. Look for Him, the same way a sailor looks for the lighthouse."

"I did."

"You did, what?"

"I did look for Him. Recently."

"Oh, Allison!" Shelby squealed as she threw her arms around the friend she'd loved since they were kids. "I'm so happy … for … you." Confusion crossed her features as she tried to diagnose Allison's gloomy attitude. "What's the matter?"

Allison related the events prior to church and how the sermon tied right into her life. She told her friend about being concerned for Hope – her future and her soul. She told about asking God to help her find her way to him. And how nothing had happened since.

"What do you mean 'nothing's happened'?"

"Just that. Nothing has happened."

"Well of course something has happened! You talked with Andrew and found out that someone is tracking you ... so you know you aren't just crazy," she explained as she began to tick off the points in evidence on her fingertips. "You got a job – and a babysitter. And now, when you began doubting, God gave me the inspiration to help reinforce your decision to ask Him into your life."

"Oh, please," Allison sighed. "Part of that was just luck."

Shelby raised questioning eyebrows, "Which part?"

"Never mind. You'll just tell me it was God moving through you all. Right?"

"Right! You've got to learn to accept the gifts God sends your way," Shelby said. "And Allison?"

"Yeah?"

"Faith in God isn't like turning on a light switch. It's more of a process. A process of learning and growing – of questioning and finding answers. There's a lot to it. You'll need help," Shelby said solemnly. "You should set up some counseling sessions with the pastor." And then brightening she asked, "Do you have a Bible?"

Allison shook her head. "I'm sure Mrs. Holmes would loan one to me. I think God has her on His team," she said with a smile.

"I think she's the local team captain," Shelby agreed with a smile before she slipped from the room to check on the babies.

Left alone for a few minutes, Allison considered the steps that had gotten her to this place in her life. She also thought about each of the new friends she had made since coming to Miller's Bend. *Is God really at work in my life? If I look for the positive, will I learn to recognize the gifts from God like Shelby said?*

As she thought about her friends, Andrew's image popped into her mind. She was certain that he struggled with his own internal demons, but his faith in God was evident. Allison had wondered about his story after the confrontations at Shelby's home. He seemed to genuinely love his brother and sister-in-law, and now that he'd shared some of his history she was hungry to hear the rest.

Since spending more time with Andrew, she had found herself thinking about him and Rori more and more. She was certain that he'd faced difficulties – that was obvious when he talked about his marriage and former wife. But, it was also obvious that his faith was helping him navigate his way through his difficulties and challenges. Since she began attending with Mrs. Holmes, she had noticed Andrew during the church activities. Being in the Lord's house seemed to recharge him mentally, emotionally, and maybe even physically. It was an intriguing idea that faith in God could make life on Earth better.

Allison had let her eyes drift closed and now she silently mouthed the words, "Please God, help me stay on the path to you. For Hope." She heard footsteps approaching and quickly opened her eyes again to find Shelby entering the kitchen.

"Here you go," Shelby announced cheerily. "You can have this one," she continued as she laid a book into Allison's hands. "Don't start at the beginning though," she advised. "The Psalms are easier reading."

Allison lowered her gaze to the book that rested in her hands. The Bible. She couldn't stop from tearing up again as she raised her eyes to Shelby's. *I just asked for help and you drop a Bible into my hand. Thank you, God.*

Cadee Brystal

CHAPTER FIFTEEN

During the ride home after church the following Sunday, with her eyes closed, Allison was digesting the morning message. She leaned her head back against the headrest in the passenger seat of the Cadillac as she noted a rising sense of déjà vu as she recalled a similar ride a few Sundays ago. The car stopped. "Mrs. Holmes? When I open my eyes, will I see a restaurant?" she asked cautiously.

"Well, I can't rightly say what you'll see. But I'm not seeing any restaurants," the old woman replied in a lighthearted tone. A delighted giggle from the back seat piqued Allison's curiosity and she peeked through the narrow slit of her left eye. No restaurant in sight. In fact, it looked as though they had pulled up beside the city park. "Hope and I thought it would be an opportune time for a family picnic. Didn't we, dear?" she asked the precious child who was strapped into her safety seat in the back.

"We picnic, Mamma!" she exclaimed in response as she clapped her hands excitedly.

Allison unbuckled and got out of the car to release her daughter. As she worked to unhook the straps, she said, "You little trickster! You and Mrs. Holmes are keeping secrets from me!"

"I sorry, Mamma," Hope said as Allison pushed the straps aside and pulled her daughter to her chest.

"It's okay, sweetie. I was teasing you. A picnic is a great idea!" The two giggled as Allison backed up and straightened. She turned to address Mrs. Holmes who she was certain had come around the car to the passenger side, but instead found herself face to face with Andrew.

The sun shown in his hair and he smiled at Hope as he reached for her. "How's my Big Girl?"

"Fine as frog's hair!" she chimed as she smiled back. Hope reached for Andrew and Allison passed her willingly to him. The hand-off was reminiscent of each weekday morning for the past few weeks. Since she'd begun her new job landscaping with Tyler, Allison would stop at Andrew's house and leave Hope with him and Rori. The school term had ended and the arrangement gave Rori a meaningful way to spend her time and earn some money, and benefited Hope and Allison, too.

After Andrew left for his office, Rori would babysit Hope during the day. Andrew and Allison staggered their lunch breaks and each would go to his home for their noon meal, giving Rori a break from the responsibility for a while. After work the adults would visit briefly, or some days the four would enjoy supper together before Allison would take Hope back to Mrs. Holmes' for the evening. The process had been working very well except … Well, it was starting to feel too comfortable.

After Shelby had convinced Allison to stay in Miller's Bend, she had sought Andrew, and together they had worked through her distress over his actions in employing Mason to investigate her. They focused instead on trying to figure out who was looking for her and Hope. They hadn't come up with any leads. They had however reached the point where they acknowledged growing feelings for each other. And Allison had discovered that the day when they spoke in the yard, when she had laid a hand to his back to sooth Andrew, she had opened the door to casual touches between them. However, she had often found herself wishing for more – more contact, more care, more support …

Hope was squirming to be released from Andrew's secure hold, "Where is Rori?" She asked the question as she leaned to the right to see past his head. "Where – Rori!" He turned and set Hope down, releasing her to run to Rori, who waited for her by the swing set.

Turning back to Allison, he noted that she was frowning slightly. "What's the matter? Has something happened?" concern laced his voice as he stepped forward and touched her arm lightly.

"No. Nothing," she said absently as her gaze followed the progress as her daughter hugged Rori and then the two headed to the picnic table where Mrs. Holmes had met up with Riley, Shelby, the babies, and Lauren.

"Hope is lucky to have so many people who care about her," he said reassuringly. "So are you." Andrew's voice was quiet, but it reverberated with a rich quality that drew Allison's attention back to the man beside her. As their gazes held, Allison realized that his eyes revealed emotions that Andrew hadn't been expressing for a long time - tender concern and caring. And, a deeper, more intense emotion that she was tempted to identify as love, but couldn't quite believe that could be true. As much as she wished he would fall in love with her, Allison always reminded herself that wishing for love from Brody hadn't worked, so she doubted it would work with Andrew.

Allison forced herself to continue to breathe, swallowed hard and said shakily, "Yes. Yes, we are lucky."

He slid his hand to the small of her back as he cleared his throat, "I suppose we should join the others ..." They began moving toward the picnic area. The spring season had progressed rapidly and the sun gently warmed the park and its inhabitants. Shrubs and perennial plants flowered throughout the area, birds whispered past on silent wings only to land in the trees and chatter loudly to the world, and bees buzzed as they went about their work gathering pollen and returning to the hives. "So what were you thinking that had you looking so serious back there?" Andrew asked while they walked alone.

The two stopped and with a nervous eye on the family group, she whispered, "It's Lauren ... she ... makes me uneasy." Allison shook her head mildly and swung a hand across in front of her face as though trying to shoo a pesky fly. Andrew had leaned in close to hear her words. Now she could smell his cologne, feel the strength that emanated from his character, and the heat from his body.

"Tell me more." It wasn't a question or a request. He spoke the words with such a powerful authority that Allison felt rebellion boil up from deep within. She shouldn't be ordered around by a man. Any man. This man.

"Maybe later," she countered noncommittally. The earnestness in his gaze intensified as he watched her a moment before opening his mouth to speak. Thankfully, Allison's stomach rumbled loudly, and she giggled. Placing a hand to her abdomen, she rubbed gently, "Guess it's time to feed the tiger in the tummy!" Using the phrase that she and Hope often exchanged lightened the mood and got the two moving again toward the picnic table which was laden with food.

Andrew's parents pulled up in their sedan and joined the get-together. Everyone greeted them warmly and the celebration continued. Plates were filled to overflowing with traditional picnic fair and the adults sat at two tables pulled together in the picnic shelter. Rori and Hope sat in the shade of a nearby tree. Shelby had taken only a few bites when baby Jake began to speak up, demanding his dinner, too. She put her fork down and moved to rise, but Riley stopped her with a touch. "I've got this," he said with a tender smile. "You eat." Kissing her lightly on the cheek he slipped from the bench and picked up his son. He headed for their car where bottles and fresh diapers were stashed.

"That's so sweet," Lauren said as Shelby watched Riley's retreating form and absently scooped a mouthful of potatoes onto her fork.

"More like survival," Shelby countered with a smile. "We have to work together or they'd have me run ragged."

"But it's just the way it should be ... I mean two parents raising their children together," Lauren continued. "It's a way better plan than those poor people who try to do it on their own. Wouldn't you agree?" she asked sweetly as she scanned the faces around the tables.

"Well, shared tasks are certainly easier tasks, Lauren," Mrs. Holmes addressed the young woman. "But people don't always have a choice in the matter." Her ghostly gray eyes drifted first to Allison and then to Andrew. "And in some instances, the child is in better care with one loving parent, that with two who are in discord."

Andrew had been keeping an eye on Allison. He had noted the sad longing in her expression when Riley had jumped to help with Jake. Then as Lauren had made her comments, Allison's spirits seemed to dip lower. With her gaze drifting randomly around the plate before her, she pushed food around, but ate nothing for a few moments.

Others rejoined the conversational flow, but Lauren fell quiet. Allison got up and started walking toward the parking area, unsure of where to go, but needing to get away from the group. She heard footsteps behind her, but didn't slow. Didn't look back. Why? Why would Lauren say such a thing, when she knows two single parents sat before her?

Allison stopped when she noted Riley, carrying Jake and the diaper bag headed toward her. Pasting a smile onto her face, she called, "That was fast."

Andrew caught up and stood beside her. He gently wrapped an arm around her and pulled her close as he whispered, "It's time. I need to know your story." She glanced up slowly to meet his gaze as he continued, "And you need to know mine." She froze.

Riley drew even with the pair. "Going somewhere?"

"Just stretching our legs," Andrew replied. "Would you ask Mom to keep an eye on the girls for a bit?"

"No problem. There are plenty of us to watch them," Riley answered as he moved off toward the picnic area.

Andrew nodded as he prodded Allison into motion again. After putting some distance between themselves and the group at the picnic area, he began, "Aurora was six when Lucy and I married. And, as I mentioned before, we were not ever in love." Allison nodded, but didn't speak. She raised questioning eyes to Andrew's face. Her heart cried out, "Why are you telling me this? Why did you marry her? Why?" But she remained quiet as she waited for him to continue.

He gave a cold laugh. "I know. Crazy right?" He scrubbed his hand through his hair as he waited but she didn't respond. "Lucy had dated a guy she thought she loved. Or she thought he loved her. Anyway, when she found out she was pregnant she went to his home to tell him. His wife answered the door. She was devastated." He laughed roughly, "Well, to be fair, both women were devastated."

"How awful! Poor Lucy! She must have been what? About 18? 19?" Allison asked with empathy.

"It would have helped if she'd been that old," he contradicted quietly. "She was a sophomore. I was younger and had a huge crush on her that school year. I offered to marry her when word got out about her pregnancy," he confessed somewhat shyly. Andrew seemed to drift back in time. "She was beautiful and popular. But there was more to her – she was smart and ... sweet." He almost smiled as he remembered the youthful Lucy that he had known in school.

"You must have been admired by all the high school girls," Allison spoke before she realized that she'd even formed the thought. "I can't imagine a man who could ..." Her voice dropped away as Andrew's gaze caught hers.

"You can't imagine what?" he prompted as he grasped her slender hands in his own. "A man who would take on that kind of responsibility? Love another man's child?" He searched her eyes – those bottomless pools of emerald wonder. "You don't have to imagine it Allison. We do exist you know."

Allison shook her head in denial. "You don't get it," she sighed. "Brody ... Hope's father ... he ...," she looked down. She saw Andrew's brown leather shoes, with their toes pointing east. She saw her own black flats, with their toes pointed west. Her own were positioned between his. What does it mean? Are we headed different directions? Headed toward each other? Is he the man to shelter me? It was a delightful distraction – considering their shoes – to pull her attention away from Brody and the pain of not knowing what had been in his heart when he had died.

Before she realized what was happening, Andrew had taken Allison gently into his arms and held her. He didn't speak for a moment, but rocked her in a subtle swaying motion. The breeze skimmed through the trees and twisted her hair. A shiver passed through her, which Andrew obviously felt. He began to rub her arms as though trying to warm her. "Want to walk some more? Or stay here?"

Allison was absolutely certain that she'd be content to stay in his arms for far too long. Instinctively she felt the need to distance herself. "So you offered to marry Lucy? And ..." she prompted as she stepped back and resumed strolling.

"And, she crushed me," he replied with a small sad smile. "Said I didn't know what trouble was or how to steer clear of it." He was in step with her once again.

"Ouch!" She said with exaggerated pain. "Must have been crippling?" she chided.

"Nah, I'm tough," he countered. "We did get to be better friends, though. We hung out together a lot. I visited her and Rori while they were still in the hospital. Other than Lucy, I was the first person to hold Rori," he announced with pride projecting in his voice and his stance.

"And the medical staff, of course," Allison interjected playfully.

"Well, yeah," he conceded with a sweet smile. "The doctor and nurses beat me to her, too."

"What happened?" Allison prompted. "I mean after Rori's arrival. Did you ... uh." Rattled by the direction her thoughts were taking, she let the question die on her lips and looked away. "Never mind. It's none of my business," she concluded with a shrug.

Andrew slid his hand along Allison's smooth cheek. She inhaled a quick breath and held it until his hand dropped away. "It's okay, Allison," he spoke quietly. "As you said, I need to deal with my past in order to have a future." His gaze bore into her, and Allison had the sensation of being totally exposed emotionally. "And recently I've been looking forward instead of back."

Allison swallowed hard. "I … uh." *Me, too!* "Maybe we should check on the girls?" she offered in response, hoping to return the focus to neutral ground.

He shook his head. "No need," he said with a smile. "They are in good hands." Allison glanced back again toward the shelter, but it was out of sight. They had rounded a bend in the walking path and the trees and shrubs, thick with foliage, obscured the view. She heard the happy shouts of the girls and a noise for which she was confident Riley could be blamed. He certainly enjoyed playing with children.

"It's okay," Andrew repeated quietly. "I know it's kind of frightening to think of a future. We have a lot in common. We both have been simply existing in the present." He paused, sighed and let his eyes follow the path of a robin that had taken flight from a branch a dozen yards away. He considered the fact that he was rapidly approaching 30, and had been in a holding pattern, at least personally, for the past two years. It had been too long since he'd look forward – to wanting to share his life with someone. He'd realized that Allison's words a few days earlier had been right on target. He had been stuck in the past. "And as you so kindly pointed out to me a while back, I have been wallowing in my past," he said with a smile as his gaze returned to Allison.

"I don't know what will happen. I don't know what our relationship will be, but right now, I value you as more than a friend," he said with heartfelt sincerity. "I need to share my story with you, if we are going to have a chance at something deeper. Better." He paused as his hand skimmed her cheek again, before adding, "And I hope you will share yours with me."

Allison's mind scrambled to recall the point in his story that they had left off. "Okay. So you were saying ... Rori was born and ..."

"I proposed again." He shook his head in disbelief. "We were still in high school. She turned me down again," Andrew snorted. "Said it wouldn't work."

"Wow," Allison breathed. "That's a lot of dedication." She skewered him with a skeptical glare, "Are you sure you're not her father?" She'd been joking, of course. Her attempt to try to use humor to lighten the mood had missed its mark again.

Andrew's frustration flared and blossomed as the words tore from his throat, "Of course I am her father! I've loved Rori forever. She's in my heart and I'm in hers. I've been ..." He turned away, trying to rein in his emotions. Andrew's hands fisted and forearms flex as he realized that he'd overreacted.

And then he felt it – the light gentle touch of Allison's feminine hand tenderly rubbing circles on his back, as her quietly spoken word reached his ears. "Just breathe, Andrew. Breathe in. Breathe out." She repeated the phrase over and over in time with the movements of her hand circling on his back. He wasn't really that upset, but Andrew enjoyed her efforts to calm him; his breathing slowed, and his muscles relaxed. Her other hand rested on his arm and she tugged gently as though trying to turn him to face her.

He gave in and turned toward her. Stepping closer, she cupped his face in her hands and whispered, "I'm sorry, Andrew." As she searched his face, with its hard planes concealing taught muscles, she continued, "I am sorry for my words. I know Aurora is your daughter. I know that you love her every bit as much as I love Hope. I know she is your life. And I'm sorry I hurt you."

Andrew had stilled as she spoke, and he regarded her with an intensity she hadn't seen in him before. She recalled that a few moments ago she had wanted distance from this man, and yet she had stepped forward and was now holding his whisker-rough face in her hands. *Step back.*

But she didn't step back. Instead, she moved forward and lifted herself slightly, to gently brush her lips against his. "I'm so sorry, Andrew," she repeated, just as his arms pulled around her waist. He returned the light kiss briefly, too briefly, she thought with dismay, before he slid his cheek along hers and dropped his face into the crook of her neck. His breath tickled her exposed skin as each clung to the other.

Allison held him, letting him draw whatever he needed from her. She felt herself supporting him emotionally, mentally, physically. Who knew that a man of such strength could need someone the way Andrew needed her right now? Who knew that it would make her feel so ... confident and empowered ... to be needed that way? Maybe there really was strength in giving.

"Well ... Isn't this quaint?" Sarcasm dripped from the lips of a woman who stepped from the shadows of the trees in the park. Allison felt Andrew's muscles tighten as he prepared to break the contact between them. He swiped a hand across his face before he turned to meet the intruder. His eyes held the old bitterness and disdain as his gaze skittered numbly past Allison's face to that of the approaching woman. He kept a hold of one of Allison's hands and tugged her close behind him as he faced the newcomer.

"Lucy." The solitary word was icy cold and hard as granite.

CHAPTER SIXTEEN

Allison thought her heart stopped for a second. Lucy! Suddenly, she wished she knew the rest of the story. She wished she hadn't sidelined Andrew's tale with her smart-aleck comment. But then he wouldn't have held her so. She wouldn't have had the opportunity to help strengthen him for the coming battle. And even with her lack of experience, she could tell that this would be a battle.

Andrew's body obscured Allison's view of the woman who had appeared, but by leaning ever so slightly she could see the whole package. Allison blinked not quite believing her eyes, "That's Lucy?!" she said in a loud whisper.

Andrew nodded in response and tightened his grip on her hand.

Allison watched in disbelief as the woman drew nearer. She sported dark, bold application of makeup and her over-dyed metallic white hair that stood in unattractive clumps. Allison recognized her as a clerk from the grocery store despite the fact that today's look was a drastic change from the one Lucy portrayed on the job.

Allison's focus dropped to the neckline of the too-tight tank top layered over the too-small tank top. A flash of artificially tanned belly showed. And then ... Allison's gaze dropped to the shorts that were simply ... obscene.

Tattoos appeared to slither around and down Lucy's legs as she walked, giving the impression that some living thing clung to her skin. Allison quelled a shudder as she thought of the woman before her being the guiding influence on a young girl – on Rori. Lucy's shoes were just the icing on the cake – fire engine red with platform soles and spiked heels that had to be at least six inches tall. The woman teetered precariously as she came to a stop immediately in front of Andrew.

"Andy, honey…" she purred. "You didn't come through for me. I'm so disappointed." She clicked her tongue and shook her head dejectedly. "How could you?" she whined as she peeked up through her eyelashes.

A wave of liquor-drenched breath swept around Andrew and hit Allison. Not having expected the nauseating scent, Allison pulled toward the center of Andrew's broad back, as if to shield herself.

"Oh, look," Lucy drawled in mock disappointment. "I scared your little friend."

Because Allison had her body pressed tightly against his back, Allison felt a slight tremor roll through Andrew's body. She knew adrenaline would have kicked in preparing him to fight, but he was trying to suppress that instinct. Her own instincts were urging her to flee, but she wasn't about to leave Andrew alone to face this woman. She was certain that he'd been forced to combat Lucy emotionally, verbally, and spiritually with no support numerous times in the recent past. At the very least, she would lend him moral support. Suddenly, another instinct kicked in – the instinct to ask for help. *Oh, Lord, please strengthen Andrew to deal with this woman. Please guide my words and actions so I can help him.*

Taking a deep breath, Allison released Andrew's hand and stepped fearlessly to Andrew's side. "No, you didn't," she declared.

"Didn't I?" the sarcasm was back in Lucy's voice as her hate-filled icy gaze traveled from Allison's face down her body and back up again. "You put on a brave front little girl, but you've never met up with anything like me in your nice clean life, have you?"

Allison didn't answer immediately. Her mind was consumed with comparing and contrasting the image she had created of a poor helpless young girl who had been taken advantage of and left to make a life for herself and her baby, with the woman who stood before her now. Allison had been feeling extremely sympathetic and empathetic toward the young Lucy of whom Andrew had spoken – the Lucy he had been willing to marry and take responsibility for. She tried to imagine what could have happened to turn her into the nightmare facing them here in the city park on a sunny Sunday afternoon.

"Lucy, you're drunk. Or high," Andrew said flatly. "Go home."

"I can't, sweetheart. You keep changing the locks," she replied as she stepped forward and reaching out as though she would touch Andrew. He shifted back to avoid the contact. Allison stepped between them with her back to Andrew, and found herself nose to nose with Lucy. Lucy seemed to lose interest in the man, at least temporarily. Her eyebrows rose as she assessed Allison again, "So you do have some fight in you after all?" She sneered at the younger woman, "Good. You'll need it."

"You need to go," Allison spoke clearly, enunciating each word as though speaking to a person of limited understanding.

Andrew's hand touched Allison's back discretely but she didn't move. He slid his fingertips around her side slightly, trying to keep the action from being seen by Lucy, and tugged lightly to get Allison to back up. Trying to get her to back off. She didn't.

"I said you need to go," she repeated to the offensive woman. "Now."

"She's kinda bossy for such a young thing, isn't she Andy?" Lucy said as she ignored Allison's statement. Dropping his hand from Allison's back, Andrew stepped around her to face Lucy and forced his ex-wife to step back. He was once again between the women.

"You need to go home, Lucy," he reiterated.

"I need that money we discussed. I needed you and you failed me again, Andy," she whimpered. "What am I supposed to do when you can't take care of me?" Emboldened, she pushed on, "I've always come to you first … I always give you the first chance to meet my needs, Andy. It's only when you let me down, that I go elsewhere." Allison kept her eyes on the woman, but felt Andrew wince from the verbal blows.

"Stop it!" Allison yelled. "Andrew is a fine, upstanding man who would never fail a woman who is deserving of him."

"He's a salesman, honey," Lucy countered. "But he's got no follow through. He cannot deliver in the long run." Her eyes filled with disgust as her gaze trailed over the man. "You never could take care of me properly. Ever."

"You need to leave, Lucy," he stated coldly. "Before …" Andrew's voice trailed away as he realized Allison was saying something. She clung to his arm whispering, but her voice was getting stronger, louder.

Allison, being at wit's end in dealing with Lucy, had searched for something she had learned in her fledgling faith that would help. Nothing came to mind, except the phrase "fear no evil". It had come to her then, that was a line from the twenty-third Psalm and she'd begun to whisper it. As the words passed her lips, she felt stronger, bolder, and had unintentionally added volume to the recitation. "The Lord is my shepherd; I shall not want. He makes me to lie down in green pastures; He leads me beside the still waters ..."

Andrew had stilled when he heard the words. He joined in, speaking in chorus with Allison when she reached the third verse, "He restores my soul; He leads me in the paths of righteousness for His name's sake ..."

"I need that money, Andy," Lucy hissed. "And make no mistake, I will do anything to get it." Then shifting her focus to Allison she smiled serenely and whispered, "I hope you have really, really low expectations."

They didn't reply to her, but continued reciting in unison, "Yea, though I walk through the valley of the shadow of death, I will fear no evil ..."

Lucy turned away and took a few steps. Allison's body immediately relaxed and with relief she let herself lean lightly against the man beside her, but Andrew stayed rigid with his eyes fixed on Lucy. She turned and called to Allison, "Hey, girlie! You have a daughter, right?"

Numbly, Allison nodded.

"You better watch out or he'll steal her away from you like he did to me!" Then she was weaving away.

Shock and fear ricocheted through Allison and she stopped speaking. Turning terrified eyes on Andrew, she spoke slowly, "What's she talking about?"

He glanced away and blinked a couple of times before coming back to her gaze. "I'll tell you later – back at the house," he replied. She looked skeptical, and cautious again. "Allison, I promise we'll talk this through. But not here. Not now."

They were silent a moment. Finally, she nodded, "Okay." She started walking slowly back toward the picnic shelter. He caught up with her in a couple of strides.

"Allison. Wait," his voice cracked. She stopped and turned slowly. He took her face tenderly in his hands – hands that trembled slightly. "Please, don't let her words take root in your mind. Or in your heart. Please," he pleaded.

She searched his face, his eyes, his soul. She had grown to believe he was honest, true and good – a worthy person to be friends with or to be aligned with in battle. But she'd been wrong before – about Brody. She couldn't risk being wrong again, not with Hope at stake. "I'll try not to," she said quietly. "I'll pray about it."

She started to turn away again, but Andrew stopped her. "And," he croaked. He swallowed hard to try to clear his throat before speaking again. "I ... Thank you for your help. I'm not sure what I'd have done if I'd have been facing her alone today," he said quietly. "It's just so ... exhausting. And humiliating," he said quietly. With his head low, he had turned away.

Allison had instinctively started to reach for him, to offer comfort, but held back. *What if Lucy is right? What if he tries to take Hope away from me?* She struggled mentally and then remembered how the phrase "fear no evil" had come to her during the fight with Lucy. Surely God wouldn't have helped if Andrew had evil intentions.

Finally she placed her hand on his back. "Andrew. I will fear no evil ..."

He faced her again, and they spoke in unison, "For Thou art with me."

From the shadows another set of eyes watched the couple. Lauren had heard the loud voices and gone to investigate, but had stayed discretely out of sight. The exchange had been interesting and the Lucy character might prove useful. "Perfect. I love it when a plan comes together," she said quietly to herself as she began moving back to the picnic area.

Andrew pulled Allison into an embrace and held her as though he truly needed her. He held her as though he would crumple to the ground without her support. "Thank you. You don't know how much it helped to have you by my side," he murmured as his whiskered check slid along her soft, smooth skin before he gently landed a light kiss there on her cheek. The movement had her lifting her face. Her eyelids drifted down, and her lips parted slightly. He didn't think. He gave in to the instinct to capture her lips in a kiss.

Allison hadn't expected Andrew to kiss her. She had felt the charge of energy coursing through him as he held her. She had experienced warmth as she heard his words and knew that she had indeed been able to help Andrew in his battle with Lucy. She'd felt elation that, as young as her faith in God was, He had answered her request to help in the situation by inspiring her words and actions, and Andrew's.

And then, as Andrew slid his cheek along hers, she'd felt the tingling sensation. Her nerve endings went on full alert ... anticipating the next touch. She'd lifted her face to look to

Andrew for guidance and had seen that look of need in his rich brown eyes. Something flared there for a second before he had lowered his lips to hers. It all felt so good and exhilarating – to be needed and wanted; and to need and want in return. Allison welcomed the kiss and responded with raw enthusiasm. And then she was consumed by confusion.

Andrew felt Allison's hands push lightly against his chest. Push equals stop – always has – so he pulled back. He was breathing hard as he took in her appearance. And then it registered in his mind that the message in her eyes was not the same as the message in her kiss. "Oh, Allison," he said quietly. "Please don't be upset ..."

She didn't respond. Those huge green eyes just watched him as emotions flashed through their depths. Andrew still held her loosely, so if she wanted to step away she could. She held her ground though, with her hands still resting on his chest. But she didn't speak.

"I'm sorry," whispered words reached her ears. "I shouldn't have ..." He had pulled her close and she had laid her head against his shoulder. She felt his heart pounding in his chest, could see the pulse jumping on his neck, and she could hear something in his voice. Maybe it was fear; maybe it was desperation. His hand softly stroked her back as he spoke quickly, "I didn't mean to scare you. I'd never hurt you ...,"

Allison finally broke in, "Just give me a minute to process this. Please."

He drew a shaky breath and waited. His hand continued its path caressing her back as he held Allison. And as he waited, he realized that he had thanked her for her help, but he hadn't thanked God. *Dear Lord, thank You for bringing Allison to my aid today. And thank You, for welcoming her into Your flock. Without You and Your guidance today, I don't know what would have happened with Lucy. I just don't know how much more I can take.*

Allison thought about the words Lucy had thrown with destructive accuracy at Andrew earlier. The idea that the woman could be so hurtful to Andrew - the person who had tried for years to help her - was beyond Allison's understanding. Lucy was bitter and nasty, and a variety of other adjectives that Allison chose to ignore. What she concentrated on was that Lucy had undoubtedly damaged Andrew's confidence and self-esteem, and Allison didn't want to compound that effect.

After long moments, she pulled back to face Andrew. He looked ashamed, emotionally drained and beaten. Allison pulled in a deep breath before speaking. "Andrew?" she asked tentatively. "Hey?"

When his gaze met hers, she saw the insecurities and doubts that he tried to mask. "That was an amazing kiss," she said earnestly and with a small smile.

For a second he looked like a little boy being praised, before his brows drew down in a slight scowl. "But?" he asked.

She licked her lips and hoped for the right words. "But, if and when we share a kiss like that again," she said as she tenderly touched his cheek, "the only emotion fueling it had better be pure, unadulterated love."

"You're not mad?"

She shook her head.

"You're not disappointed in me?"

"No, but I think we better get back to the girls."

"Yeah," he said as his gaze strayed down the path. "We should."

Allison wrapped her arm around his waist, and he laid his lightly across her shoulders, and they began walking again. "Allison?"

"Yeah?"

"Thank you."

"Anytime."

CHAPTER SEVENTEEN

Most evenings Allison, Hope, Lauren and Mrs. Holmes would gather round the table in the formal dining room for a family-style meal. Since Lauren had gotten her shifts adjusted at the restaurant, she had been joining the trio living in the main house for some of the meals.

Mrs. Holmes routinely enforced the habit of reading a devotional before the evening meal, and then the women would discuss the meaning while they dined. Sometimes Hope watched with wide eyes, absorbing the stories and discussions. Sometimes she asked questions and offered observations about God from the preschooler perspective.

On Tuesday evening, Lauren seemed exceptionally quiet and reflective. Mrs. Holmes' concern was evident as she asked kindly, "Is something the matter, dear?"

Lauren's strawberry blond hair swung slightly as she shook her head. "Just rethinking some things."

"That's good," the old woman said with a smile. "Sometimes we operate on some erroneous assumptions. Then it is beneficial to reexamine the facts periodically."

"Sometimes it's not very comfortable though," Lauren offered idly.

"Hope, honey, can you put the milk in the fridge and then go put your jammies on, please?" Allison asked as she began to clear the table and start washing dishes.

"Yes, Mamma," she replied as she slipped from her chair. She carried the milk jug to the refrigerator and placed it inside.

"I'll help her get ready for bed," Mrs. Holmes offered, as she stood.

"Thank you," Allison replied.

After Mrs. Holmes escorted Hope from the room, Lauren finished clearing the table as Allison ran the wash and rinse water in the stainless steel sinks. She started washing the glasses and placing them in the rinse water. "I didn't expect to like you," Lauren said quietly as she rinsed a glass and began wiping it.

Allison paused, "Expect?" she asked.

"You know ... when I first met you ... that night you were at the restaurant with Matt. Remember?" Lauren asked nervously.

Allison was watching the younger woman. "Is that it?" she asked. Then leaning on the sink edge, she said, "When Mrs. Holmes introduced us, I thought you seemed familiar, but I couldn't place you. It must have been from that night with Matt."

"Yeah, must have been," Lauren said as she glanced away.

"Did you guys ever hook up?" Allison asked with a smile. "He's so shy. I imagine it would take a miracle for him to call you. I tried to give him a little push the day we all were working in the yard, but I'm not sure he appreciated it."

Lauren's expression fell, "Nah. He never asked me out." She straightened then, "Doesn't matter. I don't need the distraction anyway."

Allison resumed the washing, as Lauren rinsed and dried in silence. Allison sensed a restlessness in her companion.

"What's on your mind, Lauren?"

"Can I ask you something personal?"

"Sure. But I might not answer ... I'll decide when I hear the question," Allison responded with lingering caution. When Allison had come to Miller's Bend, she'd been acutely suspicious that someone was tracking her, and although her concerns had diminished in recent weeks, she still had no answers to the questions of who or why. She reminded herself that none of her friends had known of Lauren until she moved into Mrs. Holmes' apartment. No one knew where she came from or why.

"Okay," Lauren nodded. "Fair enough." She placed the rest of the glasses in the cupboard and picked up a plate out of the rinse.

"How did your family react to your pregnancy?" she asked slowly with her focus locked on the plate in her hand.

Allison stilled, "My ... pregnancy? That's more than a little personal." She assessed the woman beside her. "Why would you want to know that?" And then a thought occurred to her, as she narrowed her eyes. "Are you pregnant? Do you need help?"

Lauren's eyes flew to Allison's and a rich blush colored her cheeks. "Me? No! I never ... I mean ... No. I'm not. Pregnant, that is," she stammered. The plate slipped from her hand back into the water and she reached for it to start drying it all over again. "I'm just curious. What's it like to be ... in the position you were ... are in," she said as she slid the plate into the cupboard and reached for the next one. When Allison didn't answer, she sighed, "I'm sorry. I shouldn't have asked."

Compassion filled Allison. She dried her hands and placed one on Lauren's shoulder. "We can probably talk about it more when we know each other better. But for now I'll tell you, I don't have a family other than Hope, and my friends Shelby and Ashley. Ashley and Shelby saved my life, and Hope's, when I was expecting. I owe them everything," she said with conviction.

Lauren swallowed hard. She didn't want to feel any sympathy for this woman. She didn't want to know that life was difficult for her, or that Brody's baby owed her life to this woman's friends. *Oh Brody! I'll get her back for you ...* Tears pooled in Lauren's eyes and she blinked them away. "What about Hope's father? Didn't you think he had a right to become your family? Shouldn't he have had the chance to be the one to protect you and her?" she challenged suddenly.

Allison felt the slap of the accusation and stepped back. Pain seared through her heart again because Brody hadn't accepted the opportunities he had been offered to do just that. But the pain was different this time. She felt more than the lost possibilities. She felt anger toward Brody because he hadn't been willing to accept responsibility for her and for Hope. Now she knew that other men – men like Andrew Wheeler – were willing to do that for women and children that they weren't required or expected to care for. Now it made Brody's resistance seem all the more cowardly.

Brody may have been scared or immature or something more complex. But in any case, he had failed to step up. And then he had died. Allison closed her eyes to block the images of the day he died. She had to get past that time in her life –

she had to move forward and leave the pain behind. And then in her mind, she saw Andrew as he struggled to move forward. It was easier for him when she had helped him face Lucy. Maybe it would be easier for her, too, if he could help her.

"You don't know anything about the chances he had, Lauren," Allison finally said softly. "He wasn't ready for fatherhood, I guess. But he definitely had his chances." She turned and walked from the room, moving blindly through the house to the room she and Hope shared. She needed to hold her baby.

Much later, after Hope had fallen asleep, Allison headed to the kitchen. A nice hot cup of tea would help settle her nerves, and she hoped to call Andrew and tell him about the disturbing conversation she'd had with Lauren. She stopped short in the doorway. Mrs. Holmes and Lauren sat at the kitchen table drinking tea and chatting. "Oh, Allison, I'm so glad you could join us," the landlady greeted her warmly.

"I'll just ... um ..." Allison turned left and right as though looking for an escape. "I ... a ... just wanted to have a cup of tea," she said as she stepped forward.

Lauren leaped from her chair and returned quickly to the table with a third cup. She lifted the antique China tea pot and poured for Allison. "Allison ..." the younger woman began. "I'm sorry about earlier. I got carried away," she said demurely. "I'm a bit idealistic."

Allison stirred honey into her tea, and thought for a moment. "Idealistic? Are you sure you didn't mean judgmental?" she asked quietly.

"No," Lauren countered as she sat up a little straighter. "I'm idealistic. I think a man and a woman should meet and get to know each other. They should date and fall in love.

They should marry before they have children," she spoke clearly. "That would be ideal."

Allison nodded in mild agreement. "It's true. That would be ideal. Unfortunately, we do not live in an ideal world," she said. "We live in the real world."

"But why can't we have the ideal? Why not?" she was asked again.

"Maybe we should just agree to avoid this topic for a while?" Allison suggested. "Mrs. Holmes? Do you have any suggestions?" she asked as she looked to the silver-haired woman.

"Well, ladies," she responded. "This is not to be the perfect world. The perfect world is in Heaven." She sipped her drink before continuing, "We must find our way through this imperfect world to get to Heaven. It is only there that things will be ideal."

Neither of the younger two spoke as they let her words sink in. Lauren looked as though she would like to argue the point, but what was there to say? Tears trailed down her cheeks, as she raised her eyes to Allison's face.

Mrs. Holmes looked from one to the other before quoting, "Trust in the Lord with all your heart, and lean not on your own understanding; In all your ways acknowledge Him, and he shall direct your paths."

"Does that really help?" Lauren asked as she shifted her eyes to Mrs. Holmes. "Does it help to trust in the Lord when someone you love is killed? Does it help fill the hole that his death leaves in your heart?"

"Yes, dear child," Mrs. Holmes spoke slowly. "Faith in God and trust in his plan does help fill the hollow places. We may never understand, but if we believe, He will guide our futures."

"I don't see it," Lauren said as she shook her head.

"I'm just starting to see it," Allison added. "Role models like Mrs. Holmes, Shelby and Riley, and even Andrew, are helping me. They can help you, too, if you let them," she said calmly.

Lauren snapped her fingers, "Oh! That reminds me … I wanted to ask you about that woman."

Allison and Mrs. Holmes both looked confused. Allison tried to recall what Lauren might be talking about. She shook her head, "Who?"

"The one in the park …" Lauren asked as her focus shifted to Allison. "The one you and Andrew were talking to."

"You saw her?" Allison began to panic and looked to Mrs. Holmes, "Did she go over by the kids? By the picnic shelter?"

"I don't know who you are talking about, dear," came a calm reply. "I didn't see anyone but our little group."

"What did you say she looked like?" the elder asked Lauren.

"It was Lucy, Mrs. Holmes," Allison spoke gently, addressing the real question. "But," she said turning her focus on Lauren, "you were watching us?!"

Lauren shrank back in her chair. "I didn't mean to … I just …" she stalled. "I heard loud voices and I thought there might be some kind of trouble, so I went to investigate. Then I saw you and Andrew facing off with that awful lady. What did you say her name is? Lacey?"

"It doesn't matter who she is, Lauren. You were spying on us!" Allison was on her feet and moving around the table toward the younger woman. "You … the one who expects a perfect world … you were spying on us. I thought you considered us to be friends." Allison slapped a hand against the table and stormed out of the room.

She came back through a moment later to clear her cup from the table. "I'm sorry, Mrs. Holmes," she said as she laid a hand on the bony shoulder of the old woman. "I'm sure you don't appreciate yelling in your home. I apologize."

"Thank you, Allison," she replied as she patted the hand that rested on her shoulder. "I appreciate your gesture."

"Me, too," Lauren offered in a subdued manner. She kept her eyes locked on the tea cup in Allison's hand, as she continued, "I mean I'm sorry, too." Then looking to Allison she spoke quietly, "I shouldn't have spied on you and Andrew. I'm sorry."

"All right then," Mrs. Holmes said. "Let's have no more of it." Rising from her chair she declared, "Bedtime for everyone over 80."

It was quiet and tense in the kitchen for several minutes as the women washed, rinsed and put away the dishes from the little tea party. Finally, Allison cleared her throat, "So ... earlier you asked about coping when someone dies. Is it safe to assume that you've lost a person that you loved a great deal?"

Lauren neatly hung the kitchen towel over the bar of the towel rack. "Yes," she choked. "Yes I did. He was everything to me."

Empathy surged through Allison as she remembered the difficulties she had dealing with Brody's death. "Did you have anyone to help you through it?" she asked. *Please, God, I hope she had friends and family who helped her when she needed it. And please, help her find peace now.* The prayer that flashed through Allison's mind surprised her, but when she thought about it she decided it had been the right request in the moment. "Are you doing alright now? Or do you want to talk about him?"

Lauren regarded Allison with suspicion. She thought carefully – she had covered her tracks well and bided her time – there was no way Allison could know her identity. She turned mournful eyes on the woman who had carried Brody's child. "I just don't think I could talk about him to you. You wouldn't understand," she whimpered.

"You might be surprised. I've lost someone, too," Allison said compassionately. "We might have more in common than either of us ever imagined."

Cadee Brystal

CHAPTER EIGHTEEN

The cell phone had gone dead in Lauren's ear. She wasn't sure whether she was the victim of a dropped call or if she'd been hung up on. But it didn't matter. She had told them that she was reconsidering the plan. The influence of the people she'd met in Miller's Bend was causing her to doubt her earlier convictions. And most importantly, the woman – the mother of Brody's child – was genuinely nice. She was a loving parent with her daughter's best interest at heart.

And all of those things were adding up to one big question in Lauren's mind, which she had voiced, "Is what we are planning really the best thing for the child?"

"What would you suggest instead?" the gruff voice had demanded. "Just pretend we don't know she exists. Just ignore her?" And then the phone had gone dead.

Andrew could hear the screaming of what sounded like a dozen babies as he approached the kitchen door of his brother's cozy home. He'd received a frantic call from Riley a short time ago. The basic message had been "Alone with babies. Help." So Andrew had left Rori home alone and headed over to lend a much needed hand to his brother.

Not stopping to knock, Andrew slipped inside, and as he dropped his jacket into a chair, he called out, "Reinforcements have arrived!" There was a second of calm before the babies resumed their chorus. Andrew enjoyed the sight of his brother trying to carry and burp a blue-wrapped squalling infant while the pink bundle in the bassinet repeatedly spit out the pacifier and her face turned brighter red.

"Not enough hands?" Andrew drawled drawing his brother's attention.

"Oh, thank heavens you're here!" he sighed in response as he passed Jacob to Uncle Andrew and reached for little Isabelle. "They're both wound up and I can't get either one to settle down."

Andrew cradled the baby close and swayed. He instinctively hummed lightly as he moved closer to Riley, "What's his status, bro?"

A blank look was all the response he got from Riley who was stripping Isabelle's diaper off with one hand while holding her securely, but gently, in place with the other. "What?"

"What does he need? Diaper? Bottle? Burp? His own room?"

Riley snapped to attention, answering with economy of words, "Fed and changed."

"Ah, come on little man," Andrew said as he turned away. "Let's find a quiet spot to work that burp out." He strolled casually into the kitchen and opened the refrigerator and pulled out a soft drink. He turned the radio on softly, all the while swaying and humming. He opened the drink and took a long swig. "Sometimes, Jake, it just helps to carve out your own space in the world."

The baby was beginning to calm, and Andrew tenderly rubbed circles on his back, adding an occasional pat on the back. The more Jake relaxed, the easier it would be to get that air bubble to break free. The process was oddly relaxing for

Andrew, reminding him of time he had spent with Rori when she was an infant. He had been young and uncertain. The first time Lucy had tried to pass Rori to him, he had backed away afraid he would break her, or drop her or something. But within a few minutes, he'd been holding the baby and falling in love with her.

Jake wiggled and stretched against Andrew's shoulder just before a rip-roaring burp erupted from the little guy. "Ah, there you go. That's better, isn't it?" Andrew kept rubbing the baby's back and moving soothingly. He took another swig of the drink before heading into the living room again. Riley looked frazzled … and he had baby powder smeared across his cheek. Andrew smiled, "Hey, you want to trade?"

Riley took in the relaxed baby snuggling on his brother's shoulder and a look of astonishment crossed his face. "How did you do that?"

Isabelle let out a screech that raised the hairs on the back Andrew's neck and he saw Riley cringe. "Hey. You've got to relax before they will. Why don't you wrap her up again and take her to the kitchen for a minute so I can get him down for the night. Then I'll spell you with her."

"I should be able to handle her, if you can get him to sleep," Riley responded with a slight smile. "Not out here though. Put him in a crib in the bedroom," he said inclining his head toward the hallway. "And, Andrew?" Riley paused meaningfully. "Thanks."

A short time later, the babies slept peacefully in the spare bedroom that was no longer a spare. It was a nursery, decorated with yellow and green and animals of all types. The men sat in the living room recovering from the recent bout of parenting. "So did Shelby run off?"

"No. She's at the gym, trying to get her … well she wants to get back in shape. So she's been working out after supper and I watch the babies for a couple hours," Riley said as he leaned back in his recliner and his eyes drifted closed. "It's usually okay, but they got away from me tonight."

"How's Shelby doing?"

"Just fine."

"Is she really?" Andrew pushed. "No baby blues? Not stressing out?"

Riley examined his brother closely, "When did you learn about post-partum women?" Then he closed his eyes again. "Never mind. I don't think I care."

Andrew laughed roughly and took another drink from his soda.

"I do want to know how you got to be The Baby Whisperer, though," Riley asked sleepily.

"Rori," the older brother stated, as if that was a full explanation.

"Rori was six years old when you married Lucy," Riley stated. "I suspect she was out of diapers by then."

"Riley. Lucy and I were friends back when she got pregnant. I visited her a lot. I held Rori the day she was born," Andrew revealed. "You really didn't know?"

"I was what – seventh grade," he responded. "I wasn't paying much attention to you. And no attention at all to the pregnant ladies."

"Ancient history anyhow," Andrew pointed out. "What's important now is that you get some sleep." He rose and patted Riley on the shoulder. "I'll let myself out."

"What's Lucy up to now?" Andrew's drowsy brother asked. "I heard she's been after you for cash."

"Same as always ..." Andrew shrugged. "She blows through it and comes nosing around for more."

"You're not supplying her are you?"

Irritation edged his words, "Thought you were drifting off."

"I don't want to see her getting her hooks into you again," Riley spoke kindly. He pulled himself up, out of the chair and faced his brother. In the earnest look from his brother Andrew saw that it was only love that drove his concern. "It took you a long time to come out of it last time. I don't want to see you go through that again."

Andrew recalled the confrontation in the park Sunday and quick, rough laugh escaped. "I think I've got a new advocate," he said thoughtfully. At Riley's curious expression, Andrew explained, "You remember Sunday, when Allison and I went for a walk?"

"Yeah," Riley's eyes danced with bedevilment. "You guys were gone so long that we thought about sending out a search party. We didn't though. We were afraid of what we might find."

"It wasn't like that," Andrew growled. "We were just talking. Until Lucy showed up."

"What? Allison met Lucy?" Riley sounded incredulous. "Shelby didn't tell me that."

"She may not know. Allison's been pretty busy with the landscaping job and working for Mrs. Holmes. She may not have been over to see Shelby since Sunday ..."

"So? What happened?" Riley's curiosity was piqued.

"She was amazing!" Andrew replied. "I still can't believe the way Allison reacted." He looked past his brother toward the darkening window as he recalled the encounter. "Lucy was drunk and obnoxious. At first I tried to shield Allison, but when Lucy started flinging insults and innuendos ..."

He paused and looked into Riley's eager face. "You should have seen her, Riley! Allison stepped in front of me and told Lucy off. She told her to go away ... She told her," his voice cracked, "that I am a man who would never fail a woman who is deserving of me." Emotion swelled in Andrew and tears brimmed in his eyes. "Do you have any idea how that made me feel? She stood up for me, Riley. She was truly astounding."

"So that's it? That's what Lucy's been doing to you all this time?" Riley stormed across the room. "She's been making you believe that you fail her?! That her condition is your fault? I knew it! She's just so ..."

"Thanks, Riley. But I'd rather focus on Allison," Andrew interjected. "You'd never guess what happened after that."

"Lucy tried to claw her eyes out?" Riley offered with a mock seriousness.

"No. Allison started reciting the Twenty-third Psalm," he recalled with a smile. "Not sure why, but it worked. Lucy high-tailed it right out of the park."

"No kidding?" Riley's surprise was clear. "It's great that she's growing in her faith. I hope it helps her."

"It has," Andrew replied with a nod. And then glancing at the wall clock, he added, "I need to get home to Rori."

"Hey, wait. Did you get to tell Allison the whole story about Rori?" Riley queried. Andrew looked away without speaking. Riley continued, "You better get all the details to her before she hears them from someone else. Like Lucy."

Andrew was thoughtful a moment before replying, "I started to, but didn't get to finish because Lucy showed up. It got pretty tense and we didn't get back to it." He paused as he remembered the kiss and Allison's request for time to think and pray about it. "I don't know that it matters," he said quietly.

"Andrew. If there is even a chance that it might matter down the road, then it matters now. You need to tell her what really happened before she gets a toxic tale from someone else," the younger brother advised.

The memory of Lucy warning Allison that he would steal her baby away sent a chill down his spine. Lucy was definitely one to tell a toxic tale if given the chance.

"Thanks. I better go," he said distractedly as he headed out the door.

Allison felt uneasy in the days following the encounter in the park. As much as she had been repulsed by Lucy and everything she appeared to represent, Allison kept hearing the bitter woman's words, "You better watch out or he'll steal her away from you ..." Allison hated the fact that the words had stuck in her mind. She liked Andrew and felt certain that if she could only hear the rest of his story, she would be relieved.

But until that time, she had changed the babysitting arrangement with Mrs. Holmes' blessing. So for the current week, Andrew delivered Rori to Mrs. Holmes' fine Victorian home each morning where she would care for Hope, under the landlady's supervision. Andrew would join the household for breakfast, and oddly, each day Lauren seemed more distant. Andrew and Allison would stagger their lunch breaks as they had before, in order to spend time with Hope and offer Rori a respite from the responsibility of caring for a preschooler. Andrew would retrieve Rori and head for home after work.

But they had lost their evening meal together and along with it the opportunity to speak privately.

By Friday evening, Allison was afraid she would lose her mind if she didn't learn the rest of the story from Andrew's point of view. She needed to talk to Andrew, to be near him, and to be reassured by him. Mrs. Holmes had a special committee meeting somewhere, and Allison had waited impatiently for Lauren to return home from work to watch Hope. The moment she returned from work, Allison met her at the door. "I really appreciate that you are willing to stay with Hope. She's watching TV, but only until eight. She should be in bed with lights out by 8:30. There shouldn't be any problems, but call me if you need me. I explained to her where I will be and that you'll be here with her until I get back. I appreciate this so much." She hugged the younger woman and hurried toward her car.

Lauren had called after her, "Don't worry about a thing. Hope couldn't be in better hands than mine." Allison didn't see the smile that curled on the woman's lips, or she might have changed her plans.

CHAPTER NINETEEN

Andrew's frustration magnified as he drove home from the daddy-rescue mission at Riley's. Feeling the weight of Riley's words, he had called home to see if Rori was doing alright. He planned to suggest that she put herself to bed and he would go see Allison. He'd get his story told and wait for the repercussions. But, there had been no answer at the house. He had tried the number repeatedly with the same response. *Please, God, let her be at home. Let there be a good explanation.*

Andrew whipped into the driveway, threw the gear shift into Park, and pulled the keys from the ignition as he leaped from the car. All the windows of the house were dark, and the front door stood open. "Rori!" he yelled as he approached the open doorway. "Rori!" He rushed inside, pulling the door closed behind him. Pure panic flowed through his veins. *Please. Please don't let her have gone with Lucy.* Andrew flew through the house, turning on lights and shouting for his daughter, but didn't find her anywhere.

He was just pulling his cell from his jacket pocket to call the police, when the doorbell sounded. Andrew dashed to the door and pulled it open with a jerk. *Come on, Rori. Be here.* It wasn't his daughter who stood before him on the porch, but it was almost as good. Allison!

"Andrew, I need -" she began, but the words died on her lips. Her eyes grew wide as she took in his appearance and agitation. "What's the matter? How can I help?" The questions rolled off her tongue as she charged into the house. "Is it Rori? Is she sick?"

"Yes. I don't know," he ground out as he spun away from Allison. "I can't find her!" He turned and headed toward the steps to the second floor again. "She's got to be here. She has to be!"

The sound of Allison's footfalls on the steps behind him was reassuring to Andrew. The reassurance that he was no longer alone helped calm his nerves as he started the search over again. "Where have you looked?" her mild voice called out to him.

"Everywhere! I've searched every room, but the basement," he said as he pushed the door to Rori's bedroom closet open. Nothing. "She has to be here!"

Allison touched his arm gently. "Andrew. Look at me."

With wild eyes he spun toward her. "What?"

She took his face in her hands. Those green eyes of hers bored into his. "We will find her. But you need to calm down. Okay?" she asked as she let her hands fall away from his face, dropping to his shoulders, sliding to his biceps. "We will find her," she repeated soothingly.

Andrew squeezed his eyes closed tightly. "You don't understand," he whispered hoarsely. "If Lucy took her, there's no telling what she'll do – or where she'll take her."

"Andrew. Rori may be hiding. She might have gone to a friend's house. We don't know where she is," she continued with a false calmness she wasn't really feeling. *What if it was Hope who was missing? How would I react?*

The panic was easing. Andrew was starting to think about his daughter and what reasonable options there were to explain her absence. He inhaled deeply. He felt the security that blossomed from Allison's touch – from her very presence. "I've got to find her!"

"And we will … First we will find her, and then we will get this cleared up. I'm sure there's a good reason she's not here." Allison's assurance was empty, he knew. But it helped to have someone telling him she would be fine. "But first, let's be absolutely certain that she isn't here." She released the hold on his arms and stepped back. "You said you didn't check the basement … Let's try there before we get carried away. How about the back yard? Isn't there a playhouse out there?"

"I'll take the back yard," he said with a nod as he started toward the steps. "Would you take the basement, please?"

"Of course."

In the dark, shadowy basement storage area, Allison peered behind a stack of boxes and called softly for the missing girl. She could hear heavy footsteps banging overhead. Apparently Andrew had come back inside the house and passed through the kitchen and toward the front door. She stopped and listened, thinking she had heard another sound – a scuffling sound nearby.

"Rori? It's Allison. If you're down here, please come out. You're scaring your Daddy to death, honey." More scuffling sounds, coupled with some sniffling, reached Allison's ears. "Rori? You in there?" she called gently. "Come on out honey. Your Dad's going to be so happy to see you." A hiccup and a sobbing sound reached her then. "Sweetie? I'm going to go get your Dad and a flashlight. Will that be okay? Or do you want to come to me and we'll go upstairs together?"

A weak answer reached her then. "Where's Dad?"

"He's upstairs. He's been searching for you," Allison said softly. "I'll go get him now." Allison deftly drafted a text to the girl's father: Found her. Basement. As she hit "send", she moved quickly and quietly toward the steps with the intention of catching him before he got to the stairway. She heard running footsteps enter the kitchen. "Andrew!" she yelled as she crested the steps. "Bring a flashlight and some Kleenex."

They collided in the kitchen. Andrew's quick reflexes had him catching Allison before she toppled. In a second, he had stabilized her and then set her gently aside as he headed for the basement steps. "Wait!" The urgency in her voice caught his attention and he paused.

"What? I've got to get down there ..."

"She's scared," Allison's gaze locked meaningfully on Andrew's. "You have to be calm so you can settle her down. She didn't say so, but I think she's afraid you're mad or upset," she whispered. "You have to regain some control, or you'll make matters worse."

Muscles flexed in the strong jawline as Andrew digested her words. He flexed his hands in an attempt to alleviate some of the tension coursing through his body.

Allison frowned. "Go on down there and talk to her, but remember to be calm and loving," she said with a wave of her hand. "I'll bring a flashlight ..." she continued as she looked around the kitchen. "If I can find one, that is."

Andrew took two strides to the refrigerator and snatched the flashlight from the top of the unit. Clasping Allison's hand, he pulled her after him down the steps. "Rori? Rori, honey. I'm so glad you're safe," he called. "I ... I can't wait to give you a great big hug."

"Dad?"

"Yeah, I'm here," he answered and Allison heard the quaver in his voice. "Are you okay? Are you hurt?"

Sniffling reached his ears as he neared the boxes which were crammed into the storage space. And then a sob escaped from his little girl. By the time he had repositioned boxes while Allison held the flashlight so he could see better, Rori was crying in earnest. Bitter, pitiful cries tore from his little girl and the sound broke his heart.

"How did you get back there, Rori?" he asked incredulously, as he pulled her up and out from her hiding place. Setting his daughter on her feet and dropping to his knees, Andrew looked her in the eye and the words poured out, "I was so worried when I couldn't find you." He whispered in her ear as he clutched the girl to his chest, "I love you more than anyone or anything, Rori. I'm so glad God kept you safe and helped Allison find you."

Allison felt Andrew's hand envelope hers. He mutely pulled her closer to him as he stood. As the three drew together, Rori slipped an arm hesitantly around Allison's waist. Allison dropped her arm tenderly across the girl's shoulder. A second later, Andrew's muscular arms encircled both of them. "Thank you, God," he whispered.

Rori's crying had begun to subside, and Allison sensed that the young girl's fear and anxiety were about to turn into embarrassment. As much as she enjoyed the feeling of being included, she didn't want to push the preteen to lash out. "Hey," she said with a smile. "How about we go on upstairs?" And then thinking of her own needs if she was in Rori's situation, and what would sooth her frayed nerves, she asked, "Do you have any ice cream? I could really use a snack."

The man looked perplexed, but the girl suddenly beamed. "With chocolate? And caramel?"

"Do you have both?" Allison responded with sincere enthusiasm. "I love mixing them."

"Me too! Let's go!" Rori answered as she raced for the steps. She stopped short and threw herself back to Andrew, hugging him fiercely, she proclaimed, "I'm sorry, Dad. I … I just got so scared. I'm really sorry."

Andrew watched in dismay as Rori clamored up the steps. And then she was gone. Frowning, he looked into Allison's face. "Will I ever understand what just happened here?" he asked quietly.

"Doubtful," she answered with a laugh. She realized that he had kept an arm discretely across her back with a hand resting on her waist. Turning to face him, she said with great seriousness, "You do need to find out what drove her down here to hide, though. You need to get to the bottom of this."

"Do you think you could talk to her? Help me out … I mean help me out even more," he said humbly. "Thank you so much for everything you did tonight. You calmed me down and made me think instead of simply reacting. You centered me." Andrew sighed and then his voice quavered as he spoke again. "Thank you so much. What would I have done without you?"

It was a rhetorical question, of course, but before she could have replied, he whispered, "You are so beautiful, Allison." He tenderly kissed her forehead before pulling her into a gentle embrace.

CHAPTER TWENTY

The mutual panic shared by Allison and Andrew during the search for Rori, combined with the relief of having found her safe and sound, had released a storm of emotions within Allison. As he held her tightly, she thought again of the terror Andrew must have felt when he realized that Rori was missing. A selfish prayer shot through her mind: *Thank you, Lord, that it wasn't Hope who was lost.*

Allison's emotions continued to roil as Andrew held her. Her mind began the cruel fantasy. She imagined what it would be like to be loved so fiercely that a person would tear the house apart – or the town, the county, the state – searching for you. She imagined being held and supported and loved through the daily crises and traumas, no matter their size or impact. Tears pooled in her eyes and she sniffled slightly, as she leaned more heavily into Andrew.

"Dear Lord," she whispered, partly to redirect her thoughts. "Thank you for keeping Rori safe." She swallowed hard, "And helping us find her." Andrew had shifted slightly, opening up a little space between them, when she began her whispered prayer. She looked up into his face and spoke to him, "You did a great job of reining in your emotions, so Rori could see your love rather than fear or anger."

Andrew's rich brown eyes seemed nearly black as he listened to her words. Moisture shimmered on their surface and his gaze held hers captive. His hands had rested on her upper arms in a light grip, but now they slid to her shoulders. He spoke with a ragged voice, "I'm so thankful that you've come into our lives. And I'm especially glad you were at my doorstep tonight."

He brought his lips to her forehead and once again kissed her delicately. A shiver ran through her as he slid his cheek along hers and his breath tickled the sensitive skin. She felt the warmth of his lips as he gently kissed her cheek before stepping back. Allison needed oxygen. She needed space. She needed to leave. With a sharp gasp she retreated a step and started to turn away. But the change in his expression stopped her. "What is it?" she asked.

A mask of concentration had Andrew scowling. Rather than looking into Allison's face, his eyes were trained lower. Not at her mouth either, more at her neckline. In a nervous motion her hand flew to the necklace she wore, and she fingered the cross absently. "What's the matter?" she asked again with rising concern.

When his focus rose from her necklace to her face, there was an eerie coldness in his glare. "Why?" he asked. "Why were you here on my doorstep tonight?" Suspicion laced his voice.

"I ... I came over to see if we could talk. To finish the conversation from Sunday," she swallowed hard. "I needed to hear the rest of your story about Rori."

With the sarcasm of a preteen, a voice from above them called out, "Hey! Did you guys get lost or fall in a hole down there, or what?" Rori appeared in the doorway. "You'd better get up here – the ice cream is melting." She disappeared again.

Stunned and confused by the sudden change in Andrew's demeanor, Allison moved woodenly to the stairway and began moving automatically up. Left. Right. Left. The fresh reminder pounded in her mind: *Caring about someone gives them the power to hurt you.* A large, warm hand closed over Allison's and tugged lightly. She stopped, but didn't turn.

"I'm sorry," he said quietly. "I didn't mean ... I've just learned to expect the worst of intentions when it comes to Lucy. And sometimes it spills over to you, too. I'm so sorry for thinking ..." he stopped speaking and released her hand. "I shouldn't have even let the thought cross my mind. I am sorry."

With a sigh, she responded, "Don't worry about it."

The evening had been a roller-coaster of emotions – twists and turns, highs and lows. Allison had felt the heady rush of working in tandem with Andrew to keep their wits about them and locate Rori. She'd experience peace as they prayed together in thankfulness for finding the young girl safe and sound. And she'd felt the pain of Andrew's obscure accusation – and relief when he realized his reaction had been unreasonable.

Allison went straight to Rori who was seated at the kitchen table absorbing a mountainous serving of ice cream slathered in chocolate and caramel toppings. Andrew saw her stoop and say something quietly to his daughter before patting her on the shoulder and moving off into the living room. Startled, Andrew began to comprehend that he liked having Allison in his kitchen, in his house, in his life.

He closed the basement door and leaned against it as he examined the thought. *Is it Allison? Or is it the idea of having a woman who is kind, loving and strong?* The thought of beginning the process of dating was less than pleasant. He grimaced as he considered just how badly that could go. He pushed away from the door and stepped close to his daughter. "I'm really glad you are safe," he said quietly and bent down to hug her. "But … I was scared to death that something bad happened to you."

The preteen swallowed the ice cream she was working on, and looked sadly into her father's eyes. "I know, Dad. I'm very sorry," she said. "I think I scared Allison, too."

Allison. "I owe her big time for helping me tonight. I better go talk to her …" he commented without thinking.

"No!" Rori wrapped herself around his arm to try to anchor him inside the kitchen. "Just wait with me."

Suspicion spread through Andrew's mind again. "Why?" He narrowed his eyes as he evaluated his daughter. "Why do you want me to stay in here? What's she doing?" he asked as he pulled away and turned toward the living room doorway.

"Why can't you just trust her?"

The words hit him like knives and he froze in mid-stride. *Why can't I trust her?*

"You know she's not like Mom. Can't you see how different they are?"

Andrew still hadn't moved. He itched to stride into the other room and see what Allison was doing in there. But somewhere deep inside, he knew that Rori was right: Allison could be, should be, and deserved to be trusted. Slowly, he exhaled and turned to face the light of his life. He looked at Rori and saw not the little girl that he had cherished and worried over for years, but the young woman she was becoming. He glanced back toward the doorway.

"She'll be right back," Rori said with a sigh. "Just chill."

"Sure." He nodded convincingly. "No problem. I'll just chill," he said as he pulled out a chair. Just as he was about to sit, Allison stepped quietly into the room. She glanced between father and daughter, looking lost – as though she didn't know if she was welcome. His heart clenched at seeing her morose expression. "Hey," he said. "Come on over here and have your ice cream. It's melting."

"Smooth," Rori offered in a stage whisper. Allison smiled and settled on the chair that he had pulled out.

"Thank you," she said quietly as she winked at Rori.

"Everything alright?" Andrew asked Allison. She turned a questioning look on him. "Well, you haven't said anything since ... downstairs. And you disappeared for a few minutes," he explained. "Did you check in on Hope?"

Nodding, she replied, "Yes. Wanted to talk to her, but Lauren said she's asleep." Her face fell as she considered something, and then shook off the thought.

"What's the matter?" Andrew asked.

She glanced briefly at Rori, who was licking the flavors from the bowl. Allison mouthed the word "later" to Andrew and then dug into her own bowl of soupy ice cream.

"So, Rori," Allison spoke quietly. "Sometimes when I used to be home alone, I would hear sounds that would kind of freak me out ... Does that ever happen to you?"

With downcast eyes the girl shook her head, and her pony tail swung back and forth.

Allison tried again. "You know your Aunt Shelby? She and I have been friends forever."

Rori looked up and nodded. "You're like sisters!" she answered. Then to her father she said, "They used to have all sorts of adventures when they were little."

"And not so little," Allison said with a sigh.

"They shared an adventure just about 18 months ago," Andrew joined in cautiously. He thought he was onto what

Allison was doing. "That's when Riley and I first got to meet Allison and Hope."

"Sometimes, when we were younger, a scary story or TV show would upset Shelby and she'd disappear for a while. Just until she felt better ..." Allison let the sentence die when she saw the insolent look in Rori's expression.

"I'm not a baby, you know," Rori declared as she raised her chin a notch. "Fake stuff like that doesn't scare me."

Andrew leaned back in his chair as he watched the interplay between the two. Allison was playing it cool, but he could tell that she knew she had an angle to get to the information they wanted. "A person doesn't have to be a baby to get a little shaken up after watching something creepy." She looked directly into Rori's gaze. "Especially if they are home alone."

A moment passed, and Rori dropped her chin to her chest. "I don't scare that easy."

"What happened tonight?" Allison asked. "Since we know you are a mature young lady who isn't afraid of fake stuff, we need to know what real stuff happened that made you go ... find a place you could ... be alone." Allison gently rubbed Rori's forearm as she waited. Eventually she cradled Rori's hand and began to massage it as the minutes ticked by.

Andrew shifted in his chair and cleared his throat, but Allison shot him a look that telegraphed the message "Just wait for it."

Rori clasped Allison's hand, but her watery gaze snagged on her dad. She drew in a shaky breath and began. "I was watching TV with all the lights out, so it was dark. Like in the theater. I heard a car pull up and went to look out the window. Mom was in the passenger seat, so I thought it was no big deal," she said weakly. She paused.

Andrew had come to attention and was leaning forward in the chair. His expression had turned flat and cold at the mention of Lucy's presence. "Who was with her?" he demanded. "Rori – who was the driver?"

"I don't know ..."

Allison recognized that Rori was pulling back emotionally, in response to his aggressive pose. "It's alright," she said soothingly a she got up and moved around the young girl to stand where she was able to place a hand on both Rori's and Andrew's shoulders. "It's important that we don't let our feelings for one person be transferred to the other, isn't it, Rori?" She patted Andrew lightly as she spoke, but her eyes were on Rori. "Do you know what I mean?"

The girl nodded up at Allison. "Sure, I do. But I don't think Dad does ..." she said sweetly. And then turning her snapping brown eyes on the silent man, she said, "It's like when Dad thinks you will act the same way Mom does, even though you are nothing alike."

Oh, Lord. She's growing up fast. "I think we are getting way off course here," he countered. "We are talking about you, young lady." Andrew didn't dare look into Allison's face. "What happened after the car pulled into the driveway?"

"They got out and walked toward the front door," Rori squirmed as she looked intently at her bowl. "I got scared and ran downstairs. Then you came home."

Andrew instinctively knelt beside his daughter's chair and pulled it around so she faced him. The abrasive scraping of the chair feet against the flooring mimicked the alarms sounding in his mind. "You know I love you and I'll do everything in my power to protect you. I'm not mad or upset with you. You know this, right?" He had taken his daughter's hands in his own and they rested on her denim-clad thighs.

She nodded and sniffled slightly. Allison saw a tear trail across the girl's cheek and hover there until a second tear merged with it and the new bigger tear dropped onto Andrew's hand. "Tell us the rest. Tell us what you left out."

"He was scary."

"How so?" Andrew asked. "Was he dirty, grungy, and tattooed?"

Once again the girl shook her head. "No. He looked like you do when you go to work."

"You mean my clothes?" he asked.

She nodded slowly.

"What else? Was he tall, short, fat, skinny? What else?"

"He was tall. He looked ... mean." She looked from Andrew to Allison gauging their reaction. "I think he was controlling Mom. She acted like she didn't want to be with him."

"Are you sure?" Andrew asked in a hollow voice.

"She kept trying to pull away from him. But he wouldn't let her go," tears were flowing freely down Rori's cheeks as she spoke. "She looked like she was crying. It just scared me. It made me think of the shows where kids just disappear." She looked at Allison with defiance in her eyes, "The real stories. Not the fake ones."

Andrew pulled his beloved daughter into his arms and hugged her fiercely. She pushed back and gazed into his face. "I figured that Mom's tough and she can handle most guys. But if she didn't want to be with that guy, then I knew I didn't either. So I went and hid."

"How did they get inside? The door was standing open when I got home."

"I ... might have left it unlocked."

"How long were you down there? Why didn't you come out when I got home? Didn't you hear me calling you?"

"I heard the footsteps, but I panicked – I was afraid the man was back," she said bravely as she leaned into her father's embrace again. Allison could tell that she needed reassurance that he wasn't upset with her. "Your footsteps were so loud … they sounded like Zeus was having a temper tantrum in the house."

"I can only imagine how loud his steps were," Allison said to Rori. "Now that you mention it, he kind of reminded me of Zeus throwing a temper tantrum when I arrived." Andrew shot a dark look Allison's way in response to her teasing.

"And then when I heard your voice, you sounded mad …"

"Oh, honey," he said as he squeezed her tightly to his chest again. "I was terrified that you were gone – that something really bad had happened to you."

"I'm sorry. I didn't mean to scare you."

"It's okay now – you're safe. That's what's important."

Allison placed a hand on Rori's shoulder and added, "You also learned to keep the door locked, right?"

"Yes."

"Why don't you go get ready for bed and I'll come tuck you in a few minutes, okay?" Andrew instructed his daughter with gently authority.

She nodded and shifted to her feet. Fresh tears filled Rori's rich brown eyes as she raised her gaze to meet her father's. "I don't want to get to be like her." She sniffled and rubbed the moisture from her cheeks. "I don't want to hang with mean people. I don't want to scare my kids. I don't want to lose you, Daddy."

The adults caught each other's gaze, and Andrew stiffened. Allison saw the flicker of alarm there in his eyes … the thought expressed by Rori had been in his mind as well. The chance that his sweet daughter could make the same choices her mother had horrified him, and luckily he remained silent rather than reinforce the struggling child's fears. He swallowed hard and closed his eyes briefly. When they flashed open again, Allison read a different response – a loving response.

"That'll never happen. Never in a million years," he choked out. "You will never lose me. I love you more than everything."

"But you and Mom …"

"That does not affect you and me." He pulled Rori back into another hug. His eyes were red-rimmed and sad.

"But …"

"No buts," his voice rumbled close to her ear. "I love you unconditionally. Forever and ever."

"You do?"

"Yep."

Serious young eyes met her father's. "Even if you would still love me, I still don't want to be like her," she declared. He paused as he searched for the right words to reassure her, when he had no guarantees in his own mind. After all, she could turn out like her mother – it's a tough world. His focus flitted to Allison briefly as he considered how to reassure the young girl.

A story she had heard long ago came to mind and in a moment of inspiration she cleared her throat. "I think …" she began. "I think the story of the old Cherokee and his grandson would help right about now."

Hope flared in Rori's expression, while Andrew's countenance reflected thankfulness. "It just might help," he said. "Go ahead."

"Well ... an old Cherokee man was visiting with his grandson, when he began to explain to the boy that there is a battle between two wolves inside each of us. One of the wolves is evil: it embodies anger, jealousy, greed, resentment, inferiority, lies and other nasty characteristics." Allison paused as she collected her thoughts. "The other wolf is good: it embodies joy, peace, love, hope, humility, kindness, empathy, truth and other fine qualities."

"What do you suppose the boy asked after a few minutes of thinking about his grandfather's words?" she asked.

Rori shrugged, "Don't know."

"How about you? Any guesses?" Allison asked as she peered at Andrew.

"Can't wait to hear," he replied with a slight smile.

"The boy asked his grandfather, which wolf wins the battle?" She continued the story. "And what do you think the answer is?" Allison looked expectantly from father to daughter. Both shrugged.

"The wise old grandfather deliberately leaned close to the child's ear and whispered the answer. 'The wolf that wins – either the good wolf or the evil one – is the one that you feed with your choice of behavior and beliefs.'"

"I don't ...," Rori began. "Oh. Oh! So the grandpa meant that if you are good, then the good wolf gets stronger."

"So you can steer who you become by the small choices you make every day," Andrew jumped into the explanation. "That's a great story. And a great plan to remember ... make positive choices every time you have the chance."

Rori threw her arms around Allison's waist, "Thanks. That story helped."

"Something else that helps is your belief in God," Andrew said cautiously. "You have a good foundation with God. And that's something you're mother never had."

"She didn't?"

"Unfortunately not," he said sadly.

"I want my good wolf to win," she said staunchly.

"Another thing you can do is to trust the Lord with all your heart," Andrew spoke quietly. "The Bible tells us that we won't always understand everything, but that we should acknowledge Him, and He will make your paths straight. That means -"

"He'll show me how to grow my good wolf," Rori said enthusiastically.

"Yeah. That's right."

CHAPTER TWENTY-ONE

Allison swiped the rich burgundy paint from the smear on the ceiling where her edging brush had gone astray as she growled in exasperation. She'd been painting in Mrs. Holmes' second story rooms since early this morning and had made such a mess that she was angry with herself. "I'm going to have to paint the ceiling again," she grumbled under her breath. Painting had seemed like a good idea to try to keep her thoughts off Andrew and Rori. And Lucy.

After the events of the preceding evening, they never did get back to talking about Andrew and Lucy, and the story of how he came to have Rori. Dipping the paint brush and continuing to work on the detailed work of the edging in the bedroom, she recalled the devastation and raw anger that Andrew had shown after he had tucked Rori in for the night.

All hope for talking evaporated when he told her that Rori had added that while she hid in the basement, she thought Lucy and her companion had gone into Andrew's bedroom. He had checked after leaving Rori and discovered that his room had been ransacked and several things were missing including a stash of a few hundred dollars in cash and his grandmother's wedding ring. It was the ring that had been Lucy's while they were married and she knew its value.

He had distractedly thanked Allison for all her help and apologized but ushered her to her car. "We'll talk tomorrow,"

he'd said glumly. "I have some things I need to take care of."
Well, tomorrow had come with no word from the man.
Allison was agitated. She backed down the ladder and
repositioned it, checked her cell for missed calls and the time
– nearly three. Why hadn't he called?

In irritation, she chucked her phone lightly onto the pile
of rags near the open paint pail. It didn't land – it bounced.
She watched in dismay as it teetered on the rim of the can and
then slid inside. "Seriously?!"

"Hi Mamma," chimed her angel's voice from the
doorway. "What you doing?"

Casting a glare at the paint can that swallowed up her
phone, Allison let out a sigh. "Going off the grid, apparently."
Then she turned to face her sweet baby girl and her spirits
lifted. "Come here and give me a hug," she offered as she
knelt down. With red curls bouncing, Hope trotted to her and
wrapped Allison in her loving arms. "Mmmm. I'm so lucky
that I have you Baby Girl," she cooed.

"We are lucky girls," Hope replied with a bright smile
and a vigorous nod.

"Yes, we are," Allison spoke with conviction. "We have
each other and we have God's love and we are a family." And
then more to herself than to her daughter, she said, "We will
be fine no matter what."

"Mrs. Holmes our family, too?" Hope spoke as Allison
pulled the preschooler into her lap and hugged her.

She nodded. "Sure, we can count her in our family."

"And Rori," Hope chirped. "She my sister – like Shelby
your sister."

Allison's heart clenched. Her beautiful loving daughter
yearned for a sister, and patterning after her mother, had
selected one to latch onto. If only Brody had made different

choices … Where would she and Hope be if he had "manned up" the way Andrew had for Lucy? It was then she realized she had always fantasized that the outcome would have been a rosy storybook ending – that they would have been a loving family, living happily ever after.

She frowned. But she wouldn't have gone searching for God – wouldn't have learned about His love, His guidelines, His expectations and His family and Kingdom, if she had been with Brody. She had seen no signs of faith in the man. The train of thought brought a question to Allison's mind: was it possible that she and Hope were better off without Brody?

Hope reached up and clasped Allison's face. "You not listen, Mamma."

"Sorry. I was thinking. What did you say?"

"If Rori is my sister, is Andrew my daddy, too?"

Allison's breath caught. "No, honey. He can't be your daddy."

"Why not?"

"Because …" *No way.* "He just can't. Besides you have a daddy. Remember we keep his picture in our room?"

"But he is a *gone* daddy," Hope's green eyes were serious as she looked to her mother. "I want a *here* daddy."

"Oh, sweetie …" Allison clutched her sweet child in a bear hug and rocked her. The paint bucket buzzed. And buzzed. She glared at it. It buzzed again and then fell silent. After a moment, Hope squirmed to be released. She scampered for the door. "It okay, Mamma. I can wait. Rori didn't get her daddy 'til she was six. It not that long."

Allison hadn't heard the front door or voices in the main floor of the house, but now as she sat on the floor among the painting supplies, her mind registered not only Hope's retreating footsteps, but another set of steps approaching. The rich baritone of Andrew's voice reached her as he met Hope. "How's my Big Girl today?" he asked in their ritualistic greeting. "Fine as frog's hair," she giggled in response.

Allison heard the rustle of clothing and pictured Andrew sweeping Hope up to hug her. She heard the clunk of her shoes as he set her down again. "What's new?" he asked.

"I get a new daddy when I'm six," she said as she blew past him and descended the stairs. A few more strides brought Andrew into the room where Allison sat curled in on herself with her face in her hands. He'd never seen her looking so small or beaten as she did just then. She sat surrounded drop cloths, painting pans, rollers and brushes. A ladder was sidled up to the wall where she clearly had been edging in preparation of painting the surface.

A strange tenderness washed through Andrew as he knelt next to her and tugged at her wrists. She dropped her hands, but kept her chin tucked tightly to her chest. She was holding it in. Every battle she'd had, every disappointment she'd endured, every wish she had suppressed was pounding on the walls of her heart trying to break free. He didn't say a word, but pulled her up to stand in the embrace of his arms.

He held her with strength and love as she drenched his shirt with tears and sobs racked her body. He would give back to her all the strength and support she had given freely to him the other day in the park and last night when he had been panicked. He would do it without reservation. Andrew's voice soothed her soul as he murmured to her and alternately stroked her hair and her back, until, at last, she sniffed definitively, wiped her cheeks with the backs of her hands and straightened her spine.

The storm was over and her need of a safe harbor had passed. She took a step back away from him and squared her shoulders. "Sorry you had to see that."

"Sorry you had to go through it." His gaze was keen as he regarded her. "Want to talk about it?"

She shook her head. "Maybe later." *Maybe never.* "How's Rori?"

"She's pretty good. Concerned about the future. But your wolf story really helped." He had been looking at Allison as he spoke, but swung his gaze around the room. "You ready to take a break?" he asked, indicating the painting project. "We could go for a walk?"

"Sure." She secured the lid on the paint can and muttered about her suicidal phone as she related the incident of the drowning phone to Andrew. Brushes and the roller were slipped into a plastic bag and the two left through the kitchen.

Lauren was in the living room playing with Rori and Hope. She called out to Allison that she'd watch them and there was no need to hurry back. Andrew caught Lauren's wink as they turned to leave.

Outdoors the birds were singing and the flowers were blooming, but Allison wasn't seeing it. She just kept seeing Hope's face when she asked if Andrew could be her daddy. Tears gathered in her eyes again as she imagined Hope's interpretation of what a daddy is and what one does for the family. Of course the little girl would want a daddy.

Andrew wrapped an arm across Allison's shoulder as they strolled. His hand slid down her arm and he felt the goose bumps on her flesh. Before she realized what was happening, he had shucked out of his jacket and slipped it over her shoulders without a word. They walked on.

She hadn't intended to tell the tale, but by the time they had covered six blocks, Allison had spilled the whole story about Hope wanting Andrew to be her daddy. And he had replied with a quiet "Hmm."

"Hmm? What's that supposed to mean?" she challenged in frustration. Her green eyes snapped as she faced him. "I just told you that my daughter has picked you to be her daddy and you say 'Hmm'!"

He smiled a half-smile. "How'd you meet?" he asked, putting the daddy question away for later.

"I carried her for nine months." Humor had been Allison's deflector for questions about Brody for years, and now she fell back on the emotional crutch.

"Not Hope. Her father." Andrew was facing Allison. He was serious and intent, but at the same time Allison sensed his genuine need to know about her past. Quietly he asked, "How did you meet her father?"

Their gazes held for a moment, before Allison blinked and looked away. Biting her lip, she began, "I'd rather not ..."

Frustration made his words sharper than he intended. "Suit yourself." He began striding again.

She jogged to catch up, grabbing his arm. Andrew tensed and stopped, but didn't turn. Allison stepped in front of him and touched his cheek. "Andrew? I was saying that I'd rather not talk about him. I'd rather not dwell on the past ..."

Finally his eyes dropped to hers and her breath caught as she saw a new pain – a fresh wound open up. His voice grated, "So you still love him?"

"No." The declaration hung between them like smoke on the air. She wanted to look away and hide, but she couldn't make herself. "No," she whispered again. Profoundly saddened by the admission, Allison knew she needed to forge ahead. Andrew had become a good friend and he deserved to know what had happened.

A portion of the tension drained from Andrew and relief flood his features for a moment. He opened his mouth as if to say something, but closed it again without comment.

"I'd rather not talk about him, but I think you deserve to know," she said quietly. "Hope's father's name is Brody Martinson. He was in one of my classes at the university," she began quietly. Andrew didn't move. He didn't even appear to breathe. "He'd smile and talk with me."

"Which class?" Andrew asked coolly.

"Psych. A general lower-level class," she explained. "He was older and very ... handsome. He started complimenting me and ... flirting. It made me feel really special to get attention from him."

"Then after you were all buttered up, he asked you out, right?"

"Yes."

"And you accepted. Just like that," Andrew concluded as he snapped his fingers. "How long did you date?"

"If you're going be hostile, we don't need to have this conversation. You are the one who wanted to know this," she pointed out. "I am perfectly happy keeping it all to myself."

Expelling a sigh and rolling his shoulders, Andrew finally looked Allison in the eye. "I do want to know your story. I just ...," he paused. "I don't like the picture I'm seeing. It's like he set out to get you. He took you to bed. And then when he found out he'd gotten you pregnant he just disappeared."

It sounded terrible when Andrew said it that way. She felt bile rise in her throat and turned away to hide her reaction. Tears brimmed in her eyes and she didn't want to start crying again. He touched her shoulder lightly. "I'm sorry. It just bothers me that anyone could use you like that and then abandon you."

"It wasn't as cold as you make it sound. And it wasn't that fast. And I wasn't that stupid," she declared defensively. "I resisted going out with him that semester. I finally broke down months later and went out with him after Christmas break - in February."

Andrew nodded thoughtfully. "So, how long did you date?"

"In April, I told him that I was expecting," she said with a nervous giggle. She pulled one hand up to cover her mouth as the giggle morphed into a gasp and finally into a sob.

Sympathy for the young, naïve girl Allison had been washed through him driving him to take her into his arms and hold her. She stood rigidly sheltered in his arms as she tried to regain her emotional footing. As they stood there on a quiet sidewalk in the sleepy little town of Miller's Bend, he wondered why God made him fall for women who had been cast off by heartless men who used them and discarded them.

As he digested that thought, another one hit him hard. *When did I fall for this woman?* The thought was an uncomfortable one and Andrew's muscles tightened. Was it fair to Allison to want a relationship with her? He had his hands full with his financial advisory firm, his daughter and his ex-wife. His friends and family kept him as busy as he wanted to be socially. He was active in the church and community.

As Andrew loosened the embrace and pulled back, Allison began to bring the tears to an end and compose herself. Swiping an errant tear from her cheek, she said, "Sorry about that. It's just …"

"No problem," Andrew replied with forced lightness in his voice.

Allison's gazed swept his features. He was a strong man – physically, morally, ethically and emotionally – and she wondered how he managed to handle not only his own problems, but to shoulder other people's as well. "How do you do it?" she marveled.

"I just have to change shirts frequently," he laughed as he pulled the front of his tear-dampened shirt away from his body.

"No, Andrew. I'm serious," she spoke quietly as the intensity in her gaze increased. "You are always there for everyone else. You look out for your friends. You take care of your family. You adore and protect Rori. And just look at all you have done to try to help Lucy over the years," she went on.

He didn't know if any one had ever noticed these things before, but no one had ever said them aloud. Andrew took a step backwards. "You're wrong," he croaked, taking another step back.

"I'm right," she said gently. Allison deftly caught up with him and placed her hands on either side of his face. "Who takes care of you, Andrew Wheeler? Who helps you? Who supports you?"

He couldn't answer. Thoughts and emotions collided in his mind and in his heart. He hadn't allowed himself to wish for someone to take care of him. At least not since it became evident that Lucy wouldn't. Oh sure, he'd had hopes in the beginning of their marriage, but they had died quickly. And now, here was Allison asking him, as though she could read his emotional need – could see the vacuum in his life – asking him "who supports you?"

His muscles twitched as his body clamored for him to reach out and grasp the woman before him and cling to her. He yearned to let her loving care envelope him and help his spirit break free from the pain and disappointments in the past. But was he strong enough to let go and trust and move forward? He doubted it. His imagination carried him forward a few years – would she end up as bitter and nasty as Lucy? Could he risk it?

He tenderly clasped her wrists and pulled her hands away from his face. He lowered her hands to her side, his eyes following their path, and tried, but failed to, drop the emotional shield into place.

"We were talking about you and Brody ..." he said as he forced the conversation back to Allison.

"Yeah," she said without enthusiasm. "Where was I?"

He snorted, and pulled one corner of his mouth into a slight smile. "You were pregnant. In April. Four years ago."

"I had imagined that he loved me," she said sadly. "I was sure I loved him. That he would be excited about the baby and we would start a life together."

Andrew turned, pretending to focus on the driver of a passing vehicle. He fought back the instinctive response that rose in him as he recalled nearly the same conversation with Lucy so many years ago. His eyes clenched closed as he battled the memories. And the fear that maybe the two women were indeed as much alike as he had originally feared when he and Allison had faced off in the kitchen of Riley's home all those weeks ago began to resurface.

Allison continued to speak, apparently unaware of Andrew's internal struggle. "It didn't go well," she whispered. "First he didn't believe me. Then he accused me of trying to trap him. Of using him to try to get money or, or something."

She paused as she recalled some of the hurtful things he had said. She felt the pain, again, but it was dulled – as though his opinion of her really didn't matter anymore.

"I told him that I loved him, and he … well anyhow," she sighed as though the memory of the conversation was unimportant. "I told him I didn't want a man who didn't love me. Then I went crying to my friends, Shelby and Ashley, about the situation." She laughed to herself. "They said I was better off on my own. Now, since coming to Miller's bend, I'm finally starting to realize they were right."

"He left me messages a couple of times. Saying things like 'I tried to call but you're not answering so the ball's in your court'. I tried returning his calls, but he never answered. Then I started getting checks from him. I sent them back. With one of them, I sent a note saying that our child would need loving parents more than periodic checks and if he was up to the task of parenting, then he should come and see me."

Allison realized that she'd been speaking to her own shoes, and that Andrew had become extremely quiet. Slowly she let her gaze slide up to meet his and what she saw there made her wince internally. Each regarded the other until Allison broke the silence. "It all sounds too familiar to you, doesn't it? You think I'm just like Lucy?"

Andrew's heart and mind were at odds: logic told him that the scenarios were identical; his feelings told him they were not. More importantly, both his heart and mind insisted that Allison and Lucy were nothing alike. Reading the desperate hope in her fathomless green eyes, he finally pulled her close once again and groaned, "No. You are nothing like Lucy. Nothing like her at all."

Cadee Brystal

CHAPTER TWENTY-TWO

His words soothed Allison as she relaxed in his embrace. Relief cascaded through her as she assimilated Andrew's words. "You're nothing like Lucy," he'd said. She let her body lean into his as she considered how lucky she was to have developed a friendship with this man. She contemplated whether it could ever grow into something more. Whether he could ever trust a woman enough to let himself love her after what he was going through with Lucy.

The sound of Andrew clearing his throat pulled her attention to the present and she looked up into his face. He spoke slowly and deliberately. "Do you think he – Hope's father – will ever be up to the task of being a loving parent to Hope?" he asked as his gaze bore into Allison's.

"No."

"How can you be certain? Maybe he's the person who was tracking you ..." Andrew's voice held a thread of dread as he continued, "I know Mason hasn't seen any new evidence, but someone had been watching you. It could have been Brody. Maybe he's decided that he wants you back – that he wants his daughter."

The insistent shaking of Allison's head brought him to a stop. With furrowed brows he watched her closely. "Tell me how you can be so sure," he asked again.

"He's dead."

"Oh?" *Good. Not good.* "What happened?"

Allison had pulled away from Andrew and had hardened her heart and waited for the pain that always accompanied the thought of Brody's death. She didn't feel the pain. She did still feel dread at the memory of the bank robbery though, and a shiver worked down her spine.

Allison turned and began walking back toward Mrs. Holmes' house. She spoke quietly and kept her eyes trained straight ahead, seeing nothing. "We didn't speak face to face again. Like I said, he left a couple messages and sent some checks that I returned. Then one day in June, Shelby, Ashley and I were out running errands and we stopped at the bank in Brookings. While we were waiting, three guys came in and …" She stopped at an intersection and waited for the car to pass before crossing. Andrew strode quietly, but attentively beside her.

When they had crossed the street she picked up the story again, "They were there to rob the bank. They had guns and they were ordering people around. It was crazy!" Allison glanced sideways to see Andrew's expression. She couldn't read what he was thinking, so she continued. "They were dressed in black and had their faces covered, but when they were yelling, I must have recognized Brody and I … well Shelby told me later … that I called out his name."

She'd startled Andrew, she could tell. He stopped walking and pulled her to a seat on a little park bench, saying nothing. His expression urged her to continue. "I couldn't believe he would do something like that! Armed bank robbery! Anyway, he turned toward me and pulled off his mask. He dropped his gun and started coming toward us … He said my name and reached for me … and then …"

"What? Then, what?" Andrew's voice squeaked a little.

"He fell. In his face, I saw pain and conflict, and then he kind of went blank. He just crumpled to the floor, right in front of me. Dead. Or dying quickly," she said as she finally shifted her gaze to Andrew's face. Confusion flickered there, and then compassion, as he wrapped his arms around her and pulled her close.

"I'm sorry," he offered in a soothing voice. Allison nodded mutely as she let her cheek rest against his chest. She let herself bask in the feeling of safety and solidarity for a moment. She'd been alone in the world for so long ... "You know you can't leave me hanging," a gruff whisper floated to her ears from Andrew. She pulled away from him slightly and sat up straight as she nodded. Andrew's arm remained draped lightly across her shoulders.

"One of his buddies – the leader of the robbers – had come up behind him and stabbed him in the back." As Allison spoke, Andrew watched her. She embodied pride, strength and fortitude that had helped her survive the trauma and the pain that had followed the robbery, and she was drawing on those reserves even now. Sympathy for the young girl she'd left behind and admiration for the woman she'd been forced to become blossomed within his heart.

She spoke again with an automatic, almost robotic, rhythm. "The guy pointed his gun at the three of us and began swearing. He pushed everyone – customers and employees – into the vault. After we were inside, he pulled Ashley, Shelby and me forward. He had heard Brody say my name, but didn't know which one I was. He ordered whichever one of us was Allison to step forward. I didn't know what he planned to do, but I stepped forward."

Andrew's arm had flexed, pulling Allison closer to him again as he listened. She lifted her gaze to his as she spoke,

"They stepped forward, too. Ashley and Shelby. They didn't worry about themselves. They sacrificed to save me and my baby. They could have been killed ... for me."

"He backhanded me and I flew to the floor. All I could think about was my baby and protecting him or her. Shelby and Allison tried to shield me. He pounded them with the butt of his gun. He aimed the gun at us and pulled the trigger, but it jammed. When it wouldn't fire, he pulled the knife again."

"He meant to kill us. And he probably would have, but the police arrived. He turned on them, but they captured him." She stopped and peered into Andrew's eyes. "You have to know about the robbery. Didn't Shelby or Riley tell you?"

Andrew nodded. "I know some of it," he confirmed. "I didn't know the details, though. I didn't know ... your ... Hope's father was involved. Or that he'd died." Andrew swallowed hard. "I can't imagine how difficult this was for you ..."

"It was very hard at first," she confirmed. "Shelby and Ashley were hospitalized. Brody was dead. The police were getting our stories over and over so they had everything they needed to prosecute. I was overwhelmed, mourning and alone."

"Shelby was injured?"

"She had broken ribs. Ashley had a concussion and bruising. But he didn't hurt me – thanks to my friends," she spoke quietly.

"So that's why you are so dedicated to Shelby," Andrew said as though some great mystery had been solved. "And I suppose you'd be the same way if you thought Ashley needed you, wouldn't you?"

"If Ashley was in trouble or needed help, I would be there in a heartbeat," she replied with conviction.

"The robbers? They were convicted?" he asked.

"Yes. And the man who attacked Shelby last year was a brother to the one who killed Brody," she confirmed.

"Did you go to Brody's funeral? Did you get the chance to say good-bye to him?"

Allison's black pony tail swung as she shook her head. "No. He ... his ... the service was in his hometown. A little town out by Rapid City. It was too far and I didn't want to go alone ... I couldn't ask Shelby or Ashley to go with me." She didn't reveal the deeper truth: that she hadn't wanted to see Brody like that. She had wanted to preserve her memory of him.

"What about his family?" Andrew's questions continued.

Allison stiffened and met his gaze. "What about them?"

"Did you meet them? Do they know about Hope?" His eyes searched her expression where he read shame and fear. He found the answer in her eyes. "You never contacted them? You never let them know that the son who had died had left them a grandchild?"

She shook her head again and her gaze dropped to her hands. "I was scared. You know – you hear stories of families trying to take children away from their parents – especially single parents. I'd never met them and don't know what they are like," she said as her gazed connected with his. "They'd raised Brody and look how he turned out – a bank robber!"

"I think – and you may not like this idea – but I think you should consider finding Brody's family and letting them into Hope's life," Andrew offered gently. "They may be fine loving people and Hope has no grandparents, no cousins, no aunts and uncles. It could really enrich her life." He tenderly cupped her cheek, his thumb sliding along the silken skin. He waited a minute before he kissed her lightly. "It could also give you more people to rely on – people who can help you and become part of your family."

Letting her face be cradled in Andrew's strong hand, Allison allowed her eyes to drift closed. "I'll consider it. But not yet."

"You still miss Brody?" Andrew asked in a low scratchy voice.

"No. I thought it was Brody that I've been mourning," Allison replied. And then she opened her eyes and searched Andrew's expression as his hand fell away from her cheek. She opened the door to the secret she'd only recently recognized and gave it wings by sharing it with him. "I've discovered lately that it isn't Brody that I lost. I couldn't have lost him because I never had him. He didn't love me. I realize now that what I felt for him wasn't love either." *Love is what I feel for you.*

Andrew's expression was open and hopeful as he waited for her to continue. His pulse pounded in his ears and he was aware of nothing else in the world, but the woman before him.

Allison had paused, but she had maintained the visual and emotional link with Andrew. "I realize that what I've been mourning was the death of the fairy tale. I lost the fantasy I'd fostered – the dream where Brody and I could be a couple; that when the baby arrived, we would be a family. I never had the loving family like Shelby did, and I wanted that so badly. And that's what I've been missing, more than the man, I've been missing the 'what might have beens'."

Andrew started to speak, but his voice caught. "And now …?" he croaked.

"And now … I want to stop wallowing in my past. I want to break free from it and move forward," she said with determination. "I want …" she finally had to let her gaze drop away from Andrew's because the intensity she saw there almost undid her.

Andrew stood and took Allison's hands in his own. He slowly pulled her up to stand before him. One hand slid up her arm, skipped to her chin and gently lifted. She saw in his expression hope and love, dedication and determination, and desire. "I want those exact same things," he whispered hoarsely. "And I want them with you."

His lips touched hers. The contact was warm and light for a second, before growing, deepening and developing into so much more. With a sense of reverence, it was a sweet promise, a quiet invitation .... It seemed to be the beginning of something beautiful, something endless.

When they parted Allison laid her head against his shoulder. She could see the pulse jumping in his throat, could feel his chest rise and fall with his breathing. Her mind flashed to their other kiss – it had embodied a viral mix of emotions some bright and good, others dark and enveloping. She had asked that if and when they kiss like that again, that it be fueled by nothing but love. Tears sprang to her eyes and her hand flew to her lips, just as the whispered words floated from Andrew's lips to her ears. "I think I've grown to love you, Allison McGuire."

Cadee Brystal

CHAPTER TWENTY-THREE

"That's odd," Allison said quietly as she and Andrew passed through the kitchen. She indicated the plate of cookies and three partially filled cups of milk. "It's not like the girls to abandon Mrs. Holmes' chocolate-chunk cookies."

Andrew agreed as she stepped through the doorway into the living room. "They probably had to get back to a TV show or something." Allison followed his steps and quickly caught up to him. "Not in here either," he said unnecessarily as he looked around the room.

"Upstairs?" Allison suggested.

"You check there. I'll check outside," he replied. "They're probably playing in the lot next door."

Apprehension grew within Allison with each step she climbed toward the room she and Hope shared. She called Hope's name and as she passed an open window, she heard Andrew's rumbling voice calling for Rori outdoors.

"Come on, girls!" she called again. "We want to go out for supper!" She was sure that would bring the children running. She had moved along the hallway, pausing in each doorway to listen for the sweet voices of Hope and Rori. Allison gave her mind free rein to run with the fantasy that the four of them could become a family one day. Maybe, just maybe, it would work out. Maybe there really could be a chance …

"Allison!" Andrew's shout jerked her out of her reverie and back to the present. "Allison!" his call had risen in pitch and intensified as he reappeared in the living room. Thrown into action by the frantic quality of his voice, Allison raced along the hallway back to the top of the stairs. She peered down at him and held her breath.

"What's the matter?" She asked as fear coiled through her.

Rori sat quietly in the back seat of the car as the countryside zoomed past her. Alternately, she prayed and worried and wondered where her dad was. Surely he had discovered that she was gone by now. He would be looking for her – for them. Rori subconsciously tightened the hold she had on little Hope's hand. *Please, God, help Dad find us. Please.* Hope was quiet. Rori figured the little girl was starting to get scared, but she wasn't putting up a fuss yet.

A short time earlier – maybe 40 minutes ago – she, Hope and Lauren had been enjoying a milk and cookie break when Lauren received a phone call and abruptly left. The girls continued to munch on their snacks as they waited for her to return. When the door opened, Rori was surprised to see the woman who appeared in Mrs. Holmes' kitchen.

Bewilderment and alarm combined to suppress Rori's reactions as the cold fingers wrapped around her upper arm with a painful pinch. "You're coming with me," the woman had declared in an unnaturally sweet voice. Rori was abruptly yanked from the chair and to her surprise, Hope had thrown herself into the mix, clutching Rori's hand and pulling mightily in a futile tug-of-war. "Get back!" Rori yelled to her would-be rescuer, "Run and hide!" Hope stared in confusion for precious seconds. But when Rori repeated, "Go – hide!" she spun and ran toward the other rooms of the house.

But it was too late. A larger hand had closed over Rori's mouth as the unseen man wrenched her from the woman's clutches. "Get the brat," he ordered in a voice that sent shivers down Rori's spine. The woman didn't hesitate as she chased through the house in pursuit of the child.

Rori sank her teeth into the soft fleshy skin of the hand and the second she could draw air she yelled, "Dad! Help!" A stream of swearing flew from the lips behind her. She could smell the vile captor although she couldn't see him and her stomach clenched. The man entangled his fingers in her hair and jerked. Tears of frustration, anger, fear and pain pooled in her eyes as Rori's mind raced. *Please let Hope stay safe. Dad – Where are you?*

"You and the brat are coming with us," the voice whispered loudly through clenched teeth. Rori's stomach lurched as she felt the spittle splat against her cheek and temple. "You are gonna be smart and behave. And you are going to keep the brat calm or we will hurt you both," he ordered. "Do you understand?"

Her mind raced for other options and found none. "Never!" she hissed to her captor. Instantaneously her head slammed into the door frame and her left arm was wrenched precariously and painfully high behind her.

The woman reappeared bearing a squirming but quiet Hope in the crook of her arm. "What do you think you are doing?!" she demanded of the man. "Don't you dare hurt her!" The tension on her arm slackened.

Rori locked her gaze on the blue eyes of the woman. "How could you?" she choked out, voice cracking and tears finally spilling down her cheeks. "How?" she wailed.

Uncertainty flared in the woman's eyes before she hardened her heart. The expression on the woman's face told Rori that she was determined to follow through on whatever this plan was. Understanding dawned on Rori – she and Hope had just become two of the country's kidnapped children. And it was up to her to leave some clues. And to try to protect Hope.

"We need our jackets. And Hope needs her stuffed bears," Rori whispered as she starred at the woman. Accusations in the young girl's face made the woman turn away.

Rori waited. Hoping someone – anyone – would come through the door, as the woman, still toting Hope rushed to retrieve her jacket and the requested stuffed animals. The man still controlled Rori with his rough grasp. Her mind worked to recall the "stranger danger" training the school had presented last winter. There was no way to overpower the two adults. Even if she could escape, that would leave Hope alone with them and she couldn't do that.

The woman and Hope reappeared with the items. She yanked Rori's jacket off the chair and tossed it to her. "Put it on." Rori complied and slid her hands into the pockets. Relief. As the girls were hurried to the waiting car, her fingers inventoried the items she found in the jacket pockets – cell phone, a few dollars, lip balm, house keys on the cross-shaped key chain. She knew the words etched on the cross, "Trust in the Lord with all your heart."

The man shoved Rori into the back seat of the car to sit next to Hope. He slid in behind the wheel as the adults argued a point in their plan. Rori took one of Hope's bears, slipped the key ring onto his outstretched arm, eased them to the open window and let them fall to the pavement while sending a little prayer that Dad and Allison would understand.

She and Hope had sat in silence as the car had moved through the town's streets. Once Rori spotted the police chief – he was the man who had taught the "stranger danger" class – and she'd silently willed him to look her way, but he had only glanced up for a second. She fingered the cell phone in her pocket. Should she wait and try to call Dad when she could talk – maybe they would stop for a bathroom break? Should she send a text? If someone tried to call her, the sound would let the captors know that she had the phone along and they would surely destroy it. If she tried to change it to mute, the sounds would chime as she decreased the volume.

Rori hugged Hope before carefully hooking the lap belt across her tiny body. "She needs a booster seat you know," she declared to the adults in the front seat. "This isn't safe at all."

The man snorted and mimicked, "This isn't safe." He concluded with a gruff, "Get over it, kid!"

"Don't worry, Hope," she said to the small child. "Your Mamma and my Daddy will find us," she said with determination. "I know they will." Hope only nodded and pulled her remaining teddy bear close to her chest.

When they'd left the city limits and began cruising at highway speeds, the sounds in the car intensified and Rori decided that she had to try to get a message to Dad. She piled her jacket loosely on her lap before pulling the phone out of the pocket. Hiding her hands under the fabric, she began to text: It's Lucy. And a Man. Headed East. Red 4 door. Help! She burst into a fake coughing fit as she hit send, willing that the noise of her coughs to disguise the chime of the phone. She waited. The man's cold eyes lifted to the rear view mirror, assessed her for a moment and then returned to the road.

She lowered her focus to the phone, clicked the buttons to delete all texts and slid the phone into her hip pocket. Wrapping an arm around Hope, she pulled the child close and whispered to her, "Your Mamma loves you. I love you, too. We'll get through this." Hope sniffled and leaned into Rori.

"What's the matter?" Allison repeated. She'd flown down the steps to stand before Andrew. She looked with confusion at the items in his hands – Hope's favorite stuffed bear which seemed to be holding a key ring that sported a cross. "Where did you get those? What are you doing?"

With his eyes locked on hers he pulled his cell from his pocket and without glancing at the phone he hit the button to pull up the keypad. She watched with growing terror as he hit the keys, 9-1-1, and pulled the cell to his ear. Allison's world stopped when she heard his choked words, "I need to report a kidnapping."

When she came to, Andrew was kneeling beside her with a cool wet cloth pressed to her forehead. Concern and fear battled with anger in his features. She struggled to get reoriented, "What happened?" she asked.

"You fainted," he replied hoarsely as he gently pulled her into a sitting position. "Did you hurt your head when you fell?" he asked as he tenderly felt along her scalp.

"No," she said as she shook her head and pushed his hands away. "The girls?"

"Gone," he whispered. "The police are on the way over now."

A commanding knock at the kitchen door had the two racing through the rooms to the let the police officers in. "Mr. Wheeler. Miss McGuire," the officer said as he stepped into the kitchen. "I'm the Police Chief, Jeff Schuster," he said to Allison because he and Andrew had been acquainted for years. "What happened here?"

Allison listened mutely as Andrew presented the bear and the key chain to the officer and explained the afternoon's events. She was reeling from the very thought that someone had taken her daughter. *Why God? Why did you let this happen?* Her mind raced to try to understand what reason anyone could have for kidnapping her daughter. Her earlier fears – the ones she'd had when she first came to Miller's Bend – resounded in her thoughts, and the conclusion became clear: *someone followed us here specifically to take Hope from me.*

Lost in thought, the words from the chief startled her back into the present. "So this Lauren woman was the last person you know to have been with the girls?" he asked.

"Lauren!" Allison interjected. "It had to be her – she's been acting suspiciously all along."

Andrew's scowl deepened. "No, Allison. This feels like something Lucy would do."

"We'll get an APB out on both women," the chief spoke calmly. "We already have all of Lucy's info, but what can you tell me about Lauren?"

Andrew shrugged. "Not much. She rents the apartment downstairs from Mrs. Holmes. Came to town about ... what? Two months ago? Maybe three?" he looked to Allison for confirmation.

She nodded as she remembered the conversation with Mrs. Holmes and Riley. "She moved into the apartment downstairs just days before Hope -" she gasped a little sob, and Andrew moved to her side and pulled her close. Glancing into his face, she continued, "... just before Hope and I moved in upstairs."

"Do you know her last name?" the chief asked as he looked expectantly from one to the other. Other officers were on the scene, moving through the house, taking notes, collecting evidence. Andrew suspected there were others combing the yard and adjoining areas. He shook his head indicating that he didn't know.

"Martins," Allison croaked. "Lauren Martins is what Mrs. Holmes told me."

"What?!" Andrew's sharp response had Allison spinning toward him.

"Martins," she repeated. Confusion furrowed her brows, "So?"

"Hope's father's last name is Martinson and her name is Martins? And you didn't question that coincidence? Even when you felt – you knew – that someone had been tracking your movements? You didn't question her identity?" he demanded.

An officer appeared in the kitchen doorway and spoke quietly with the chief for a moment. "I need you two to come downstairs and look around with me, but don't touch anything," he cautioned.

As they began to follow Schuster, Andrew tightened his hold on Allison's shoulders. He dropped his lips close to her ear and said quietly, "I'm sorry. I didn't mean to make you feel worse. Lauren might have nothing to do with any of this. I'm just suspicious, as you well know."

"But she might have everything to do with this," anguish twisted her voice as she leaned into him. "I could have prevented it."

"We don't know that," he countered after a moment. "I still feel in my gut that this is Lucy's doing."

They had descended the steps and entered the apartment. "Look around," Schuster instructed. "See if there's any sign that your girls have been down here." He watched the two move silently through the rooms. "Remember not to touch anything."

Allison's gaze snagged on a composite photo and she froze as a gasp escaped her lips. She closed her eyes tightly. "Brody," she breathed the name more than spoke it, but Andrew instantly materialized by her side. Her hand drifted toward the photo of a young man with curling blond hair and crystal blue eyes. He smiled at them from the photo in which he held a much younger Lauren in his embrace.

"Chief," Andrew called, as he captured Allison's hands to keep her from touching the photo. "I think we have a link here."

"What's that?" Schuster was beside the couple as his gaze swept the photos. "Who's who here?"

"This woman," Andrew said, as he pointed to Lauren's image, "is Lauren Martinson." He emphasized the "son" as he was confident now that she'd been using an alias. "And this …" he continued slowly, indicating the man. "This is Hope's father. Brody Martinson."

The chief nodded as he scribed information into the notebook he held. "And where can we find him?" he asked without looking up.

"You can't," Allison finally spoke. "He's dead."

The chief sent the two up the steps, ordering them to go to the seating area in the yard and wait. He called an officer to forward the woman's likeness to all law enforcement statewide with an APB on her, as well as Lucy. He ordered Lauren's prints run for a positive identification and he ordered a check of local hotels for anyone named Martins or Martinson. He dispatched one of the officers to issue an Amber Alert for the two missing girls.

Andrew took Allison's hands in his own and discovered that they shook with the effects of adrenaline and emotion. He finally captured her gaze and tried for reassurance in his voice as he spoke. "We will find them," he said as he swallowed his own fear. "I won't let you lose Hope," he declared with conviction.

His touch quieted her emotions, but not her mind. She was terrified at the thought that her daughter was alone with strangers who had taken her. Hope was alone and afraid. But she wasn't really alone, Allison remembered. She was with Rori. "Rori's my sister," Hope had announced earlier that very day, "Like Shelby your sister." Allison flinched as she realized that Andrew had lost as much as she had today – his daughter was gone as well. Surely his heart bled and cried out just as badly as hers did, and yet, he was trying to comfort her.

Allison stiffened her spine and looked up into his face. He was afraid, she could see it there in the depths of chocolate brown eyes, but he wasn't panicked. Faith. She realized in a flash that his faith in God was sustaining him, so he could offer support to her in this awful time. She pulled one hand free and placed it with extreme tenderness to his cheek. "I won't let you lose hope either," she whispered. "Our girls will take care of each other until we find them," she offered with a sniffle. "Dear God, help them stay strong. And help the police find them," she prayed aloud.

"Amen," Andrew's voice cracked.

Allison didn't know whether she held Andrew, or whether he cradled her, but they were together in this. Each giving strength and taking comfort from the other.

After long moments, Andrew said, "It has to be Lucy. It's the only thing that makes sense. She wanted money and I refused her. She broke into my home and stole from me." He closed his eyes and leaned back on the bench. Eyes clenched shut, he shivered. "She said she needed the money and she'd do anything to get it. I should have just given it to her."

"That wouldn't have helped," the chief's voice boomed from nearby startling both Andrew and Allison. "A person like Lucy never goes away if you start giving in to her demands. The demands just get higher."

"What now?" Andrew asked.

"You wait. We work," the chief answered. Softening, he said, "You probably want to call your family ..."

His radio crackled, breaking off the thought. "Martinson has a room at the Super 8," an officer's voice announced through the static. Andrew and Allison bolted for his car, but an officer blocked the path.

"We are going with you," Andrew announced as he turned to face the chief.

Schuster regarded him carefully before responding, "Ride with me."

CHAPTER TWENTY-FOUR

Lauren sat rigidly in an ugly orange chair. Disheveled. That about summed up the image she portrayed, Allison thought. An older couple sat on the bed. The man resembled an aged version of Brody and the woman looked lost. Tears streaked the older woman's cheeks; her breathing wheezed as she held the oxygen mask over her mouth and nose. An officer stood guard over the trio.

"What do we have here?" Shuster asked in an almost too-friendly manner as he stepped into the room.

"The abductees are not present here, sir," the officer responded.

"Have the Martinson's vehicles been checked?"

"Affirmative. Not here, sir," the officer reiterated.

"How could you?!" Allison broke past the officers and rushed toward Lauren. Just as she reached the cowering woman, a firm grasp manacled her in a tight embrace. *Andrew.* Even in her frenzied state, she knew his touch in a millisecond. He pulled her against his solid chest and waited for her to succumb. "How could you?" she whimpered again as Andrew silently guided her to the other side of the cramped hotel room.

"It's Lucy, Chief," Andrew asserted. "Don't waste your manpower here. You have to find Lucy to find the girls."

"The girls?" Lauren spoke for the first time. "What's wrong with the girls?"

No one responded to her question. The chief turned to the other officer, "Cancel the APBs on the Martinsons and get me an update on Lucy's whereabouts." With a nod, the officer disappeared through the open doorway.

"What is your name miss?" Schuster asked as his gaze pinned the younger woman.

"Lauren," her voice quavered. "Lauren Martinson." Her gaze flitted to Allison's face as she made the admission. "Brody was my brother," she admitted, and her eyes filled with tears.

"And, you ma'am? Your name?" Schuster asked of the woman with the oxygen mask. She breathed deeply before lowering the mask slightly, but before she could speak the man raised it again to cover her mouth.

"I'm Brody and Lauren's father, Christopher Martinson," he offered. "This is my wife, their mother, Sheila. She has emphysema. This stress isn't good for her."

"It isn't good for any of us," Andrew added. The chief shot a quelling look his direction to silence him.

"Do you know the location of Aurora Wheeler and/or Hope McGuire?" Schuster asked the trio of Martinsons. The older couple shook their heads in denial and turned questioning eyes on Lauren.

"They were in Mrs. Holmes' kitchen just a little while ago," Lauren answered.

"You left them alone!" Allison accused, "Or you took them somewhere. They are ... gone!"

"I didn't take them anywhere!" Lauren countered as she rose to her feet. Allison advanced on the woman, only to be stopped by the chief.

"Now, ladies. It won't help if you get into it," he said soothingly. "When and where did you last see the girls?" he asked Lauren.

"We were having a snack, when I got a phone call from my parents," she glared at the elder Martinsons. "They said they had arrived in town and they were coming to my apartment. I couldn't let them do that," she explained. "So I told them to meet me at the hotel and I'd get them set up in a room until we could figure out what to do. I left the girls," she added as she lowered her focus. "Andrew and Allison were nearby; they had just gone for a walk. What could possibly happen to them?"

"They could be kidnapped!" Andrew snapped in response. "Now they are missing."

"Missing?" Sheila dropped the mask. "But I have to meet her! I have to see my Brody's baby!" Christopher quickly slipped the mask back into place and pulled his wife close.

"We had nothing to do with their disappearance, I assure you," he offered. "We just arrived in town this afternoon."

"I'm having you all moved to Lauren's apartment and placing an officer with you until we have the girls back," the chief announced. "You two," he said as his gaze swung back to Andrew and Allison, "back in my car."

Andrew watched from the back seat of the cruiser as the chief gave orders to the officer at the door of room 21 of the motel. On an impulse he pulled the phone his pocket and thumbed the speed dial for Rori's cell. It rang. It rang. It stopped. He heard a shuffling sound and a distant voice saying, "What was that?"

A sniffle. "Nothing, Mom."

Andrew's heart stopped. His breathing stopped. He focused every fiber of his being on picking up background sounds.

Lucy's voice: "Don't be smart with me! What was that sound?"

"Where are we going, Mom? Can we stop in Benson to go to the bathroom? Please? Hope needs to go …"

"No! She'll have to hold it," the woman replied.

"What about your friend. He must be getting hungry?"

"Why are you talking?" a man's voice snarled. "I told you to be quiet and keep the brat quiet, too!"

Allison stared at Andrew. Whatever he was hearing had clearly at once traumatized him and enraged him. He'd first paled and then reddened as he listened. He paled again as he held a finger first to his lips and then to Allison's, he changed the phone to his right ear and leaned close to Allison so she could listen too.

"I want to go home," they heard Hope's timid voice. "I want my Mamma." Allison bit back a gasp, as Andrew touched her lips again in a silent reminder.

"Dad will find you," Rori challenged her captors. "And when he does …"

"Stop talking! I told you to shut up!" the anger in the man's voice was increasing.

"Eric – They aren't hurting anything by talking," Lucy's voice quavered slightly. "And I don't want to have to clean up any messes. Maybe we should take a break at a Casey's Store or something."

That was the last thing they heard. Andrew looked at the display on the phone: call dropped.

Chief Schuster dropped into the driver's seat and he turned to face the passengers, about to say something that died on his lips. Glancing from the infuriated expression on Andrew to the hollow look in Allison's eyes he demanded, "What happened?"

Together they rushed to explain the phone call. The information they related to the chief made him smile. "That's a smart girl, you have, Andrew." He grabbed the mic on his radio and relayed the new information to the dispatcher. "Notify the Minnesota authorities, but first get ahold of the Benson city police and get the photos of Rori and Hope to them ASAP. Maybe they can intercept the girls when they make their pit stop. And start tracking Rori's cell phone signal."

Schuster was holding Andrew's cell phone as he spoke. After signing off, he reached to hand it back to the girl's father. "You've got an unread text," he noted. Andrew's adrenaline surged as he grabbed the cell.

He opened the text. "It's from Rori. She said, 'It's Lucy. And a Man. Headed East. Red 4 door. Help!'" he quoted for Allison and the chief. "Sent at 4:47 p.m. Over an hour ago! We could have been on the right track an hour ago!" Agony and regret swirled together as he groaned and threw the phone into the front seat. Why? Why hadn't he checked for texts?

In silence Andrew and Allison rode to the police offices with Schuster. After they were escorted to a private room, Andrew stared blankly. His fears were coming true – Lucy had stolen Rori away and was running with her. But worse than he'd ever imagined in his nightmares, a second child that he loved was gone as well. And poor Allison. Her treasured daughter – her only family – had been taken in the same evil sweep of events. He turned tortured eyes on her and spoke quietly. "I'm so sorry for this, Allison. I can't believe my screwed up life has spilled over on you and caused you this pain."

After a strained moment of silence, she spoke softly, "I don't accept."

"What?"

"You can't apologize for this, Andrew," Allison said with deflated quietness. "I won't let you take responsibility for Lucy's actions. She did this. Not you."

"You don't blame me?" he asked incredulously. Feeling his spirits buoying, he studied her. He saw sadness, pain and worry. But he saw no anger, no hate. "I just don't know how we are going to bear this ..." he said as he dropped into one of the hard plastic chairs. Elbows on his knees, forehead in hands, he let the anguish take him.

After a few minutes, he felt Allison's gentle touch on his back. His mind told him he didn't deserve her compassion – he didn't deserve her support, but his body welcomed the touch and the caring that she offered. He leaned into her as she rubbed his shoulders without speaking for a few more minutes. With a heavy sigh she finally asked, "Could you finish telling me about you and Lucy, please? I think I need to have all the information here."

Andrew nodded without looking up. He knew she was right – she did deserve the whole story and he also knew deep down that he should have found the time to tell her sooner - as Riley had advised him to do. He stood and walked away from Allison without looking at her. *Will she hate me? Fear me?* "I don't remember where we left off," he said absently as his eyes searched the room for a focal point other than the beautiful woman who had come to mean so much to him.

"You were the first to hold Rori," she reminded gently. "Lucy denied your marriage proposals twice."

"Oh, yeah," he said as he appeared to forget the present and slide into the past. "After she graduated, I would see her around. I graduated and went off to college. When I'd come home, I would see her and Rori."

"You'd see her?" Allison asked timidly. With a sad note in her voice, she asked, "You were dating?"

"No. We didn't date," he replied. Andrew made a visible effort to pull his mind from the memories to the present. He locked on her gaze and moved close to Allison, "I told you before that Lucy and I never loved each other."

"Lucy was making bad choices," he said as he returned to the story. "I would plead with her to change her ways. I was too attached to Rori – I loved her like she was my own," he said as his voice caught. "I was so scared for her. Lucy was going through men like there was no tomorrow. I was afraid one of them would hurt Rori. Lucy was drinking more and more. And I was afraid she'd started doing drugs."

Allison's mind flitted ahead, imagining the relationship and drawing conclusions. *Oh my – he married the woman to save the child?*

"Then one night – I was at school studying for finals – I got a call from the police in a little town two counties over," he spoke raggedly and gestured in a generally westward direction. Andrew's eyes had left Allison and his gaze bounced crazily around the room. Finally he gazed at the mirror on the wall, knowing it was really a one-way observation window – knowing that anyone passing in the hall could be watching, or even listening. He refocused his thoughts to continue his explanation for Allison.

"Lucy had been out with one of their local bad boys and he had assaulted her." As he recounted the incident, his eyes told her of the terror he'd felt that night. "She'd been beaten and was unconscious. The police found my number in her purse, so they called me."

"Dear Lord," Allison gasped. Questions raced in her mind, but she kept them corralled. Andrew would tell her what he could.

"I asked about Rori, but they said there was no child with her," he choked. Allison read the emotions in his eyes, but couldn't tell if they were today's or those from the day so long ago. "I was scared to death that we wouldn't find her … or …," his voice trailed away as he struggled to control his roiling emotions. He straightened and swallowed hard. "They located her the next day. She'd spent the night alone, hiding in the shed in the backyard of a house a block or so away from the hovel Lucy rented. She'd left her six-year-old child alone and driven more than an hour away to party."

"Lucy was hospitalized in Aberdeen, so I went there, thinking that they would bring Rori to where her mother was when she was found," he explained. "They didn't though. Lucy was still unconscious, and there were charges pending against her for child endangerment, among others. I learned that it wasn't the first time, either."

"Where was Rori taken?" Allison asked. Needing to know, but not wanting to hear the answer.

"Lucy had no family. Child protective services put Rori into a foster home," he answered. "I wasn't allowed to see her. Besides her mother, I was the only other person that the little girl really knew, and they wouldn't let me see her!" His voice roared at the cruelty to the terrified little girl who must have felt confused and abandoned.

"I vowed then that I would find a way to protect her," his voice resounded with sincerity and his eyes snapped with conviction. "I made a promise to myself, Rori, and God that she would never feel that way again."

"And you've done that," Allison spoke reassuringly. "She knows that you are doing everything you possibly can to get her back safely." The woman moved to stand in front of Andrew and gently placed her hands on his shoulders. "We both know it. We all know it."

He shrugged away from her. "Maybe today, but not the day Lucy woke up. You have to know what I did back then before you decide to stand by me now," he said ominously.

"Then tell me," she challenged. "Tell me the awful thing you did to save a helpless child." Her heart wrenched for the man before her. He clearly blamed himself for some misstep so long ago.

"I twisted the facts. I pressured her into marrying me," he answered as he turned away. "I told her that she would lose Rori. I told her they would put her up for adoption and that Lucy would never see her again, unless she married me and let me become Rori's adoptive father. I forced her to give me a legal claim on Rori."

Lucy's words spoken with venom in the park that day resounded in Allison's mind: *You better watch out or he'll steal her away from you like he did to me.* She looked away for a moment as she realized that if she'd heard this story weeks ago, she would have taken the revelation as a threat. She would have felt the bite of suspicion and the uncertainty of wondering whether Andrew could intend to take Hope away. But no more – Allison had changed since then. She was learning to trust and have faith.

A warm calm feeling washed over Allison – a certainty that Andrew's spirit wouldn't allow him to ever intentionally hurt anyone. Not quite a voice, and not quite words, but

Allison knew with confidence that she could trust him completely.

A quick reminder of the time they'd spent together had Allison shaking her head. "You did what was necessary to protect Rori. And," she spun to face the man, "you didn't deny Lucy her daughter. You improved their lives – both of them." The vehemence in her statement surprised both Allison and Andrew. The solace was a balm to his frayed nerves for a moment, but he wasn't through. There was more she needed to know.

"You'd better wait until you hear the rest before letting me off the hook," he stepped hesitantly toward Allison. *I don't want to lose you and Hope.* His arms ached to hold her, his fingertips tingled with the pull to touch her silken skin, but his mind warned him off. She might never talk to him again. She might grow to loathe him as Lucy did. And it would hurt so much more ... because he'd never truly loved Lucy.

In tormented misery he forged on, watching Allison closely for signs of how she was taking this all. "I couldn't help her get clean and stay that way. She eventually was sentenced for her drug use. The divorce was finalized while she was in prison," he said quietly. Dropping his voice to barely above a whisper, he continued, "About nine months later, the courts stripped Lucy of her parental rights."

Neither Allison nor Andrew moved, spoke or even seemed to breathe for what seemed like an eternity.

The door burst open. "We've got them," Schuster declared. "Let's roll."

CHAPTER TWENTY-FIVE

Tension coursed through Andrew as he and Allison sat in the back seat of county transport SUV driven by Chief Schuster, speeding toward the small town of Benson in the neighboring state of Minnesota. Andrew's mind grappled with the implications – Lucy and her associate, Eric, had kidnapped two minors and crossed state lines as they fled – there would be charges and trials and endless battles with Lucy. But the biggest battle Andrew would face, appeared to be the one to win Allison's trust again. In the last hour, since they'd begun the journey to reunite with their daughters, she had looked at him blankly for a long moment before turning to look out her window. He glanced at her again and his heart ached.

He thanked God over and again for keeping the girls safe, and helping the police find them. They hadn't been told the details – only that the Rori and Hope were safe and looking forward to seeing their parents. "Their parents." It was implied that the four of them belonged together, and as much as Andrew harbored that desire before disclosing his secrets, his mind assured him that all chances for that had dissipated like dust in the hot July wind.

Allison tried to wrap her mind around what had happened. Since first meeting Andrew nearly two years ago, and especially in recent months, she'd seen him react through a variety of situations, but nothing had prepared her for the scene in the interrogation room. He had laid all of his fears and secrets – the demons that he had hidden for six long painful years from his family and friends – at her feet and waited for her response. She sensed his vulnerability and his need for reassurance. Prior to that moment when he revealed that he had coerced Lucy into marriage, they had divorced and Lucy had lost her parental rights, Allison had thought she might love the man.

In the moment when he had entrusted her with what he perceived to be his darkest deeds – she had frozen. Locked up. Failed him. If she couldn't be trusted to come through for him in his moment of need, then what good could she be to him? Did that mean she was weak? Would there ever be a chance to make up for this missed opportunity to let Andrew know that she was a woman who would stand by him if given another chance?

Allison tried to turn in her seat, fighting with the seat belt for the space she needed so she could face the man she had grown to love. In frustration, she released the clip which alerted Chief Schuster. "Hey," he called over his shoulder, "buckle up."

"Sorry," she replied. Settling in her new position with her body facing Andrew, she pulled the seat belt around her again. Her hands shook and the belt slipped away from her. Grasping it again she yanked it forward so hard that it hit the end of its slack and ratcheted back, which would lock it tightly in place if she clipped it now. In exasperation, she let it recoil and began pulling it once again, but much more slowly, toward the clip. Lost in concentration on the belligerent seat belt, she was surprised when Andrew's hands captured hers and the seat belt.

He tenderly guided the seat belt hasp into the clip. He continued to hold her hands but didn't look into her face where he might have seen the truth. Andrew tightened his grip on Allison, willing things to have been different, wishing he'd done things differently years ago, wishing the past wouldn't taint the future. He could feel Allison's gaze on his face, but he didn't dare respond – if he looked into those emerald pools of emotion again he would surely flounder and drown – he would be lost. If he wasn't already.

Something landed on his hand. He knew instinctively that it was Allison's tear, warm and wet. And in a fanciful twist he thought of it as a representation of his dreams; her dreams; a shared dream. The tear was a symbol for a wish for family and love that fell and crashed and splintered in all directions – gone. Loosening his grip, he readied himself to let go. Let go of her hands. Let go of Allison. Let go of the dream he'd fostered for years, buried, and recently resurrected. Now his own rash acts were forcing him to give it up for good. *Why can't she accept and forgive what I've done? Why can't we have the love, the family that we crave?* A single tear hung in his lashes as he let her hands fall and, with his eyes tightly closed, pulled back to sit quietly on his side of the car.

Andrew imagined that if Allison loved him, although she had never spoken the words, she would cross the invisible canyon between them, and tell him so. He'd forgotten about the tear drop that had clung to his lashes as he squeezed his eyes tightly against the fantasy. No, she could never risk that he would do to her and Hope, what he had done to Lucy and Rori. The tear slipped silently from his lashes onto his cheek where an angel's touch whisked it away.

The angel spoke softly, "I'm so sorry, Andrew. So very sorry."

He nodded, his mind in a twisted dream. In his imagination, Allison was before him, hair upswept, long flowing white gown and the beautiful children beside her. "It's okay," he whispered. "I know it's too much to forgive. Too much to ask you to trust me. Too much to wish that you could love me."

Road noise met his waiting ears, but otherwise all was silent. Perhaps it was just a dream, a wicked tormenting dream. He hoped he hadn't said the words loud enough to reach Allison's ears. He heard a click; felt a rustle of movement; Schuster's voice reached him again, "I said buckle up." Then a chuckle. "Ah, what's the use? Nothing will keep you two apart."

The divider between the front and back seats slid closed.

Curiosity got the better of him and Andrew slowly peeked. He found Allison perched on the edge of the seat facing him, as close to him as she could be. Their gazes caught and his resolve was undone. His hands moved of their own accord to cup her cheeks, his thumbs tenderly wiping away the tears that shimmered there. "That's not safe," he warned in a husky whisper. "You could be hurt."

"I've been hurt before and I lived through it. Came out stronger for it," she countered. "As did you."

"Can you trust me?" The words had slipped past his lips before he could catch them.

"With all that I am, all that I have, and all that I ever hope to become. Yes, I do trust you," she affirmed.

"Can you forgive me?" he choked. He knew he could never bear it if Allison grew to despise him.

"No, I can't."

His heart clenched. Andrew rolled his head to stare out the window. "Oh."

Gently, hands touched his cheek and tenderly pulled his focus back to her. "I cannot forgive you because you have done nothing to be forgiven. You love a child enough to have sacrificed your own happiness to assure her safety. That is a noble act."

Just as his heart swelled with the possibility that they could make it together, Allison let her focus drop, pulling her hands into her lap and shifting away from him. He couldn't let her go, couldn't let her pull away from him. "What?" he asked. "What's the matter?"

"Can you ever forgive me?" she whispered.

Bewildered, he carefully asked, "For what?"

Tears filled her eyes as she straightened and faced him. "I failed you. When you shared your past, you needed my love and support. You needed me to be strong and reassuring," she said. "And I froze. I failed to give you what you needed."

"You didn't fail me," he countered with a smile. "You scared me. A lot. But you didn't fail me." He pulled her forward and kissed her lightly on each cheek. He held her for a moment, and then urged her to get back into her seat so she could be belted in.

Reluctantly, she did as he asked. And then searching for a tissue in her jacket pockets, she pulled out a piece of paper. She read the message there and silently passed it to Andrew. Confusion crossed his features before he opened the folded paper and read: "Show me your ways, O Lord, teach me your paths; guide me in your truth and teach me, for you are God my Savior, and my hope is in you all day long. Remember, O Lord, your great mercy and love, for they are from of old. Remember not the sins of my youth and my rebellious ways; according to your love remember me, for you are good, O Lord." Psalm 25:4-7

Cadee Brystal

CHAPTER TWENTY-SIX

A chorus of "Daddy!" and "Mamma!" pealed through the open foyer of the Benson Police Station the second they stepped through the glass doors. The interior was intensely bright, accentuating the shadows of fear that lingered in the children's faces as they bolted from their chairs to rocket toward their parents.

Andrew knelt to catch and hold Rori as Allison rushed to meet Hope. As he clasped Rori tightly to his chest, he whispered phrases of love and reassurance, and tears flowed down both their cheeks. "I knew you'd find us," Rori whispered. "I knew it in my heart." He noted in a corner of his mind that Allison had lifted Hope into her arms and was also crying.

"Why do you cry, Mamma?" Hope's sweet voice carried over the sounds of the reunion.

"I was scared, sweetie," Allison said as she wiped her eyes. "I was so scared that ..." She let her eyes trail to Andrew and Rori. *That you were gone forever. That I would never see you again. That you would be hurt or killed.* She realized the exact fears that Andrew had faced alone six years before when Lucy had been hospitalized and Rori hadn't been found. And he had held no legal rights – he had no avenues of recourse. When the girl had been found, she'd been kept from him.

She refocused on her own child, whom she now held safely in her arms. "I'm so glad you are safe," she said quietly. And then with passion she added, "Thanks to God, you are safe."

"Rori make me safe," Hope spoke with intensity as her serious green eyes were drawn to her mother's.

Allison hadn't realized that Andrew and his daughter had come up beside her. She startled when his deep voice rumbled, "How's my Big Girl?"

Hope beamed in response and leaned sharply toward Andrew, extending her arms in a plea to be held. When Allison let Hope pass to his caring embrace, Hope chimed, "Fine as frog's hair!"

Allison bent to look into Rori's worried expression. "Thank you," she said to the child that she had grown to love. "Thank you for keeping my baby safe through this."

Rori's focus was low, not meeting Allison's. Andrew watched as the woman tenderly raised Rori's chin and the girl finally met her gaze. "What is it?" Allison prompted. "We are so thankful to you for your quick thinking. You saved yourself and Hope, too."

Denial. Rori stubbornly shook her head. "It's my fault. It was my ... It was Lucy. She only wanted to take me, but Hope tried to help me, so they took her, too." Her shoulders shook as she tried to hold back the torrent of emotions that battled to break free. "If Hope hadn't been there with me – if she hadn't tried to help me – she wouldn't have had to go through this."

As Andrew held Hope, he and Allison dropped to their knees and mutually embraced Rori. She stood rigidly as if to ward off their expressions of love until Hope spoke. "We goed together. I knowed you love me," Hope said as she slipped from Andrew's hold to wrap her arms around Rori. "I love you. We sisters." Finally, Rori accepted the support that was offered and collapsed into the loving arms that surrounded her.

"I love you girls. All of you," Andrew spoke reverently as his eyes scanned the faces of the trio. Then he lowered his head, "Thank you, Lord, for bringing us safely back together. Thank you for second chances, and for teaching each of us to love and trust each other."

Many long hours later, Andrew stared into the cup of coffee on the table in front of him as he sat alone in Mrs. Holmes' kitchen. The vivid colors of dawn were just beginning to streak the skies when he'd given up on trying to sleep and slipped into the kitchen. He'd had a rough night, to say the least, as he worked over all that had happened – and what remained to be done. This morning, he was faced with telling his daughter that her mother, Lucy, had died yesterday. He was having enough trouble dealing with his own swirling, dancing, diving emotions over the woman's life and death. He didn't know how he could help Rori through the loss, but he was certain that he would be relying on God's love to do it.

After their emotional reunion in the Benson Police Station, an officer had taken the children so Andrew and Allison could be updated. They had learned that Lucy's accomplice was a known drug dealer to whom she owned tens of thousands of dollars. The tips that Rori had managed to relay to Andrew had helped the Benson police be ready when the foursome had stopped at a convenience store.

The police said the abductors had sent the children inside so Rori could take Hope to the restroom, but instead she had slipped Hope into the "employees only" area and hidden her with instructions to talk only to a police officer. She began to return to the car to face whatever her fate would be with Lucy and the man, only to be intercepted by a plain-clothes officer. Squad cars immediately swarmed the area, but the kidnappers had decided to make run for it.

They sped from the parking lot and headed for the open road, leaving both children behind. The highway patrol reported that the two died in a fiery one-car accident about 20 miles east of there, when the driver failed to negotiate a sharp curve in the roadway.

"God rest her soul," Andrew said quietly, not even realizing that he'd spoken the words allowed.

"Lucy's dead?" Rori's voice seemed timid and strained.

Andrew's head snapped up in response to his daughter's voice. He hadn't heard her enter the room. He hadn't heard anyone moving around the house in the early hours. When the four had arrived back in Miller's Bend, the chief delivered them to Mrs. Holmes' place. Hope, groggy with sleep had held fast to Rori's hand. They'd put the two girls to sleep in the room normally shared by Hope and Allison. And Allison slipped in beside them so they wouldn't be alone.

Andrew had crashed on the couch, unwilling to leave.

Words now clogged his throat as Andrew tried to respond to his daughter's inquiry, but they wouldn't pass his lips. *What do I say to her?*

"Dad? Is Lucy dead?" she reiterated with rising voice.

"Yes, honey," he finally answered as he moved to her. "I'm sorry, but she died in a car crash after they left you yesterday. I'm so sorry."

She pushed him back and stepped out of his embrace. Watery eyes implored him for understanding. She exhaled a shaky breath and whispered, "I think I knew that she had died.

The police acted funny when I asked about her." After a long pause she added, "Is it bad to be relieved?"

"God help us – I hope it's not bad," he said as he pulled his daughter onto his lap and sat holding her. "Your mother's life here was so tormented ... I tried to help her. But ..." Andrew's voice faded.

"Maybe she'll finally be okay," Rori whispered. "I told her God would help her, if she would only ask. Maybe she finally asked."

CHAPTER TWENTY-SEVEN

Rori was nervous. Nervous and excited. She flanked her dad, and Hope had slipped in beside Allison as their parents faced the pastor and prepared to take their wedding vows. Uncle Riley stood behind Rori and rested his hand lightly on her shoulder. Aunt Shelby was beyond Allison, and kept smiling at Riley. Surrounded by love, Rori knew how lucky she was.

She glanced out over the faces of the congregation where she saw Grandma and Grandpa Wheeler who had been so accepting and loving to her for six years now – almost seven. They held Jacob and Isabelle who were now beginning to try to walk and making a lot of noise. Mrs. Holmes was next to Grandma and was all dressed up. She smiled broadly as she scanned the group at the altar.

Hope's grandparents – the Martinsons – and Lauren smiled up at the wedding couple from their seats in the first row across the aisle. Rori thought of how she loved her grandparents, and was happy for Hope to have gained not one set, but two sets, of grandparents.

Two ladies that Rori didn't know sat next to the Martinsons. When Rori had been introduced to the older one, Allison explained that the woman was her aunt and Allison had lived with her when she was growing up. The other was Allison's friend, Ashley, who had barely arrived in time for the ceremony. There hadn't even been time for her to be introduced, Rori remembered. Ashley had appeared in the doorway of the church as the bride and maid of honor were waiting to walk up the aisle. The three had squealed and hugged and cried just a little, before Matt had ushered the new arrival to the seat in the front pew.

Rori felt her eyes burn and tingle before the images began to blur and waver.

The wedding would change her life, yet again. Some old fears began to rise in her mind as she remembered how life had been when Lucy and her Dad had tried to live together as a family. A shiver slithered through her at the thought. Andrew must have sensed it, because he turned slightly and dropped his gaze to look her in the eye. He sent her a reassuring smile and a wink as he reached for her hand. Allison caught Rori's gaze and mouthed the words "I love you" to her before the pastor cleared his throat to begin speaking again. Hope slipped from her mother's side to Rori, who picked her up and let her settle on her hip.

Andrew lovingly nestled the girls close in the embrace of his right arm while his left scandalously slid around Allison's waist and pulled her close. The pastor's next words were, "Well, Mr. Wheeler, it certainly looks like you have your hands full!"

The laughter died down and the ceremony proceeded quickly. Much of it was traditional but there was a twist at the end before the pastor would normally introduce the couple as man and wife. The pastor spoke with Christian love as he said, "I have been honored to counsel this couple in recent months. I have met with them singly and together. I have met with each of them with the children. And each time I am left in awe of the love and understanding they share – not just as a couple, but as a family. If you know their stories, then you will understand that I have learned a great lesson from these people and I want to share it with you. Take it to heart because it is simple and true: Don't hold on to anger, hurt or pain. They steal your energy and keep you from love."

The sanctuary was quiet for a moment before the pastor announced, "I now present the Andrew and Allison Wheeler family."

LOOK FOR
SETTLING DOWN,
MATT AND ASHLEY'S STORY,
COMING SOON!

Cadee Brystal's next novel is also set in Miller's Bend, where you've already met and grown to love the characters. Get to know Shelby and Allison's friend, Ashley when she shows up in the small community. Ashley and Matt each come to the realization that they are ready to make some serious life changes in *Settling Down.*

EXCERPT

Ashley was aware that they hadn't known each other long. Not long at all. But she also felt a soul-deep certainty that she did know him and had formed a strange connection to him. She couldn't explain it – didn't want to examine it. She surely didn't want to explore it. But she knew it was there.

The wind whipped loose snow around them, pulling the crystals from the roof and sprinkling them over the pair as they stood facing each other. His blond curls danced in the breeze as he regarded her. Gazing up into Matt's face, watching as the hard shadows played across his features, Ashley had a flash of another image. Like a photo that she'd meant to capture, she saw it clearly in her mind – in her memory.

Ashley closed her eyes tightly as her mind gave her a glimpse of the night she'd fallen and hit her head. She'd crashed to the hard concrete patio and smacking her head against the wall as she'd careened out of control. When she had opened her eyes, this man had been kneeling at her side regarding her intently. The lights from the windows had battled with the shadows of the night, and she had reached for her camera then to capture the effect.

"Are you okay?" his voice was laced with worry as it registered. Past or present, she wasn't sure, but the sound was soothing. "Ashley. Are you okay?" he asked again with growing concern. And then his hands closed around her shoulders. She felt his strength through her winter coat and leaned toward him, but still didn't answer. He pulled her close, tucking her into the crook of his arm and simultaneously taking the key from her gloved hand. "Come on," said with authority, "I'm getting you inside."

He'd guided her into the apartment, helped her out of her coat and settled her on the couch as he'd wrapped her in a blanket. She knew it wasn't fair, but she still hadn't answered whether she was alright or not. Since she wasn't certain herself, how could she tell him? Now she watched as he brought a cup of tea to her and settled next to her on the couch.

"Here, if this doesn't help, I'm taking you back to the ER," he threatened with a smile.

"Thanks, Matt," she said as she looked up into his bright blue eyes. "I don't think it will come to that. I think ..."

"What?"

"I think I just had a shimmer of a memory from the night I fell," she said uncertainly. "You were kneeling beside me ... my head hurt like a ... and my arm and my ... well, where I landed," a self-conscious laugh escaped from her lips as she spoke. "And you were there ... the light dancing on the contours of your face ..." her fingers lightly touched his forehead, traced his brow, trailed across his cheek, and then followed the planes to his lips before he pulled back. She continued to speak as though in a trance, "The passions played in your eyes. You were hurt, and angry, but you still could show such compassion and caring for me," she said before falling silent.

Matt's heartbeat raced as she'd laid a gentle hand to his face. But now it felt as though his heart had stopped cold: Ashley's memory was back. Would this change her mind about staying in a small town? Would she leave Miller's Bend? Everyone always left. He surged to his feet and backed away. "That's great. I'm glad for you," he said, trying to convince her – trying to convince himself. "What happens now?" he added as he tried to focus on anything but the feelings she had started churning within him.

She watched Matt's retreat a moment. Confusion and disappointment replaced the wistful look of wonder Ashley had borne as she had spoken of the night she fell. "No, Matt," she answered. "I'm not ready. It was just a picture in my mind – without context. This was a millisecond out of missing weeks." She dropped her gaze to her hands which clutched at the blanket in which she was wrapped. "It's not enough ... I don't have my memory back."

Emotions swirled through Matt as he watched her. Joy swept through him when Ashley declared that she wasn't ready to leave. The feeling was followed, of course, by guilt for being happy that she wasn't healed. He felt sad for her because she'd lost a part of herself with her memory; he felt sad for himself because he was certain he would lose part of himself if she decided to leave.

She'd come to stand before him, wrapped in the blanket that trailed behind her like a robe worn by royalty. She'd glided to him while he'd been immobilized by his feelings and now she gazed at him with curiosity and caring. "What's the matter?" she asked quietly. "Did I get it wrong? Is it a dream instead of a memory?"

"No," he said gruffly. "You got it right. Your memories are in there," he whispered, as he tapped a finger lightly to her temple.

Made in the USA
Middletown, DE
08 September 2015